OXFORD SHADOWS

Veronica Stallwood

HEADLINE

First published in 2000
by HEADLINE BOOK PUBLISHING

10 9 8 7 6 5 4 3 2 1

British Library Cataloguing in Publication Data

Stallwood, Veronica
  Oxford shadows
  1. Ivory, Kate (Fictitious character) – Fiction
  2. Women novelists – Fiction 3. Detective and mystery stories
  I. Title
  823.9'14 [F]

ISBN 0 7472 7205 0

Typeset by Avon Dataset Ltd, Bidford-on-Avon, Warks

Printed and bound in Great Britain by
Clays Ltd, St Ives plc

HEADLINE BOOK PUBLISHING
A division of Hodder Headline
338 Euston Road
London NW1 3BH

www.headline.co.uk
www.hodderheadline.com

For Sally and Jasper
with love

I should like to thank the Imperial War Museum, and in particular Roderick Suddaby, for helping me to find letters and diaries giving background material for this story. All mistakes, however, are my own work.

PART 1

OXFORD, 1945

1

I still wonder whether I should have seen what she was up to right from the beginning. Does that make me partly to blame for what happened?

It's a painful thought to live with in the small hours of the night when sleep is harder to come by than a new laid egg in Rye Lane market. It's easier for me to believe I was just another of her dupes. I lie awake in bed, with the curtains flapping in the open window, and even with my eyes closed I can see her face looming out of the darkness, just the way it looked that last time, with her hair loose and that smile of hers lighting up her eyes. She didn't blink or drop her gaze, not even then.

And yet the question that slips most often into my head is this: in another time and place, could we have been lovers?

Don't be daft, Alan, I tell myself. She wasn't your class, or even your age.

At the time, I didn't even know her first name.

2

I saw Chris and Susie just the once while they were staying down there in Oxford, even though I was entitled to a monthly rail ticket. Perhaps I should have made the effort to see them more often, but I thought the kids were really lucky, tucked up warm and well-fed in a comfortable billet while the rest of us were roughing it back in Peckham.

This was in early January of 1945, and as soon as I clapped eyes on him I could see Chris hoped I'd come all that way just so's I could take him and Susie back to London with me.

'No can do, Chris old chap,' I told him.

'We want to go home,' he whispered again. He had hold of my arm, and his grip was so hard it hurt. I didn't have much meat on my bones in those days. 'She doesn't really want us here.'

He was referring to Miss Marlyn, of course. But I'd just met her, and I couldn't see what he was getting so worked up about. Sure, she was taller than most of the women I knew, and had the easy authority of people of her class, men and women both, but she'd seemed pleasant enough. Her face was made up of straight lines, sharp angles, and had the hard sheen of ivory – and Chris and Susie probably thought she looked like a witch out of one of their story books, but she smiled at me in a friendly way and offered me a cup of tea with sugar, and even a currant bun to go with it. The kids are just homesick, I thought. They don't know when they're well off. There's nothing more to it than that.

And Susie appeared happy enough, even if Chris didn't.

'Danny Watts has a new puppy,' she told me, holding on tight to my other hand. 'He says I can take it out for a walk one of these days.'

'That's because he's getting bored with it,' said her brother. He could always see through other people, our Chris.

Miss Marlyn's eyes were on a level with mine and she didn't bother to look away when I stared at her. They were hazel eyes, and I found myself snared by them. Ocean-green, flecked with brown. And she had the black lashes and eyebrows that seem to go with that colouring. She looked straight at me all the time we were speaking, as though interested in every trite phrase I uttered.

I drank the tea she handed me, sitting at the kitchen table. I watched it pour from the pot, a rich mahogany colour, not the pale stuff we'd been reduced to as we reached the end of the week's ration. I helped myself to two heaped spoonfuls of sugar – she didn't blink at my extravagance – and topped up the cup with milk from a blue and white jug. The currant bun was plump and stuffed with fruit and even had a smear of marge on it. When I'd drunk the tea and eaten my currant bun I scraped out the bottom of the cup with my spoon to reach the last of the damp, sweet sugar grains. If I'd been on my own I'd have licked out the cup like a dog, but I'd learned to control myself, though the effort I was making must have shown in my face. I could feel a nerve jumping at the corner of my mouth, but I knew how to behave in civilised company. When I'd done with the cup, I licked my index finger and ran it round the plate, picking up every last crumb, sucking my finger to make sure I hadn't missed a single one. I caught Chris giving me a funny look, but he dropped his eyes when he saw me watching him. There was a flash of pink across his cheekbones as though my behaviour

embarrassed him. You don't know the half of it, Chris! I didn't
care what he thought, I wasn't going to waste food. I'd learnt
its value the hard way. I didn't waste it then and I don't waste it
now.

Susie was bouncing up and down on her chair and smiling at
me, revealing the gaps in her teeth where the baby ones were
starting to fall out. Chris was showing the first signs of the
moody adolescent he would soon become, I thought then. I
suppose kids grow up faster during a war, but he'd been easier
when he'd been a carefree little kid like Susie, learning to kick
a ball around in the park with me and Harry on Sunday
afternoons.

I needed the little snack Miss Marlyn gave me. I'd walked all
the way, most of it uphill, from the railway station to her house
in Armitage Road, Headington. The journey from Paddington
had taken more than three hours in an unheated railway carriage.
The train chugged through the dishevelled London suburbs at a
bare fifteen miles an hour, only picking up speed once we had
reached the sad brown countryside. And then it sat in unmarked
stations for no reason that I could see, while the cold and damp
seeped through to my bones. The compartment smelled of
damp serge, unwashed bodies and stale cigarette smoke. People
spoke in a desultory sort of way, as though they had a duty to
be friendly. You could hear them thinking, 'Have to make an
effort. There's a war on.' They spoke of yesterday's raid and
swapped their favourite bomb stories. Then someone repeated
a joke from last night's *ITMA*, and everyone joined in the
laughter.

'Soon be over, now,' said a man in RAF blue.

I don't know whether he meant our journey or the war, but
both seemed to be drawing to a close.

Most of the other passengers were in uniform and they

7

looked at me as I entered, as though wondering why I wasn't, and then looked away again quickly. I suppose they could read in the lines of my face that I had done my bit and now was judged unfit for service.

At one of the anonymous stations a woman in a green uniform wheeled a trolley stacked with cartons labelled *Lunchboxes. One shilling.* With difficulty I stopped myself from leaning out of the window to buy one, though two of the other people in the compartment did so. You never knew when you'd get your next meal in those trains with no buffet car. But I was meeting Chris and Susie for dinner, I reminded myself. I didn't need two meals at midday.

A young woman entered the compartment after that and squeezed into the seat opposite. She had the smooth oval face and gash of scarlet lipstick that they were all wearing that year. Rows of them, all the same, standing in queues, sitting in buses, in railway carriages. Identical and interchangeable. This one wore a navy coat with square shoulders in a shoddy cloth that looked much too thin for the bitter weather. Then I saw that she sat with a bulging shopping bag balanced on her knees. I suppose she, too, was visiting her children, taking them whatever little treats she had managed to save from her rations, and which were too precious to remove from her sight for a single moment. I had a knapsack myself up on the rack, stuffed with comics and sweets and carrying the letters which Sheila had laboured over at the kitchen table the previous evening. You wanted to take them the moon from the sky to make up for the long separation, but this little bag full of trinkets would have to do for now. I smiled at her to show I understood her, but she primmed her mouth and turned her head away as though I had made an obscene remark.

I tried to settle my gaze on the other men in the compartment, to save her embarrassment. The faces around me looked exhausted, their fatigue etched on to the greyish skin. Did they look so ashen-faced from the grime that filmed everything that passed through Paddington Station, or was it more permanent than that? It looked to me as though they could never wash it off. I'd noticed this uniform drabness as soon as I got back to England – as soon as I was well enough to notice anything at all, that is. Apart from the exhaustion, it was due to a lack of soap, and of time to clean things properly. Maybe cleaning things was the lowest of people's priorities when they had to struggle hard just to survive. I don't suppose I'd have noticed it, either, if I'd spent the past four years in this country.

After half an hour I was getting restless. I'm not good in confined spaces and the compartment was just too full of other people's bodies. I wanted to open a window, but knew it would make me unpopular with the other passengers. I tried looking out at the passing countryside but the rain and the gusting wind made all seem shifting and impermanent. Hills and fields, hedges, houses, were alternately hidden and revealed until I gave up trying to make sense of what I saw. Maybe I dozed off, but the landscape turned into a nightmare one where nothing was what it seemed and enemies might lurk in any copse, hidden by the mist.

When we finally arrived in Oxford, and I'd taken my rucksack down from the rack, helped the woman in the thin coat on to the platform and pushed my way to the outside of the station, I found that it was wetter than ever. Sky, air, buildings all blanketed in grey. Bare trees dripping. Muddy water swirling down the gutters. I shouldered my pack, checked the directions I'd been given for Headington, and set off through the town, aiming north-east.

Just another provincial town, I thought, as I looked around

me. I couldn't see much of its vaunted colleges – just the
occasional archway and sturdy oak door, firmly closed against
the likes of me. I crossed a bridge over flooded water meadows,
heard the mournful quacking of ducks, then followed a road
leading to the outskirts of the town. I could have taken a bus,
but I'd been shut in for long enough, sitting in that railway
carriage. I needed the open air, even if it was cold and damp.
The air smelled of wet, rotting cabbage: the smell of January in
the country. London smelled of the smoke from coal fires,
escaping gas and fractured sewers.

I looked over the hedges at the suburban redbrick houses:
all those respectable households had dug up their neat lawns
and tidy flowerbeds and planted potatoes and carrots, Brussels
sprouts and cabbages where once the asters and roses had
bloomed.

They hadn't seen any doodlebugs out here, but the people
didn't look any the happier for it. Sour faces on the passers-by.
Army trucks, their loads covered with painted camouflage
tarpaulins, passed me on the way up the hill. Then a tradesman's
van, delivering to one of the posh houses. The driver was an
old, wizened man who looked as though he'd learned to drive
in the last war. Then a Jeep. You don't see many Americans
about since they went off to Normandy, but they say there are
dozens of aerodromes in the county and he must have come
from one of them. Apart from the van, they were all driving
fast. Bloody Yank showing off to the local girls, I reckoned,
and the English speed merchants all would-be Malcolm
Campbells. A motorbike zoomed past at sixty, so close that it
splashed through the swirling water in the gutter and covered
me with a thick, muddy spray. Dispatch rider! Hurrying home
to his dinner, more like.

The wind was blowing straight into my face and I think it

10

carried flakes of sleet, but maybe my memory's just added that for the effect. I do know I would have preferred it if it had snowed. At least the sun might have come out afterwards and cheered us all up instead of hiding behind the bank of cloud. Even at midday you could tell that it wouldn't stay light much longer. The dark, sullen day would drift downwards into dusk by three o'clock.

I reminded myself that this little trip wasn't for my own benefit. I'd come to see Harry's kids and bring them cheerful news of their home, even if most of it was made up for the occasion.

3

My shoes were sodden and water was dripping down inside the collar of my mac by the time I got to Armitage Road – High Corner, the house was called. The first thing I noticed was two white ovals at the window. Chris and Susie. When I saw those two anxious faces pressed to the glass, I stopped regretting that I'd ever agreed to visit them. Poor little buggers must have been there for hours, looking out for me, hoping I'd get there. And yet, if I'm honest, I resented it! I wasn't ready to take on so much responsibility for their happiness. They shouldn't have asked that of me.

Susie spotted me first and her whole face widened into a smile. Chris had his hand on her shoulder as though keeping her under control.

I hitched the rucksack into a more comfortable position and walked up the front path, fixing a smile on my own face. *It's being so cheerful that keeps me going.* The memory of last night's wireless programme turned the made-up smile into a real one.

I heard a chicken squawking from somewhere out the back. They'd have fresh eggs, then. Back in Reckitt Street someone had tried to keep ducks – bigger eggs, she said – but the buggers all died of heart attacks when the air raids started.

This front garden was a good size, with a herring-bone pattern path leading to the front door. On one side of the house someone had built a small garage, its bricks still raw red next

13

to the weathered fabric of the house itself. The garden might once have boasted a neat lawn and some venerable shrubs, but now the grass had been dug up and the plot was a miserable sight with clumps of yellowing Brussels plants and a few winter cabbages whose outside leaves were a lacework of holes left by the slugs and snails. Not all the shrubs had been rooted out, though. There was a cotoneaster and something fernlike and evergreen. It wouldn't take long to get it back to its pre-war splendour once this show was done with. Not much like South London, it seemed to me. We wouldn't get back to normal in Reckitt Street for a good few years yet.

I waved at the kids and rang the bell. The white faces disappeared. I waited. Water ran in a small stream from the gutter on to my head and so I moved forward a foot or two until my face was only inches from the door. When it opened I was eye to eye with the woman who stood there. She was no longer young, but with a striking face and a gaze that took in my bedraggled appearance and made me feel no more important than the drowned rat I must have resembled. I didn't like that. I forced myself to stare straight back at her, and I saw the approval in her face. No scarlet lipstick for her, either.

She had pulled her hair back from her face and tied it in a knot at the nape of her neck, as though she didn't care what she looked like. But I could tell that it was thick, and wavy, and probably difficult to keep tidy. There were a few grey hairs among the dark brown, but you hardly noticed them. I wondered for a moment what she would look like with her hair undone, massed around her shoulders, framing that arrogant face with the gleaming skin and the hazel eyes that stared at me from under the black lashes. Deep grooves were incised from nostrils to chin, and vertical lines between her eyes gave her an air of disapproval. But then she smiled and the smile lit up her face and took years off her age. There was something in her expression that made me think she was quite aware of the effect on people of her smile, and she wasn't averse to using it to her own advantage. It turned her into an attractive woman.

'I am Miss Marlyn,' she said, just like that, as though it was all anyone needed to know – and it probably was in those parts. She looked as though she was used to being the queen of the neighbourhood. Certainly she made me all too aware of the shabbiness of my mac, the way my hair was plastered over my forehead, and the shoddiness of my shoes. I realised then that I should have been wearing a hat.

'Alan Barnes,' I said after a moment's silence. 'Christopher and Susan's uncle,' I added.

When had I last called them by their full given names? That was the effect she had on me, though she was hardly a fashion plate. She was wearing corduroy trousers and a plain v-neck pullover in navy blue, with a shirt in the colour I think they call biscuit; her shoes were well-polished brogues. She had a mannish, upright figure and the masculine clothes suited her: a plain enough get-up, and nothing fashionable about it, but still it shouted quality. The pullover looked so soft I wanted to stroke it with my fingers; it could have been cashmere. She must have bought her clothes up Piccadilly way, back in the thirties, before the war.

She opened the door wider and stepped back to allow me to enter. She smelled of carnation-scented soap and it wasn't until some time later that I realised I hadn't smelled anything like it since before the war. There was a lobby behind the front door where the kids had left their gumboots and where a faded black umbrella leant dripping against the side wall. On the other side was a bentwood coatstand with a patched tweed jacket hanging from it and beside it a brass bucket just for holding walking

15

sticks. In front of us another door with fronds and petals of coloured glass in its panels stood open on to a square hall.

The kids hadn't come out into the hall when the doorbell rang: I imagine they were feeling shy. They hadn't seen me for a long time, and I was no oil painting in those days. When I got up close to the windows, where they could see me properly, I'd probably terrified the little blighters. I stood in the hall, aware of the pools of water forming by my shoes on Miss Marlyn's polished wooden floor. I half-expected some minion to appear with a mop to tell me to clean up the mess, but Miss Marlyn just went on smiling that brilliant smile of hers and pulled a small, plain mat across for me to stand on. She must have kept that scrap of rug handy for just such occasions as this.

I could feel the wealth that lay behind that hallway like a solid object. Maybe it was the warmth that seemed to enfold us and wrap us around, so different from the small, sharp flames from the coal fire in the living room back in Peckham whose heat never penetrated further than a foot or two away from its heart. Or maybe it was the smell of good food – meal upon meal with meat and vegetables, or toast, bacon and eggs, and coffee (yes, I could smell coffee!) – breathing out from the polished wood and gold-and-white striped wallpaper. Everything was clean and bright, as though it had just been redecorated. I daresay I'm letting my imagination rip, filling in details that were never there, or reading too much into those few minutes in the hall of High Corner. All I know is that at that moment, I didn't feel resentment at her moneyed comfort, rather was I relieved that the children had fallen into such a good billet. We'd heard lurid stories about kids who'd been sent to villages where there was no electricity or running water and no lav but a bucket in a shed at the bottom of the garden. This place was as civilised as London and I could tell they would be warm and well-fed, even if they'd been homesick for Peckham at first. They couldn't be unhappy for long in a house like this.

What is no twist of my imagination is that Miss Marlyn gave me a look as though amused at my pinched face and dripping coat, and switched on the lights.

'That's better,' she said. 'Isn't it, Mr Barnes?'

It was so much better that it hurt my eyes.

The hall was completely closed in. Quite private, I saw. No one on the outside could see what she had just done – flicking a switch and shaming the dull winter's day. The show was just for the two of us.

I turned round slowly while she watched me, pleased as a child with the effect her action had on me.

There were wall lights, like candles with brass shades. There were lights that showed the pictures to their best advantage. There was a standard lamp and a hard chair in one corner in case you wanted to sit and read your newspaper. And from the centre of the ceiling hung a chandelier, and every bulb on it was blazing. Someone had cleaned the dangling flakes of glass so that they shone and sparkled like gemstones. They shivered in the slight draught from the door and gave off a musical, tinkling sound like distant sleighbells.

She was burning enough electricity to light the whole of Reckitt Street and beyond. I know you wouldn't look twice at something like that these days, but then, such a short time after they'd relaxed the blackout regulations, it seemed as though she was simply tearing up five-pound notes. I think it was that wanton waste of electricity – and it was hardly past midday – that brought home to me what sort of house the children were living in.

The hall wasn't just brighter than the winter sky outside, it was brighter than anything I'd seen since Italy. We had nothing

17

stronger than 40 watts back in Reckitt Street, and we switched off anything that wasn't strictly necessary.

I tried not to show my surprise. I can't say I was disgusted at the waste because inside I was as pleased as a kid to see the show. And I could tell it gave her pleasure, just to show off her wealth. It wasn't simply a question of the money: it was a kind of defiance, as though she was standing back from the years of denial and telling us all that she didn't give a damn.

'I'll fetch the children,' she said, and disappeared through a door to her right.

I was left standing there in the hall. I'd never before been in a house where space was used so extravagantly. The house in Peckham had a narrow corridor running from front to back, with the stairs rising up just a couple of feet inside the front door. But this hall was large and square, with a rug in shades of dark red and russet on the polished wooden floor. There were pictures on the wall – oil paintings of trees and lakes and purple mountains, mostly. And not exactly a row of ancestors, but a few dull paintings of men who might have been aldermen or something in the Chamber of Commerce. There was just one portrait of a woman amongst them, a commanding old witch who looked enough like Miss Marlyn to be her sister. On sunny days, when someone opened the front door, the coloured glass in the panes would have scattered bright jewels of light across the floor, like in a church. No one would dare to throw their coat and hat down here the way we sometimes did at home.

There were several doors leading off the hall, and I was just wondering where on earth they could all lead to when Chris and Susie came in with Miss Marlyn. The children holding on to her hands slowed her down and she had to take small steps instead of her normal long, rapid ones. They're anchoring her to the ground, I thought. She can't fly while she's holding on to them. They came to a halt right underneath the chandelier and the three figures, under the moving discs of light, were posed like a picture in a book. Not an illustration from a fairy tale, but one of those grim Civil War scenes, perhaps, with the children being led in for interrogation. It's just your imagination, Alan, I told myself. They were all as friendly as anything together.

She was urging the children to approach me, but they seemed reluctant, hanging back. She looked amused by the situation, but spoke to them gently enough.

'It's your Uncle Alan,' she reminded them. 'You're not going to play shy with him, are you?' And then Chris finally moved away from her and took a step towards me. Susie followed, but more hesitantly.

Someone had recently scrubbed them. Their skin shone pink and their hair was flattened into a semblance of good order. Chris was wearing the grey flannel shorts that he wore for school, and a navy belted gabardine mac. Susie had her hair scraped back into wispy plaits tied with navy ribbons, and she, too, had on what looked like a grey pleated school skirt and her navy mac. I guess they had dressed themselves in their best, as they saw it.

'Hello, kids!' I said in my jolly uncle voice. Chris gave me a half smile, but Susie was still po-faced. She was always shy.

It was at this point that Miss Marlyn invited me into the kitchen for that cup of tea. She must have noticed how awkward we looked. I was relieved: it might help to break the ice. The children had been staying at High Corner since the previous July and it probably seemed more like home to them than our place in Reckitt Street by then. I wouldn't have blamed them if they'd never wanted to leave this warm, comfortable house.

Miss Marlyn led the way, I followed her, and the children trailed behind us. As we passed the picture I thought was her sister, she said, 'My Aunt Margaret. She left me this house in her will. It's belonged to my family since the day it was built.'

'It's a fine house,' I said lamely. But Miss Marlyn had walked on as though she had already said too much. I followed her through one of the doors leading off the hall and down a passageway to the kitchen. As the children and I settled ourselves at the scrubbed wood table, she hung my mac up by the range so that it would warm up a bit, even if it was still wet when I put it back on. Considerate of her, I thought. She didn't look the domesticated type, but we'd all had to change with the war, and the likes of Miss Marlyn were no exception.

The kitchen was a gloomy enough place, with stone-coloured walls, a high ceiling and tiny windows, but the range kept it cosy and there were aluminium pans hanging up on hooks on the wall, and what looked like copper jelly moulds and strainers. The floor was made of quarry tiles and there were old rag rugs to add a bit of cheer. It might not have been very posh but it was still a lot different from our little kitchen at home with the American cloth on the table and the draught from the back door cutting your legs off at the knee. There hadn't been much coal to feed our poky range, and we didn't light the fire in the lounge until six o'clock in the evening when we went in to listen to the news on the wireless.

'I'm afraid you'll have to take the children out for their lunch, Mr Barnes,' Miss Marlyn said, watching me as I dealt with the currant bun. I realised that she was referring to our dinners. 'I have one of my committee meetings in an hour's time, and then I must go and check my allotment.'

She looked as though she'd be more at home on the allotment than she would in the committee meeting – though goodness

knows what you could do on an allotment on a wet day in January. Then I imagined all those ladies sitting round the table in their costumes and hats while she lorded it over them in mud-spattered corduroy trousers and I smiled at the thought.

'Good,' she said, seeing the smile and misunderstanding its cause. 'It'll be much more comfortable for you all to go off on your own and get to know each other again. I believe there's a very nice municipal restaurant just a short walk down the road. Back towards the town,' she added. 'You can have a good lunch there for ninepence, they tell me. And only fourpence each for the children.' I wondered fleetingly whether she had ever eaten there herself. She was more likely to patronise the big hotel I'd passed in the centre of the town. Three and six your lunch would set you back if you ate there, I reckon.

I said, 'I think the bank can afford one and fivepence,' reverting to my jolly uncle voice, and with an encouraging smile at Chris. He'd been having trouble with his arithmetic, his letters had informed us.

The children had taken a seat each at the table, too, though they hadn't removed their macs. I had a chance then to look at them properly. If they hadn't been my niece and nephew I don't think I'd have been too impressed. Chris's bony knees poked out from under his mac and were covered in bruises and scabs. His face was winter-white and he had a couple of ugly cold sores in the corners of his mouth. His hair was cut as short as a squaddie's and Brylcreemed down against his scalp so that he already looked like a rainsoaked ferret, even before we ventured out into the winter's day. Then I noticed that his ears stuck out, just like his Dad's, and for some reason the sight of them made me want to cry. Harry's gone, I thought, and all that's left to remind me of my young brother is this kid's ears. I blew my nose and returned to my currant bun.

21

If Chris was a skinny little kid, Susie made up for it by being on the podgy side. Her mother was quite plump before the TB got to her. I couldn't see much else of Sheila in her, though, or of Harry. I suppose it was because she was sort of unformed, the bones of her face hidden under the soft layer of fat. Her ears were covered by a woolly hat, but I expect they stuck out just like Chris's, and Harry's, and mine. Her face was as pale as Chris's, except for her button of a nose, which was pink. The poor girl had obviously just got over a cold. Her short, plump legs bulged above the garters in her socks and she was swinging them so that they banged against the chair. It wasn't till I noticed her hands with their short fingers, the tips with thick pads and the nails bitten right down, nearly to the cuticles, just like Harry's – and mine too, if it came to that – that I saw that she was every bit a part of my flesh and bone as Chris was. The cold hadn't quite left her, for she sniffed, hard.

'Use your handkerchief, Susan, the way I showed you.' Miss Marlyn spoke quite mildly, but I didn't like it all the same. Harry and Sheila had taught their children how to blow their noses, hadn't they? She wasn't talking to slum kids, I wanted to tell her. But Susie was pulling a handkerchief out of her pocket and blowing her nose obediently, so I didn't say anything.

If the Barnes family had run to ancestral portraits, I thought as I watched the children, what would they have looked like? Pale, peaky faces and ears like jug-handles, stubby hands with bitten nails, and handkerchiefs raised towards the pink button noses. I found myself smiling, and my heart filled with – I was going to say 'love', but who am I to use that word?

Susie was perking up a bit, getting used to me again. Her face seemed more used to smiling than Chris's did.

'Remember the way I used to take you for rides on my shoulder?' I asked her.

'Yes,' she breathed, though I doubt whether she really did remember.

'I remember playing football,' said Chris, and I'm sure he was thinking about his father.

'And how is their mother?' asked Miss Marlyn, as though the children had no ears. Sheila didn't want them to know just how bad she'd been this winter and I wasn't going to disagree with that.

'She's getting along just fine,' I said brightly.

'Then we can go home soon,' said Chris. Miss Marlyn looked as though she would have liked to say the same thing but was too polite to do so.

'Give her a chance to get her strength back,' I said. 'Being poorly's taken a lot out of her.'

'We should go to the seaside,' said Chris earnestly. 'That's what the doctor said.'

'That's not on the cards. Think of all the barbed wire they've put up to keep Jerry out,' I answered, not meeting the lad's eyes.

'They say it will be over by the summer,' put in Miss Marlyn. 'Perhaps you could all go away then.'

'Perhaps,' I said. Perhaps we could all go away to the South of France, did she mean? That was where the likes of her would go. Or up on a Swiss mountain. The likes of me and Sheila just stayed and festered in South London.

'I like it here sometimes,' said Susie, getting bolder.

'I hope you're not forgetting your Mum,' I said.

'It must be hard for you and your sister-in-law,' said Miss Marlyn. 'Still, I'm sure you'd both rather be up there in' – she'd forgotten the name of our suburb – 'er, London, instead of running away to the country like these hysterical women we've been asked to deal with. They turn up on the outskirts of the town, pushing a pram and carrying half their household with them. How are we supposed to cope? They're just lacking in moral fibre, I tell the Billeting Officer.' She looked quite fierce for a moment but I had no sympathy for her. What did she know of air raids and casualties? I just nodded and chewed on the last mouthful of currant bun.

'Here,' I said, suddenly remembering the kitbag of tuck I'd brought the kids from home. I pulled it up on to the table and handed over comics and a blue paper bag each full of boiled sweets. Not much, but the best that Dobson's could do that week. The kids fell on them eagerly enough.

'And your Mum made you this,' I said to Susie. 'It's a new outfit for that teddy bear of yours.'

Just made out of scraps, but it looked really good. Susie's eyes widened with pleasure, then brimmed over. 'I wish she was here,' she whispered. So I suppose she hadn't really forgotten her.

'It's not a bear, it's a rabbit,' said Chris. 'She calls him Betsy.' I didn't ask whether the rabbit was a girl or a boy.

'And I think you asked for a penknife,' I said to Chris. 'Your Mum found you this one.' Actually it was an old one of mine, and I hadn't shown it to Sheila. She was funny about knives.

'It's smashing,' he said, and his voice, too, was all choked up. I suppose it brought their Mum nearer and yet reminded them that she wasn't there.

'Christopher would have found a new pair of socks quite useful,' said Miss Marlyn. I'd forgotten her for the moment, but now I looked at her again. I wasn't sure I read her expression right. It was almost as if she was jealous of the few little treats I'd brought for the children.

'I'll send him a pair,' I said quickly. 'Two pairs, maybe.'

'And they'll be needing new shoes, both of them, before long.'

'They'll have everything they need,' I said firmly. I wasn't going to be put in what she thought of as 'my place' by her.

'It's as well to keep your priorities straight,' she added.

'And that's what Chris and Susie will always be to me. My priorities,' I said. That silenced her. And when were *you* last someone's top priority, I could have asked her, but there was no need to be cruel.

There came a rap at the door at the back of the kitchen and I realised it must lead to the outside world. We were so well cocooned in this house that I had nearly forgotten that another world existed outside its walls.

Without waiting for any invitation, two men walked in.

'Arthur and Danny,' said Miss Marlyn. 'You're earlier than I expected.'

'Van's in the garage,' said the younger man.

'And we saw Pescod, like you said,' said the other.

Miss Marlyn interrupted him. 'Why don't you pull up a couple of chairs and pour yourselves a cup of tea.' She spoke pleasantly enough, but the atmosphere in the kitchen had changed. The two men stared at me as though wondering who I was.

The older of the two was thickset, with a lot of very black hair, not just on his head, but sprouting from nostrils and eyebrows and the backs of his hands, too, I saw when he took his gloves off.

'The rest of the news can wait till later,' he said, taking the teapot and pouring out tea for himself and his companion before dragging over a couple of chairs. The legs grated on the stone flags, setting my teeth on edge. Before sitting down he opened his coat and I could see that underneath it he was wearing a suit

– a formal kind with a waistcoat and a shirt with an old-fashioned, stiff collar. The suit was old, and shabby; it could have done with some cleaning, and didn't fit his body, as though some fatter, softer man had owned it before him. He smelled of the outdoors and of beer.

The younger man was thinner and dressed more casually. He had a small black dog, just a puppy really, on a string. He made it sit by his feet, but the animal kept jumping up to explore the kitchen and the people who sat round the table.

'Bonnie,' said Susie, showing the gaps in her teeth. 'It's Bonnie.' And she climbed down from her chair without a 'Please may I get down?' and started to make a fuss of the animal.

I thought Miss Marlyn would tell her off for her lapse in manners, but she ignored it and all she said was, 'This is Alan Barnes, the children's uncle. And these are Arthur and Danny Watts, who work for me.' There was something in her voice that made me think she was giving them instructions rather than stating a simple truth.

We didn't say much to each other. Maybe we all felt inhibited by Miss Marlyn's presence, or maybe there was something going on between them that I didn't understand.

'Time to be going,' I said, when I'd licked my forefinger and chased the last of the crumbs round the plate. I put my damp mac on, Susie petted the dog for one last time, and we traipsed in a procession back through the house and out of the front door. Miss Marlyn pulled a curtain across the glass panes in the door so that passers-by couldn't see the blaze of light in her hall.

4

In spite of the rain, which was coming down harder than ever, and the cold, which seemed keener than it did in London, I could feel the eagerness in the children as they pulled me outside and down the brick path. Even the gate closed with a well-oiled click that spoke of money. I put their eagerness to be away down to their pleasure at seeing a familiar face, one that belonged to their own family. Not so many of us left now. Just me and Sheila really, since Harry was posted 'missing, believed dead'. Sheila still hoped she'd hear from him, or see him turn up at the front door, but I knew my brother was dead all right – probably blown into so many pieces that they never could identify him. But I wasn't going to tell Sheila that, not in her state of health.

We turned towards the town centre and when we'd walked a hundred yards or so I suggested we should sing a song to help us on our way. It was then that Chris asked me if I was taking them back to London with me.

'Are we going home now, Uncle Alan?'

Susie's face, round and white, framed by her leaf-green pixie hood, was turned up to mine. She looked as though someone had switched on a lightbulb behind her pale blue eyes.

I saw the disappointment in his eyes when I shook my head, but he was a brave kid, and he just took Susie's hand and held it tight. The light in her face switched off again as she clutched Chris's hand.

We walked back down the hill, trying to find somewhere to shelter from the rain and warm our frozen fingers. I started them off singing 'One man went to mow', and they sang out gamely enough. I ignored the pleading in Chris's face and reminded myself that they were being properly looked after, safe from the daily raids on South London. It was only natural that they should miss their mother, but the war couldn't last much longer, and then they'd be home again. Better a little homesickness now than risk their lives. Kids are resilient. They soon get over things. Don't they?

There was none of the bomb damage here I was used to seeing in London, but the place looked dingy and uncared-for. None of the houses had had a lick of paint for the past five years, and it showed.

I suppose that any walk with an unhappy child seems slower and longer than it really is. We dragged along the wet streets, singing endless verses of 'Ten green bottles' once we'd done 'One man went to mow' to death, until we reached the scatter of shops and offices where Miss Marlyn had told us we would find the restaurant. Restaurant! That was an inflated term to use, I realised, when we found the place. The authorities had done their best, painting it inside in cheerful shades of yellow and green. But that had been three or four years ago, and now the walls and ceiling were stained with tobacco smoke and even the jolly pictures of smiling girls in apple orchards, or overloaded with unlikely sheaves of corn, were hazed and bleary. The floor was of lino in a wood-block pattern, scarred with discarded cigarette butts and traces of spilled food.

An arthritic waitress with grey curls under her jaunty white cap laboriously scrawled our order down on her pad. She took obvious pleasure in telling us that 'sausages were off', so we settled for roast mutton, boiled potatoes and Brussels sprouts, followed by jam tart and custard. The mutton was grey and striped with yellow seams of fat. The sprouts were cooked to a khaki mush and the potatoes tasted old and earthy, and were spotted with black eyes. But the pudding was pretty good: steaming hot and very sweet. The jam was red, but I couldn't tell whether it was supposed to be strawberry or raspberry. The rumour was that they made it from turnips or swedes and added small wooden pips to make it look like fruit. I just remember it as wonderfully sugary, and the custard of the right, thick consistency, with no lumps.

At one point in the meal I noticed that Chris was looking at me strangely again. I realised I was back with my old habits: running my finger round the plate to pick up the crumbs of pastry, licking it, longing to pick the bowl up and lick that, too.

'That's Susie's,' he said, and I saw that I'd taken the last lump of tart from her bowl while her attention was on what her brother was saying.

'Sorry,' I said humbly. But I could hardly take it out of my mouth and put it back, could I? We swallowed without chewing, back there in the camp, and it's a habit that's hard to get out of. 'Sorry,' I said again, and this time it was as though I was apologising for the whole bloody shooting match and the fate that kept these two kids away from their mother for the last few months of her life.

'It's good though, isn't it?' I said.

They both nodded their heads. Going out to lunch was a real treat for them, and I don't suppose they noticed how lousy the food was. You couldn't expect kids to remember back over five years to better times. This was how their life had always been. They didn't know any different.

After lunch we found a cinema in Headington. The seats

were more expensive than I was used to, and from the grumbling by the other customers I wasn't alone in thinking I was being overcharged. But what else could you do with two kids on a winter's afternoon? It was hardly the weather for strolling in the park.

They were showing some sort of comedy flick. It didn't mean much to me, but the kids seemed to enjoy it and at least we were warm. We'd missed the newsreel, thank God, and we didn't wait to watch it when it came round again. I'd had enough of reality. I'd rather try to understand the humour in the Will Hay film.

Afterwards we went back to the restaurant for a cup of tea for me, orangeade for Chris and Susie. They asked me about Sheila and I told them a load of fibs.

'Why doesn't she come and live here?' asked Chris. 'We could get a place for the three of us.' He remembered his manners and added, 'Sorry, the four of us. I've seen the sort of place, and it would only cost a few shillings a week.'

How to argue with that? It made perfect sense to Chris and Susie, But Sheila didn't want them to see her the way she was now, didn't want to become dependent on her children the way she was on me. She would hate them to be woken in the morning by one of her coughing fits. Graveyard cough, I called it, but not to her face. She was sure the disease was going to abate again, the way it had before, that she'd be feeling right as ninepence in no time. That's what she said she believed, anyhow. In those days I thought that the children should be protected from the sights and sounds of their mother's dying weeks. I'm not so sure now. Who was it we were protecting from the truth – the children or ourselves?

'She needs warmth and good food,' I told Chris as gently as I could.

'There's good food here in the country,' he said earnestly. 'I've seen it.'

I remembered the fatty shaving of roast mutton we'd had for our dinner, but I didn't want to disagree with the lad. He was trying so hard. 'She'll find food and warmth easier to come by in London,' I said. 'It's always cold out here in the country, and back in London the local shopkeepers know her and do their best for us.' I could have been right, at that, but if I'd done what Chris wanted at least we would all have been together for those last few months.

It's hard to forgive myself now, at this distance of time, that I didn't go down to see them again a week or so later. I might even have found myself some digs for a few days. I would have understood the situation better if I'd been on the spot and ready to listen to what they had to tell me instead of being so keen to believe what was convenient. And we ought to have had them back at Christmas for a week or two, but then Sheila was in no condition to look after a couple of kids, and I was little better, recovering from my weeks on the run. I still wasn't getting much sleep at night, listening out for the arrival of imaginary Germans, while the all-too-real V2s sent me cowering down to the shelter. The doctor said I should try some newfangled tonic, but a half-bottle of whisky from under the counter at Dobson's did me more good, I reckon. At least it allowed me to forget, even if only for a few hours. That brief oblivion was all I asked for.

Miss Marlyn opened the door to us when we got back to High Corner. She didn't invite me in this time, but stood there for a moment, with a hand on each of the children's heads, as though giving a blessing, or telling me that they belonged to her now.

'Say goodbye to your Uncle Alan,' she said.

And, 'Goodbye, Uncle Alan,' they chorused dutifully.

'I'm sure everything will soon be sorted out at home,' she said bracingly. 'And then you'll all be back where you belong.'

I was getting used to her manner by now, though it grated on my nerves when she spoke to me as though addressing a meeting.

I stood on the step for a few moments after the door closed, neither wishing to stay nor wanting to go. The children must have rushed into the front room to catch sight of me as I walked down the road.

So I left them, just as I'd found them when I arrived, with their white faces pressed against the window, watching me as I disappeared out of their lives. I turned and waved, and I believe they waved back, but maybe my imagination's adding that as some small consolation.

5

I still have the first letter you wrote home, Chris. I keep it to console myself, and to convince myself that there was nothing to get worked up about, nothing that Sheila and I should be worrying about. There was no clue to what would happen in that brief page, was there?

Dear Mum,
    This is just to let you know we arrived safe and sound all right yesterday. We ate all the sandwiches you made us for the train, though Susie wouldn't finish her grated carrot even though I told her it would make her see in the dark. We are settled into our billet. We went on a bus as well as the train and then we had to go to the Baptist Hall where Miss King the Billeting Officer told us where we were to go next. She said to call her Auntie Naomi but we didn't. Luckily it wasn't very far from the hall and I carried Susie's suitcase for her though she looked after her own gas mask just like you told her.
    The billet is very nice and so is Miss Marlyn our foster mother and we are very well. Hope you are well too and there have been no more doodlebugs I hope. Will write again soon.
    With lots of love from your son, Christopher. XX
    PS. The second X is from Susie. She would have signed

her name too only she's already gone to sleep and I don't want to wake her up again. I think she was very tired after the journey.

The billet is very nice and so is Miss Marlyn our foster mother. Is that what you really thought, or did you write it because she was looking over your shoulder, Chris?

But I'm running ahead of myself, reading too much into your polite little sentences. I daresay you were just relieved to have the long journey over and to find that you were in a house with a clean bed and a meal on the table. I don't suppose Susie stayed awake for the meal. I can picture her sitting there at the table, her head drooping and her eyelids closing. I hope someone tucked her in and gave her a goodnight kiss, but then I expect you'd do that if no one else would. You're a good kid, Chris. *Were* a good kid, I should have said.

What can I say in my own defence? At the time I was too wrapped up in my own troubles, trying to adapt to life in England after the camp. And my major concern was to look after my brother's wife – widow, I should say – while she coughed her way through the final stages of that dreadful disease.

I thought the children were safe and well-looked after in that warm, prosperous house. It reminded me of a cat purring by the fireside, up there on its hill. A cat that had just drunk the top of the milk and eaten a whole tin of sardines. How was I supposed to know any different?

PART 2

OXFORD, 2000

1

'Look, sweetie, I know you haven't been well and you've been feeling a bit off-colour these last few months, but it's time to snap out of it. If you want a career as a writer you've got to get down to work.'

When her agent called her 'sweetie', Kate Ivory knew that she was due for some bad news. Estelle was trying hard to sound sympathetic – or *simpatico* as she would call it – but the effort she was making not to shout at Kate in rage and frustration was all too evident in her voice.

'You can't afford to stay away from the marketplace for much longer, Kate dear. People will have forgotten all about you and it will be hard for me to persuade an editor to read one of your manuscripts. You'd have to change your name and pretend you were someone young and exciting. You don't want to do that, do you?'

Kate had to admit that she would find it difficult to reinvent herself as a young and exciting person.

'Now, why not get down to some hard work? You'll feel much better for it. And ring me back in an hour with a really good idea for your next book.'

That was Estelle for you: find an idea – like that, out of the blue! – and phone her back. As though it were that easy.

A dreadful lethargy had come over Kate in the months since the near-fatal attack in Christ Church Cathedral. It wasn't only the ugly pink scar on her ribs, the ache in her side, or the way she got tired if she tried to walk for more than a few minutes at her usual brisk pace; it was as though someone had thrown a switch inside her head. During the weeks in hospital and the months of convalescence that followed, her personality had changed, and the bright, confident, active person she had once been had disappeared, and this pale, passive woman had come to take her place. She felt a stranger to herself and could understand why others grew impatient with her.

Recently she had made an effort to write, had stared at a blank computer screen for minutes on end before succumbing to Tetris (the only computer game a writer would admit to playing). She had even tried writing longhand in a pretty notebook, usually a surefire method of persuading the creative juices to flow, but could get no further than yet another description of the view from her window before reverting to an analysis of her own feelings. Once she had admitted on the page that she was frightened, of anything, of everything – even of her own words as they crept across the page – there was nothing left to say. After a page or two she had given up. No bright ideas, no vivid images, no riveting storylines. No point in trying to say anything. And she didn't fancy getting out to see new sights and talk to people so that she could spark off a plot or a character. She didn't want to leave the house, or even stir from the room where she had settled herself with a cup of coffee and a good novel. *If you stay here you're safe.* No need to make an effort. This chair was the only place to be. Never again should she go out into the streets and risk being attacked. The world was a dangerous place, even this small, apparently civilised corner of it.

She often thought about the woman who had tried to kill her. It wasn't as though she had looked like a monster – not at first glance, anyway. An insignificant woman, one you would pass in the street without noticing – though you might have to step aside to accommodate her bulk. And she had eyes that stared straight into yours. Anger stirred inside Kate: a small yellow flame that threatened to grow into a ravenous blaze that would consume her if she let it. If she carried on with this thought she would lose control of her feelings, and then what might she do? She knew she was capable of anything if once she allowed herself to erupt into a murderous rage.

Luckily the phone rang again. It was her mother, Roz.

'Kate?'

'Possibly,' she replied. For a moment she wondered if she could pretend to be out, or even to be someone else.

'Don't be silly,' said Roz briskly. 'I know it's you, Kate, and I bet you're sitting there with a mug of tepid coffee, wondering whether to read your library book or give up and go back to bed.' Roz knew her too well. That was the trouble with mothers.

'What was it you wanted?' she asked cautiously. Roz was not the sort to fuss, but even she had been showing signs of concern over her daughter's protracted convalescence. Kate wished she would go away and leave her alone.

'I was wondering how you were getting on with your new book,' said Roz. 'You have started on it, haven't you?'

'Have you been speaking to Estelle?'

There was a brief pause. 'Estelle? Who's she?'

So she had. Things must be serious if Estelle had sunk so low as to phone her mother.

'You've been talking about me behind my back. Discussing my private affairs.'

'Estelle phoned your old number by mistake. It was out of habit, not from some dark motive. Since I'm living here, I answered and we drifted into a conversation about you. She's concerned about your health. We both are.' She means my

39

mental health, Kate translated. They all think I'm losing my marbles. 'There's nothing sinister going on,' Roz continued bracingly. 'Stop making a fuss and answer the question. Have you started on your new book yet?'

'No. I'm not sure I'm ever going to write anything again.'

Roz sensibly ignored the dramatics. 'So what are you going to do with your life? You aren't going to lie on a sofa for ever like the Récamier woman, are you? Even the lovely George might grow tired of seeing you lazing there for another month or two.'

Lovely George would never grow tired of her. Would he? 'I might get a part-time job,' she said.

'Really? It might lead to something, I suppose, if you're lucky. I'm not sure what qualifications you've managed to pick up over the years, but perhaps you've learned some little thing you could use to earn a living. Working in a shop, perhaps. Or would that be too demanding? Doing a little copy-typing in an office might suit you.'

'I'm a writer!' Kate retorted.

'Not unless you write,' replied Roz crisply. 'Lying around feeling sorry for yourself doesn't count, I'm afraid. So what are you going to do about it? You were never short of ideas before.' That 'before' hung in the air. Neither of them referred to the attack in the cathedral.

'I did sketch out an idea for something set during the French Revolution, rather along the lines of the Scarlet Pimpernel stories but with a young woman as heroine. But now Estelle tells me there's no longer a market for historical romances like that,' said Kate, trying to keep the note of self-pity out of her voice and failing. But even as she spoke it aloud she realised what a crap idea it was.

'So what *does* she want you to write?'

'Something modern.'

'You can manage that.'

'All about thirty-somethings with colourful sex lives wondering whether they should commit themselves to a relationship, then settle down and have babies,' said Kate gloomily.

'Something you obviously know nothing about,' said Roz drily.

'It's no good winding me up,' said Kate. 'I'm too tired to respond.'

'I'm about to say something unforgivable like "snap out of it".'

'I've tried snapping but it didn't work. Have you any other brilliant suggestions? If not, I'll hang up.'

'Wait a minute. Tell me, when Estelle talks about "modern", what does she mean, exactly?'

'I've told you. Thirty-somethings—'

'No. I understood that part. Tell me more about the setting. It occurred to me that the part of writing a book that you've always enjoyed is the research,' interrupted Roz quickly, before Kate could spin herself into a downward spiral of self-pity and depression. 'And you could cope with a little gentle background reading at the moment, even if you can't face the empty page with Chapter One typed at the top of it.'

'So?' But at last Kate felt a prickle of interest – more than she had a moment or two before.

'Why can't you set your story in the recent past: some time during the last fifty years, say. Hasn't everyone been writing their World War One novel? I'm sure Estelle would be delighted if you wrote yours.' Roz's perception of dates was as bad as ever, Kate noticed.

'She'd only tell me there's no market for it,' she said.

'You're being negative again. But even if you don't want to

write about trench warfare at the moment, you could set something in the thirties, couldn't you? The fifties?' There was still no response from Kate. 'What about the sixties?' Roz was sounding slightly desperate by now.

'I'll think about it,' said Kate, putting her mother out of her misery before she ran out of decades. 'You may have something,' she added grudgingly. 'I said I'd leave it for an hour and then ring Estelle back. Perhaps there's an idea there. Goodness knows I need one.'

In spite of herself, Kate felt her spirits rise an inch or two. 'Bye, Roz.'

She pushed her novel aside. She hadn't managed to get into it, somehow – just couldn't concentrate on anything these days. She took the cold coffee out to the kitchen. When she had first moved into George's house in Cavendish Road, this was the room which had been hardest to get used to. Nothing was ever quite where you expected it to be in someone else's kitchen, and you couldn't put your hand on exactly the right saucepan the way you could in your own place. But that's what moving in with someone's all about, she told herself. Adapting, fitting yourself around their life.

She tipped the coffee down the sink and rinsed the mug under the tap, scouring it out with the blue brush that she had bought last week. Now at last it was starting to feel as if this kitchen had always been hers. It was the one in Agatha Street that would feel strange if she went back there. Doubtless Roz had brought in *her* own favourite washing-up liquid by now, and her own favourite brand of soap. Not that Kate was thinking about returning to Agatha Street. The arrangement with George felt permanent, and she was sure he thought the same. And it had been working pretty well for a couple of months now – which was six weeks longer than she had ever lasted before in a live-in relationship.

She'd told Roz and Estelle that she'd think about her next novel, and she would. But she could do that just as well when she was doing something else, preferably something practical. If she was honest, she didn't really do much thinking about her writing, and even less in the way of planning, once she'd completed her background research. She just let her stories well up out of the sludge that was her subconscious, following the storyline wherever it decided to travel. But she wasn't going to admit that to Estelle, or even to Roz. It would only interfere with their stereotype of the well-organised author.

She put the mug back in its place in the cupboard. Now that she was upright and walking, she might as well keep going, she thought. If she sat down again in her favourite chair she might not get out of it for the rest of the day.

She went to find George.

Lovely George, as Roz had called him, was a lecturer in Geography at Brookes, Oxford's other university. They had met the previous November and were just starting to get to know one another when Kate was attacked and injured. George had spent days sitting by her bedside, alternating with Roz, while she drifted in and out of consciousness. Roz had looked after her for a while when she came out of hospital, but once Kate was on her feet again, her terraced house in Agatha Street had become too small for the two of them, and they started to bicker. At that point, George had suggested that Kate should move in with him and leave Roz to live in Agatha Street. It was an arrangement that appealed to both mother and daughter as they could put off making any decisions about the future. They both liked to act on impulse. Kate called it 'being decisive', but Roz, with the wisdom of relative age, knew it was a sign of their incurable immaturity.

Yes, George was something special. He was the sort of man who warmed the croissants for breakfast in bed on Sunday mornings. And found apricot conserve to go with the croissants. And made real coffee, and remembered which was your favourite mug, and how you liked no sugar, but a dash of skimmed milk. And he was just as considerate about other, even more pleasurable, aspects of their life together. She drifted off into a reverie involving the most recent one of those . . .

But what had Roz said? That she must snap out of her fit of depression or even the lovely George would abandon her. That couldn't be true, could it? Her hands began to tremble at this thought. And this fear was even worse than the one that gripped her when she had to enter a crowd of people.

Maybe she'd better follow her mother's advice, because she didn't want to find out the hard way that it was true. She tried a smile, but felt it freeze into something unattractive. Better stick with something easier, like correcting the droop of her shoulders and lifting her chin off her chest. She willed the tremor in her hands to stop and eventually it subsided.

George was in the upper part of the house, engaged in something he called necessary maintenance. Kate's maintenance of her former home had involved nothing more onerous than choosing new colours to paint the rooms, but George believed in undertaking more substantial work.

The house in Cavendish Road had come to George Dolby from his Aunt Sadie. When she died, George, grateful for the bequest, had organised a quietly opulent funeral for her, complete with incense and tuneful hymns, and then had converted the property into two flats. He might have divided it into bedsits and made more money from the rents, but he liked the idea of having a base that he could come back to after his forays into the wider world. And, besides, he didn't want the hassle of chasing half a dozen students for their rent every month.

The lower flat was on the ground and first floors, the upper on the top floor. The latter consisted of a sitting room, bedroom, small bathroom and galley kitchen. Just right for a modestly-sized couple or a large single person. George had used this upper flat himself in the early years but as he had acquired more possessions and a more settled lifestyle, he had moved into the lower flat himself and let the upstairs to a succession of quiet professional tenants. ('I didn't mind noise when I was younger since I was rarely at home, but these days I like some peace and quiet, so I look at the size of their feet,' he told Kate only half-jokingly. 'Anything over a size eight shoe and they're turned down, however good their references.')

It was just as well they had two floors to themselves, thought Kate, commandeering the second bedroom for her own study. Not that she had achieved much in the way of study, or even of writing, if she was honest. She had sat in the upright chair at the plain wooden table and stared at the blank screen of her notebook computer for a while. Then she had stretched out on the single bed and stared at the equally blank ceiling for a while longer before returning to the kitchen to make herself another pot of coffee.

'Don't think of it as a study,' said George cheerfully. 'Why don't you just call it your boudoir, then you can sulk for as long as you like.'

'I never sulk,' said Kate, closing the door firmly behind her and lying down on the bed with her eyes closed to recover from the insult.

She wasn't sure why George put up with her.

And now the most recent tenant in the upper flat had reached the end of his lease and had left after several years' occupancy. 'Time for some refurbishment,' said George, without any great enthusiasm. Although he liked to dress expensively, he didn't seem to care too much about his surroundings as long as they were neat and moderately clean. He tried to interest Kate in choosing wallpaper and curtains for the new tenants, and in replacing some worn-out kitchen equipment, but she soon lost interest in the project and retreated back to George's half of the house to read a book or watch some undemanding programme on the television, while he pottered round making lists and wondering what colour to paint the walls.

But now, invigorated by her conversation with Roz, Kate went looking for George to discuss the idea for a new book with him. The division of the house meant that the front door led into a small hallway containing two more doors, one for each flat. The one on the right led into Kate and George's; the one on the left opened on to an enclosed staircase belonging to the tenants. This second door was ajar and Kate pushed it open and started upstairs.

The walls were scuffed and the carpet on the stairs was wearing thin. She wrinkled her nose: there were memories of frying fish and Indian takeaways lingering like ghosts around the landing at the top of the stairs. The whole place needed a coat of paint – hyacinth blue and aqua would look clean and inviting. Much better than the dreary faded green that had been laid over everything for what appeared to be the past twenty years. Watch it! she told herself. You might find yourself getting interested, or even involved. Are you ready to give up your total preoccupation with yourself? Perhaps not quite yet.

To her left were the bedroom and bathroom, to the right the large sitting room looking over the front garden and the leafy suburban street. There were a few other big old houses like the one she was sharing with George, but newer, smaller boxier ones had eaten away at their rambling gardens and brought a younger generation of house-owners into the neighbourhood. The kitchen was a small galley off this sitting room. She noticed that the cooker and the floor both needed a good scrub, but she was in no mood to volunteer to deal with them.

A couple of electricians were updating the wiring in this top flat, and she looked into the bedroom where they were working to see if George was there.

'Sorry, love,' one of them said. 'Haven't seen him for a bit.'

'George!' she called. She knew he was around somewhere.

'Up here,' he called back and she looked up to see that the folding ladder used to get into the loft had been pulled down. She had forgotten about the loft. Her little house in Agatha Street didn't run to such things.

She climbed up and, still standing on the ladder, peered into the space under the roof.

It was like looking at a stage set, perhaps for a child's model theatre. A central hanging light, fitted with an old-fashoned shade, cast a triangular yellow beam on to the centre of the stage. The rest of the loft was in darkness, giving only an impression of cobwebs and dust draped over heaps of unidentifiable objects from a family's past. In the centre of the light beam George Dolby sat cross-legged on the floor, facing to the right, so that he was in profile. A perfectly self-sufficient figure. Yet she knew that when she spoke to him, he would listen. He would listen intently, as though she was the one person he wanted to hear, even if she was only asking him whether he wanted his tea now or would rather wait until later.

To each side of this central figure stood stout, lidded cardboard boxes, their labels peeling and barely legible. On the floorboards in front of him lay an untidy pile of notebooks and photographs. He was holding one of the latter up to the light so that he could see it better.

Kate hesitated for a moment, balancing on the rung of the ladder. She felt like a member of the audience, not an actor in the piece. George was waiting for the curtain to rise, and she had the feeling that the playwright was still hovering there, as though no decisions as to the nature of the play to be performed had yet been taken. Tragedy. Comedy. Farce. Any one of them might begin to unfold in the next second or two.

George looked across at her. 'Are you coming in?' he asked. In spite of the dust, there was a slight echo from the ceiling and the bare boards of the floor which made his voice more resonant, deeper. Older, thought Kate. The light cast hard shadows over the lower half of his face, taking away the humorous lines and putting something uncompromising in their place. It made him more attractive in her eyes rather than less so.

One more step and she would enter the stage and set the production in motion. She would move from audience to cast, take on a role, progress from passive to active. And she was being too fanciful. It was all in her imagination. She stepped off the ladder and into the loft.

'What's happening? Are you planning to convert this into a studio flat? It might work really well.'

'It's not a bad idea. Come on in,' said George. 'But actually I was just clearing out these boxes. When Aunt Sadie died I got rid of most of her clothes and things at Oxfam. I used her furniture to furnish the two flats, kept the books I wanted and sent the rest to the charity shop. But there was the usual collection of papers and mementoes that I didn't like to get rid of and yet I wasn't really interested in them at that time.

And I have the Dolbys' sentimental attachment to objects belonging to the family, however trivial. So I put them into cardboard storage boxes and shoved them up here in the loft. I'd forgotten all about them till now, but it's about time I dealt with them. I'll need to hire a warehouse soon if I don't stop hoarding them.'

Kate climbed through the opening and knelt down beside him. He had rigged up a light, and although the bulb was only 40 watts, she could see that he had opened two or three brown boxes and was sifting through the contents. A few old letters, their paper greying, their ink faded, lay scattered on the floor. Kate picked one of them up.

' "Dear Sadie," ' she read. ' "I'm having a delightful time here in Bournemouth. I have already spent many pleasant hours rambling along the footpaths, while refreshing myself when necessary with blackberries from the hedgerows." Yawn, yawn,' she commented rudely. 'Why did anyone keep them? They're written to your Aunt Sadie, I assume.'

'You keep your e-mails, don't you?' said George reasonably. 'It's the same thing. My Aunt Sadie kept letters from her friends.'

'And postcards. And birthday cards. And theatre programmes,' said Kate, sifting through another pile. Probably bus tickets, too, she thought, but had the grace not to say this aloud.

'Pass them over,' said George. 'I'm collecting them up to burn later.'

Kate suspected that instead they'd be returned to their boxes, as soon as she turned her back, as too precious to destroy. They'd all stay up in the loft until the floor caved in.

'I could spend hours up here, looking through all these things,' she said. In fact, she could imagine finding the plots for half a dozen novels. An exaggeration, perhaps, but at least there would be plenty of local colour. Background, as we novelists call it.

There was a large torch on the floor near George and she switched it on and started to investigate the shadowy corners of the loft outside the cone of George's light.

'A bentwood coatstand,' she said. 'Why don't we take it downstairs?'

'Because it's large and ugly and would take up too much space,' said George. 'What's wrong with the hooks behind the kitchen door?'

'Oh well. And I don't suppose you'd let me take this brass bucket to hold our umbrellas.'

'What umbrellas? You never use one.'

'Fair enough. But it would do as a wastepaper bin.'

'In your own study,' said George firmly. 'I'm not having it cluttering up my sitting room.'

'*Our* sitting room,' corrected Kate quietly. 'But I would like it in my study.' She placed it near the entrance. 'I won't forget it if I put it here.'

'You'll fall over it if you put it there,' he warned her.

Kate was still exploring. 'Look, George – ancestors!'

'Dead or alive?'

'They're portraits. They must be of your family.'

'Let's have a look.' He joined her, stooping so that he didn't crash his head against the rafters. 'Oh, yes. I like these. I'm sure they used to be on the walls downstairs when I first came to this house. Perhaps we could have them in our dining room,' he suggested.

'When we have a dining room,' said Kate. 'But they're not a very attractive bunch, are they?'

'What do you mean? They're a fine, upstanding collection of Dolbys.'

'Who's this one? She looks as though she's swallowed the vinegar bottle.'

'Now that is the great-aunt, or maybe great-grand-aunt, who was the first owner of the house. Her name was Margaret Marlyn.'

'And you think she'll aid digestion in the dining room?'

'A fine figure of a woman,' agreed George, smiling.

'Do you know who these others are?'

'Not really. I expect I could find out. But they're great uncles and second cousins and people like that.'

Aldermen and other such worthies, thought Kate. And I don't want them in my dining room. She quietly turned their faces to the wall and left them in the gloomy corner where she had discovered them.

George went back to his place under the light.

'Look! This is rather a nice carpet,' called Kate.

'It's just a rug, and its hem is unravelling,' said George.

'It's a good colour, though. Can't we get it mended?'

'I suppose so. One day.'

Kate rolled it up and put it back.

'And here's a notebook,' she said, picking it up off the floor. 'Old-fashioned quarto. A school exercise book, by the look of it, but it's missing its front cover.'

'I'd forgotten you were a connoisseur of notebooks.'

'I used to be. I've lost interest now.'

The *now* sat on the floor like a grenade with its pin extracted.

'Rubbish. Of course you're interested. I can see you're longing to read all through it.' George spoke mildly as though he was getting into the habit of not upsetting her.

'Let's see,' he said, taking the exercise book from her. 'Oh, I don't think this one's very interesting.'

'Why? Is it one of yours?'

51

'No, it's much older than that. It came out of this box of rubbish. I was just going to throw it away.'

'I'd like to look at it first,' said Kate, and put it to one side. George didn't argue.

'And I suppose you want to see these photos before I throw *them* out, too?'

'Of course!'

George passed across a handful of black-and-whites.

'Not a talented photographer,' commented Kate, looking at the first few. 'And why didn't she put them in an album? These are getting dog-eared.'

She started to turn them all the same way up. 'Who are these people?'

'The one guaranteed to instil fear into small boys is my great-aunt, Elinor Marlyn. At least I always thought of her as my great-aunt. She was Aunt Sadie's aunt on her mother's side. Does that make her my great-aunt? I'm not good at working out these relationships.'

'I expect so,' said Kate vaguely. She had no aunts or uncles of her own and had never tried to work out the precise nature of any relationship.

The woman in the photograph was glaring straight at the camera, and Kate wondered who had been bold enough to point it at her in the first place. Her hair was drawn back into a bun, but a few strands had escaped from their severe treatment, softening the effect. The hair looked likely to wave in profusion over her shoulders if Aunt Elinor ever set it free. There were deep grooves running from nostrils to jaw, pulling her mouth into a severe expression. No, I think it's because she's discontented with her life, thought Kate, and I bet she's making everyone around her miserable.

'The story in the family is that she had a beautiful smile

52

which transformed her face and made the most unlikely people fall over themselves to help her,' said George.

'I bet they were men,' said Kate.

'I expect you're right.'

Kate was leafing through the old exercise book. The owner was even worse at arithmetic than she was. She had a feeling that George and his brother Sam had been quite competent at science and maths, so it couldn't have been theirs. Maybe some visiting child had left it behind. Without the cover it was hard to tell.

'You don't want to take any more of this old junk, do you?' asked George.

'I shouldn't think so. What did you come up here for originally anyway?'

'My tool-box.'

'I can't see one up here. Though I suppose it could be hidden away in a corner.'

'Apparently not,' said George, looking around at the heaps of junk, all of it obviously old and useless. 'I'd better get downstairs and leave the repairs to men who know what they're doing.' He rose to his feet, dipping his head to avoid hitting it on a beam. 'Are you coming?'

'Yes,' said Kate, throwing the exercise book back into the rubbish box. Before following George she looked round regretfully. She would like to come back with a proper light, a duster, and a whole day in which to explore the loft *all on her own*.

She picked up the brass bin and took it down to her study. Now that she had it in the daylight she could see that it needed cleaning. She'd get round to that later.

2

'I have good news and bad news for you,' said Roz.

These telephone chats were becoming a daily habit with them. Although neither would admit it, even to themselves, they both enjoyed the regular gossip sessions.

'Start with the good news,' said Kate. 'You can lead up to the bad very gently, or even miss it out altogether.'

'The good news is that your noisy neighbours have left.'

'Trace and Jace? Harley and Shayla?'

'Together with Baby Toadface and Dave the dog. All gone.'

'That was very sudden. What happened?'

'Tracey booted out Jace and his headbanger music and has returned to Ken. Or "My Ken" as she calls him.'

'Her husband,' elucidated Kate. 'The father of all those children.'

'Apparently he has been doing very nicely without them, making lots of money and investing it in a property in one of those places beginning with a "K" that one never visits. Kennington or Kidlington or somewhere like that.'

'I shall miss young Harley,' said Kate. 'And who will make sure he does his homework?'

'He's of an age to find himself a strong-minded young woman of his own who'll bully him into passing exams and making something of himself,' said Roz cheerfully. 'You set him on the right road, I doubt he'll stray far from it now.' She managed not to point out that Kate was no longer living in

55

Agatha Street and Harley had fended for himself quite well these past months without her.

'Oh well, I suppose they were rather noisy,' said Kate sadly. 'Though I did get used to them, mostly.'

'I hadn't told you that Shayla had taken up the saxophone, had I?'

'You're making it up.'

'I'm afraid it's all too true.'

'If that was the good news, I'm not sure I want to know what the bad news is.'

'You have new neighbours,' said Roz carefully.

'Morris dancers? Satanists? Enthusiastic supporters of the Tory Party?'

'A retired headmaster and his wife, a nurse, who is currently on long-term sick leave.'

'They sound ideal. Quiet, cultured people. I imagine they spend a lot of their time reading books or playing Scrabble. They probably go out to concerts and belong to the National Trust.'

'Probably,' said Roz. But she didn't sound convinced. However, she quickly changed the subject and Kate soon forgot about what was happening in Agatha Street. It was, after all, on the other side of the city and nothing to do with her at the moment. The way things were going, she would be staying here with George for the foreseeable future. Roz would sort it out, whatever the problem was – and she couldn't imagine that it was anything very serious. A retired headmaster, an invalid wife – really, Roz just needed something to worry about.

'It's extraordinary to think of this house standing here for a hundred years and owned by your family all that time,' said Kate.

She and George had taken a sofa each and were sprawled out lengthways, pretending to listen to music on the CD player, idly turning the pages of the Sunday papers, and in Kate's case, dipping into a packet of chocolate biscuits and dropping crumbs down the front of a black T-shirt.

'What's so extraordinary about it?' George helped himself to the *Lifestyle* section and stared at a picture of a made-over garden which featured much blue paint and very few green plants.

'Oh, all this family of yours –'

'Only the women, till it came to me,' put in George.

'– not just living in the house, but leaving bits of their lives embedded in the walls, just waiting for us to tune into them.'

'Drifting about like fluff underneath the furniture,' added George. 'Scrabbling like mice behind the skirting board. Don't put down a mousetrap, that might be Great-Aunt Elinor.'

'They're all around us,' went on Kate, ignoring him. 'And particularly they're up in the loft.'

'Loft. Attic. I thought such places were reserved for mad-women.'

'History,' continued Kate, warming to her theme and brushing aside George's interruptions, 'and not just the dry, impersonal kind you read in books, that happened to people *out there* as it were. No, this is real history, happening to people we knew.'

'You wouldn't want to know my female ancestors, from what I've heard. Or my great-grandfather, John Marlyn, who built this house and settled it on his sister, Margaret Marlyn.'

'That was decent of the old boy.'

'Anything rather than having Margaret installed at home, hogging his own hearth. I believe she was a New Woman and had Advanced Ideas.'

'Excellent!' exclaimed Kate. 'Just the way in I was looking for.'

'I thought you were considering World War Two.'

'I am. But I like to research the background.'

'You like to research, full stop,' said George.

'Don't be so repressive. This is the key to my new book. It's historical, so I can research it and get my teeth into it, and yet it's about people living recently, who have a link to us in the present day.'

'You want to go fossicking around in the loft?'

'Got it in one,' replied Kate. It was always a good idea to get someone's agreement before nosing around in their affairs. Sometimes you have to work quite hard to get it, she had found.

George turned another page of his magazine. Succulent chunks of lamb glistened in a red, herb-strewn sauce in a way that real meat could never quite achieve.

'Time for lunch,' he said.

After lunch (prepared by George), Kate tidied up the morass of newspapers in the sitting room and made coffee for them both.

'About the house,' she began, when they were both installed on their sofas.

'You want me to tell you its history,' said George.

'Yes.'

'Are you lounging comfortably?'

'Yes.'

'Then I'll begin.'

'This house was built, as you've probably worked out by now, in the mid-1890s by a John Marlyn. Have I mentioned that the women on the Marlyn side of the family were a strong-minded lot? Yes, well, the first of them to come to our attention is Margaret, John Marlyn's sister. Born in the 1860s – 1865, if I remember it rightly – so by the mid-1890s she would have been around thirty. There's a photo of her somewhere. Yes, possibly up there in the attic, and I'm sure you'll unearth it before long. A tall, thin woman with a prominent nose and a strong belief in the superiority of her sex. Don't interrupt or I'll stop telling you about her. But yes, I expect she did see herself as a New Woman. And she has the mad light in her eye of a woman who would chain herself to railings or throw herself under the hooves of a racehorse in order to achieve the vote. (Or perhaps that was just the time it took to expose the film in those days.) Now, where was I?

'Margaret . . . Margaret Marlyn. She moved into this house when it was new – a house of raw red brickwork, orange roof tiles and a bare garden. There's another photograph somewhere, showing the house in the 1890s, and it's odd to see it looking like something on a modern housing estate.

'You want more detail? Things you can use in your book? I don't know that I'm going to be much use to you. And neither is poor old Margaret. She wasn't really the stuff of which romantic heroines are made. John Marlyn gave her the house because he could see she would never find herself a husband. Apart from her looks – and the woman was certainly plain – she didn't have the gift of pleasing men. Don't snort like that, I'm sure John Marlyn would be horrified if he could hear you. She didn't, according to my Aunt Sadie, listen in a submissive manner to whatever they chose to tell her. She probably didn't laugh at their jokes. Maybe she corrected them when she found they were wrong in something and pointed out their mistakes. So, she decided to be an independent woman at a time when this was not common, and she trained to be a lady typewriter.' He looked sternly at Kate. 'You needn't laugh. I'm sorry, but that's what they were called in those days.'

Then: 'Isn't that the phone ringing in the kitchen? I'd better get it. It could be someone from Brookes. It's just as well we've been interrupted,' George called over his shoulder as he disappeared. 'I could have carried on for hours about my family's glorious past.'

It was next morning that one of the workmen from the upstairs flat put his head round the kitchen door.

'Bill found this under the floorboards in the bedroom,' he said. 'Must have been hidden by some kid years ago.'

'This' was covered in grime and cobwebs. George put it down on the kitchen table, well away from their toast and marmalade.

'An old biscuit tin,' said Kate. 'Or maybe it once contained a Dundee cake. Does it look familiar?'

'It's just old rubbish,' said George dismissively.

'I'll find a duster,' said Kate.

'The tin's so corroded you'll never get it open,' he warned her.

Kate wiped off the worst of the dirt. A picture of roses and forget-me-nots appeared from beneath the dust, speckled with rust.

'It probably contains a dead mouse,' said George.

Kate searched through a drawer until she found a screwdriver then started to prise the lid open.

'Or even a rat,' added George.

'If you don't want me to look at the things you buried under the floorboards as a child, just say so,' said Kate. 'I can take a hint.'

'I never stayed here as a boy,' said George. 'Anything I buried is in Sam and Emma's house, where I grew up.'

The lid of the box sprang open, showering the table with crumbs of rust.

'Then who did this belong to? I thought you said this house was passed down from maiden lady to maiden lady for a hundred years until it reached you.'

'I have no idea,' said George.

The interior of the box smelled a bit musty, but the contents were clean enough. On top was an exercise book and some loose sheets of paper. Kate picked up the exercise book and read the cover. The writing matched that inside the coverless one in the loft, though she had to admit that children's writing often lacked individuality and so she couldn't be sure.

' "Christopher Douglas Barnes. Age 10. Private Diary." '

'I told you it wasn't mine,' said George. He dipped into the box as though it were a bran tub at a village fair. 'Oh,' he said.

He had come up with a child's soft toy, so old and battered that it was difficult to tell whether it was a bear or a rabbit. It wore a blue gingham shirt, sewn by hand with small, neat stitches. Sawdust leaked from a split in a paw and one black button eye dangled from a thread.

'And I don't suppose this was yours, either,' said Kate, taking it from him and sniffing at it. It smelled of mildew and extreme age.

'No,' said George, brushing grime off his fingers. 'I've never seen it before.'

'Tell me again about your ageing spinster aunts.'

George grinned at Kate's raised eyebrow. 'All of impeccable morals, and pillars of the local Anglican church. I can't think how these things got here.'

Kate was turning over the oddments that remained in the box.

'Drawings,' she said. 'And these must have been done by

Christopher Douglas Barnes, too. I don't think they were done by a girl.'

The paper was cheap and thin and had grown yellow over the years. How many years? she found herself wondering. The drawings had been made with thick wax crayons – the sort they gave you at primary school, that you could never do anything really good with. The first one showed a series of outlines of aircraft – side views and the view from the ground looking up. They were marked with swastikas and had been named in a childish hand, in purple indelible pencil: *Me 109, Me 110, Junkers 87, Junkers 88, Heinkel 111, Dornier 17.* In the bottom right-hand corner were the initials *C.D.B.* in firm capitals.

'Christopher Douglas Barnes. Are you sure the name means nothing to you?'

'No. I told you.'

The next drawing showed more German aircraft, this time with thickly-pencilled-in black bombs dropping from their bellies on to a conventionally-drawn house beneath. The house was exploding – the roof with a gaping, ragged hole; there was broken furniture on the surrounding ground, and broken bodies with detached body parts and gory pools of blood. At the bottom of the page the caption read, *High Corner, Armitage Road.* That's just round the corner, thought Kate. Only a matter of yards from here. Again, the boy had marked the corner of the page clearly with his initials: *C.D.B.*

'Perhaps Elinor Marlyn or your aunt – Sadie, wasn't it? – had a little friend to the house to play,' she suggested.

'I think they're the wrong ages. This must come from the 1940s, but Elinor was born back in 1900 and Sadie in 1920.'

Kate did some rapid arithmetic. Unless Sadie had produced an infant when she was about sixteen or seventeen and then had him to stay with her in the house (unlikely from what she knew of George's family), then *C.D.B.* must be someone outside the family. She would probably never find out who he was and what had happened to him.

George was packing the drawings and notebook back into the box. He placed the bear (or rabbit) on the top and snapped the lid down firmly.

'Is that all that was in there?' Kate asked.

'Just a few more bits of old junk,' said George dismissively.

'I'd like to see the rest,' said Kate.

'Take the box if you want it. I was going to throw it away.'

'I want to know who Christopher Barnes was and what he was doing in your aunt's house.'

'I've no idea. But I'm sure you're going to find out.'

Research, thought Kate. I can call this research, can't I? This box is old, but not too old. A woman with imagination can soon turn it into a thrilling story that will astound her agent and delight her editor. She took it quickly into her study and stowed it in her desk drawer before George could put it out with the rubbish.

'What on earth are you doing with that handbag?' asked Roz. She maintained that she had walked in a brisk and healthy manner from the other side of Oxford, but Kate thought that something very like a taxi had whisked round the corner as she opened the front door.

'This? What's wrong with it?'

'I'm used to seeing you with something the size of a suit-carrier, that's all.'

'This is my latest attempt to appear ladylike,' said Kate.

'Positively dainty,' said Roz. She didn't make it sound like a compliment.

'Small, neat, organised,' said Kate, stowing a clean tissue into the tiny green leather case.

'Where do you keep your keys, your sunglasses, your hairbrush, your—'

'I leave them at home. I do without.' Kate looked dubiously at the bag. There was barely room in it for a biro and a very small notebook. Still, in this day and age, image was everything.

Judging by Roz's expression, she was preparing herself to say something difficult. 'Does this mean that you're planning to leave the house?' she asked.

'Of course!' said Kate.

'Oh, good.' She paused for a moment as though wondering whether to continue this line of questioning. 'Only I thought you might be having problems with the outside world.'

'You don't need to come with me, if that's what you were going to suggest,' said Kate.

'You're sure?'

Actually, she wasn't sure at all, but she would have to face the world on her own some time. She wasn't convinced that it would be today, but she was working on it. She decided on a change of subject.

'What can you remember about the war?' she asked.

'Are you asking me about the view from my pram?'

Kate did some rapid mental arithmetic. 'You can't have been in your pram for the entire war. It lasted for six years.' She didn't mention the fact that Roz was well out of her pram before the war even started.

'I was *much* too young to remember anything. Perhaps just the waving of Union flags on VE Day. I have a hazy recollection of little rectangles of red, white and blue, bobbing up and down. And distant cheering.'

Roz must be in one of her age-reducing moods, Kate deduced. It was no use trying to push her into admitting that she could remember something that happened more than fifty years ago. Quite a lot more than fifty years ago, now she came to think about it.

'Let me know if anything emerges from the mists of time,' she said.

When Roz had left, Kate dialled Estelle's number. It was, admittedly, considerably more than an hour since her agent had exhorted her to come up with an idea for her next book, but then, Kate had never been one to take her agent too seriously.

'Livingstone.' Estelle was in one of her terse moods, obviously.

'I think I've got it,' said Kate.

'Yes?'

'A story of children in wartime.'

'Sounds a bit grim.'

'Children separated from their parents but sent into the safety of the countryside,' improvised Kate.

'I hope you're not thinking of doing something about child abuse. That's last year's story.'

'It might have a bit of a mystery to it.'

'Is there a love story?'

'Of course.'

'Sounds promising, but make sure you put in plenty of exciting sex scenes.'

'But I don't do explicit sex,' objected Kate.

'I know. It's been a great disappointment to your fans,' said Estelle.

'Has it?'

'Of course.'

'I'm not sure—'

'Try reading a book or two if you've forgotten.'

'I don't need to read a book.'

'Good. Well, I'll expect to hear you've finished the first draft in six months' time.'

Estelle put the phone down and Kate let out an audible breath. Six months. She'd better get her skates on. And she hadn't confessed to Estelle the difficulty she was having in leaving the house. Perhaps this was the day she would confront her fears. She was alone in the house. No one would see her attempts. She knew it was time to do something. She didn't want to be a prisoner in George's house for ever. And she certainly didn't want to stop being a writer.

She would get back to CB's box from under the floorboards after she'd been out.

For the moment, confronting her fears seemed to be the most important thing she had to deal with.

3

Kate stood with the front door behind her, very aware that it had clicked shut. Of course she had the key with her, didn't she? A moment of panic, then she slipped her hand into her pocket to feel the cold metal and reassure herself that she could go back inside at any time. She could turn round and go straight back inside *now*, if she wanted to. George was at college, busy with a committee meeting, so no one would know that she had chickened out. But no, she wasn't going to do that, not yet.

She took a deep breath and walked a few steps forward, then stopped again. This was ridiculous, but it was the first time in weeks that she had left the house completely alone. Up to now there had always been someone, at first helping her with a hand under her arm then, later, hovering more discreetly in the background or finding that they, too, had an errand to run in the same direction she was taking. And she had been out in her car, sealed well away from other people, and managing to get from vehicle to friend's house in under ten seconds. But not this morning. Her car was shut away in the garage at the side of the house and she had promised herself to do without it for one whole week. She would walk everywhere. She was tired of convalescence. She was tired of being frightened of everything and everyone. She was going to restore the bits of her life that had been stolen from her by Ruth's knife.

She looked down the road to the right: a couple of small children squabbling over a bicycle. Their mother appeared and shepherded them back into the safety of their own substantial garden. To the left a woman in jeans and T-shirt and an expensive haircut was climbing into a four-wheel drive fitted with tyres that could have crossed the Alps without bothering with tarmac. Probably about to drive sedately to Sainsbury's, thought Kate.

Everything normal, then.

It was, too, a lovely day, with small, fluffy clouds being chivvied across the blue sky by a light breeze. She took one more step forward. The air smelled of the usual mixture of mown grass, exhaust fumes and the white-flowered shrub by the gate that Kate couldn't put a name to. She inhaled the faint memory of the beef burgers that number 70 had char-grilled on their barbecue yesterday evening, then sneezed. The air was heavy with summer pollen.

Well, it was no good standing glued to the brick path like this. Time to get moving. She walked resolutely towards the gate and opened it. Which way? Left or right? The Daihatsu had moved away down the road, so she turned left.

She walked down the middle of the pavement, the sun behind her. If someone should approach from behind she would be warned by their shadow overtaking her own. But in the middle of a Monday morning, the street ahead of her was deserted. She had gone about ten paces before she realised she was holding her breath. She released it and looked around her. She must make some sort of decision about where to go.

As she drew nearer, the grey wall and dark green trees on her right resolved themselves into a churchyard. Forgetting her fear for a moment, she crossed the road to take a look. The wall was low, but solid and comforting. She rested her hands on the time-worn stones. They felt cool and heavy and the mortar was grainy. Durable. Reassuring. In front of her stretched crowded headstones, and grass that someone had kept mown and weeded. Small bunches of flowers adorned well-tended graves. Nothing here but dead people. She wasn't afraid of ghosts, it was the living who terrified her. In the background stood the church. It was low and grey, with a squat, crenellated tower, and looked old to Kate. Norman? Saxon? She was vague about church architecture, but this one could have been standing here for ever.

She pushed open the gate and walked up the path towards a substantial wooden door. Should she brave another of her demons and go inside? She remembered a candlelit interior, the sound of choristers, the rolling notes of the organ. No, she wasn't ready to face the nightmares. And in any case, the place was probably locked. In fact, she could see that there was a key pad in the porch, the code doubtless known only to vicars and flower-arrangers. Absolutely no need to attempt to go inside. She could just wander round outside, looking at fading flowers and reading inscriptions on tombstones. It wouldn't get her very far with her new book, but at least she was out of earshot of the telephone and Estelle's insistent voice.

The grass had been cut in the past day or two so that it was easy to walk around the graveyard, winding her way through the plots. They were, she found, in groups more or less according to their age. The oldest – splashed with grey and orange lichen, the soft stone blackened and pock-marked – bore inscriptions that were illegible. The next group, from the 1800s, she could just about make out. *Thomasine, relict of Arthur Brown*, she read. Thomasine had been a relict for nearly twenty-five years after Arthur's death, she calculated. Was that how the poor woman was regarded? But maybe she wasn't so poor. Arthur was described as a *Farmer and Countryman* and had probably left her well-off and independent, for the first time in her life able to make her own decisions instead of doing what her father or husband told her. Kate hoped so. Being burdened for life with the name Thomasine had to be enough of a handicap for any woman.

She moved on. She was entering the part where the more recently dead lay under the dusty green yew trees. Beneath her feet, a generation of brown needles softened the paths. And still the women seemed to outlive their spouses by twenty years or more. There were vases of flowers here, many of them plastic, or mounds planted with bedding plants. In front of one granite headstone someone had placed a pink geranium in a pot. The wind had freshened and Kate saw it pitch over and roll down the small slope. She walked across to retrieve it and place it upright in front of *Edgar White, Passed Away 15 April 1998.*

As she bent down, she saw the small plaque set unobtrusively into the grass at her feet.

Christopher Douglas Barnes. Aged ten years. 1934–1945. What?

Ordinary enough names. But she had seen them before, and quite recently. She stared at the small black plaque with the plain white letters. It told her nothing more. In this section, with its recent dead, there were more bunches of flowers than elsewhere, but none by Christopher Barnes's grave. An old coffee jar lay on the grass a couple of feet away with a brown residue of water in its base. Maybe it had held flowers for Christopher. Maybe not. After all, he had died more than half a century ago.

She began to walk back towards the gate, past the door of the church. Why had he died at the age of ten? *And was there a story here for her?* Was he a civilian casualty of the war? But the war was coming to an end in 1945, and surely she had read somewhere that this area was largely spared from enemy attack because Hitler had wanted to keep the city for himself. So Christopher couldn't have been killed in the Blitz. And, come to think of it, surely the Blitz took place earlier, and in London. Roz might remember more about it. Or maybe she'd get herself a book on the subject.

A figure loomed out of the porch, moving towards her. A woman.

Kate stopped. Her heart thudded. Her mouth felt dry. Her hands were clammy. She wanted to scream. She wanted to run. She could do neither.

'Hello,' said a cheery voice.

Not Ruth. Someone younger-looking, about Kate's age, someone not quite as tall as Ruth. And how could you be terrified of a woman wearing an electric blue tracksuit? She was only a few feet away now. She was offering a hand in Kate's direction. Kate noticed that the fingers were tipped with lime-green nail varnish. The woman smiled, and she saw a wide mouth painted with scarlet lipstick, then a round face, very short black hair, and a straight nose embellished with a diamond stud.

'Oh, hello,' Kate said warily.

'Are you looking for a particular grave, or just looking?' The woman sounded friendly, not at all scary.

'I was just looking,' answered Kate. She indicated the plaque dedicated to Christopher Douglas Barnes.

'Ten years old,' said the other.

'Yes. Do you know anything about him?'

'A bit before my time, I'm afraid.'

Kate decided to give away a little more. 'Only I came across his name quite recently in a different context.'

'Really?' She waited for Kate to say something more.

'Does the church have records, do you think?' persisted Kate. 'They must take details down when they bury someone, don't you think?'

'There's a register of funerals. And one of burials.'

'Oh, good. Just what I was hoping for,' said Kate. 'Do you think they'd let me take a look at them?'

'I don't see why not. But they only go back to 1979, I'm afraid.'

'Bother.' So close to the church, Kate was more careful than usual with her language. And who was this woman, anyway? Some sort of caretaker, or verger or churchwarden or whatever they called these things. For a moment she wondered whether she could be the vicar's daughter, or even his wife, but glimpsing again the shiny scarlet lipstick, she pushed the unlikely thought from her head.

'There's just one thing we could check,' the woman was saying.

'Yes?'

'I could look out the plot register for you. It should be in the safe.'

Plot register? Did someone keep a register of all possible plots? Was this what other novelists knew and no one had ever told her before?

'Graveyard plots,' explained the woman, perhaps wondering why Kate should suddenly look so pleased and surprised.

'Ah!' Oh well, better than nothing.

'I'm Elspeth Fry,' the woman threw over her bright blue shoulder as she walked towards the church door. The hips inside the tracksuit trousers were wide and rounded. The blue cotton jersey did not flatter her figure.

'My name's Kate Ivory,' said Kate.

'The one who writes the—'

'Yes.' *Or at least I used to be* – but no point in saying that aloud.

She followed Elspeth into the porch.

'Are we allowed in here?' asked Kate.

'Oh, I think so. They usually let me in,' said Elspeth. 'Maybe it's because I'm the vicar.'

Oh yes, of course. With a diamond nose-stud? But that would be why she was so familiar with the church and churchyard.

She followed Elspeth into the church, pausing briefly before setting off into the dimness of the aisle. *It's all right. You're quite safe. There's no one waiting for you with a knife.* She found she was forgetting to breathe, and walking on the balls of her feet so that no one could hear her. She forced herself to place her feet squarely on the floor and to breathe evenly.

'Are you all right?' asked Elspeth. She had stopped and was looking at Kate with concern on her face.

'Yes, of course.'

'Only you were looking a bit odd.'

'I'm fine.' No doubt vicars were trained to notice when visitors to their church were likely to pass out, throw a fit of hysterics or bring their breakfast up over a hand-embroidered hassock. She hoped they were trained not to ask intrusive questions, too.

They were walking into the vestry, which was better than the body of the church as far as Kate was concerned. She could pretend it was just an office. Elspeth was clattering a bunch of keys and bending down to the safe, and eventually came upright with a red-bound book in her hands.

'Nineteen forty-five, wasn't it?' she asked, leafing back through the pages. 'Here we are.'

'Christopher Douglas Barnes,' prompted Kate.

'Of High Corner, Armitage Road, Headington.'

'Anything else?'

'The date. Tuesday, 27 February, 1945.'

'Nothing else?'

'I'm afraid not.'

'That's really helpful, though. Thanks.'

Elspeth put the register back into the safe and locked it. The two women walked together out of the church and into the sunlight.

'I could try the local paper,' said Kate, thinking aloud. Now that she'd braved the interior of a church, the Central Library should be a doddle. 'It might suggest some reason for his death.'

'Or you could just use your imagination,' said Elspeth.

'As a last resort.'

They had reached the gate. 'I'm going this way,' said Elspeth, indicating the direction of George's house.

'I'll be going into town,' said Kate, feeling brave. 'But thanks again.'

She stood uncertainly, looking down the road. She could see no one, just a small dog lifting its leg against a gatepost and then returning to its own garden. But who knew what lurked behind the lushly green trees or the trimly-curtained windows of its solid houses?

'Are you sure you're all right?' asked Elspeth, who hadn't, after all, walked away. 'I've just realised it must have been a bit of an ordeal for you going into the church.'

'You read about the attack?'

'Didn't everyone?'

She was probably right. Those curtains were twitching at this very moment. Kate thought the experience existed only inside her own memory, but of course it must have been the gossip of the neighbourhood for weeks. All those people, feeling sorry for her. She cringed inside at the thought.

'Why don't you come back to the vicarage for a coffee? It's not far.'

Kate wasn't sure she wanted the vicar to practise her pastoral skills on her, but on the other hand, Elspeth was right: she did feel shaky and she would be glad of some company for the next half hour. Elspeth was cheerful and solid enough to dispel the shadow of Ruth from her mind. At least for the time being.

'Maybe I can help you with some of your research,' said Elspeth, setting off up the road. They turned left after fifty yards or so, into a narrower street with the houses set closer together. Kate noticed that the vibrant blue of the tracksuit was set off by the brilliance of the white leather trainers. She caught a glimpse of emerald sock as her companion strode along. A colourful woman, Elspeth Fry.

The vicarage turned out to be a bungalow set in a scrubby patch of yellowing grass. A buddleia waved purple cones, surrounded by a halo of cabbage white butterflies. Kate hoped the vicar didn't try to grow her own vegetables.

Inside, the bungalow had the look of a place where someone else had chosen the furniture and the wallpaper, aiming at an effect that would offend no one's taste. The result was beigely depressing.

They sat on opposing oatmeal armchairs and leant against identical brown and orange patterned cushions.

'Coffee?' asked Espeth.

'Could you make that tea?' answered Kate, who had already drunk a pint or two of strong coffee while talking herself into leaving the house that morning.

When they were settled with their mugs of tea, Kate decided to take Elspeth into her confidence. The other woman was looking sympathetic and receptive. Being a vicar, she was probably expecting to join Kate in exploring the inner recesses of her soul. Kate believed that such recesses and crannies, together with their motley contents, should be left strictly alone.

'I'm thinking of writing something more modern than usual,' she began. 'My agent wants me to tackle something contemporary, but that's not really my thing.'

'You enjoy the research,' suggested Elspeth.

'It's easier than writing the story,' agreed Kate. Though now she came to think about it, libraries weren't any safer than churches, in her experience. 'World War Two,' she continued firmly, putting such thoughts behind her.

'Which is where Christopher Douglas Barnes comes in?'

'Exactly. I hadn't intended writing about children. I don't know much about them, really. I like the idea of women in smart uniforms driving lorries, and dashing pilots in Spitfires. Maybe add a few slick GIs in sexy Jeeps. But then I came across a couple of old notebooks and drawings that belonged to a child in the house I'm staying in at the moment.' Better not to mention her relationship with George when talking to a vicar or she might call down a sermon on her head.

' "Staying in at the moment",' repeated Elspeth. 'I thought you and George Dolby had a permanent arrangement.'

Trust a vicar to know all the gossip. Trust a vicar to notice how she gave away her lack of commitment, even before she had noticed it herself.

'Of course we're committed to one another,' insisted Kate. 'At least, we will be when I make my mind up about it.' Elspeth had her eyebrows raised as if waiting for further enlightenment. 'Back to the war,' said Kate, growing tired of the silent interrogation. 'I suppose I'd better find out what was happening in this area.'

'So you're going to set it in Headington?' Elspeth drank some of her tea. When she placed the mug back on the table Kate saw that she had left an arc of scarlet lipstick, like a miniature slice of watermelon, on the white mug.

'Headington, perhaps. Or Oxford. Or the surrounding countryside.' Or maybe just Cavendish Road if she couldn't face travelling further than the corner of her own road. Was that why she was getting interested in Christopher Barnes? It seemed from the plot register that he had lived and died here. *And what sort of story will that make?* She could hear Estelle's sharp voice dismissing the whole idea before she even got started on it.

'How do you begin researching a subject that broad?'

'I'll find a few general background books and read them, then I'll go down to the Centre for Oxfordshire Studies and see what they have. The local paper's always a good source of information. Come to think of it, now I have a date for Christopher's death, I could see if they reported it.'

'That's the date for his burial, strictly speaking,' said Elspeth. 'He probably died about a week before that.'

'Good point. I'll start a month before and work forwards.'

'And there are still people living around here who remember the war. Christopher would only be sixty-five or six if he were here today. There must be plenty of his contemporaries still alive.'

'Can you suggest any?' asked Kate, never one to let an opportunity slip by.

'You could try old Mrs Watts. She lives in one of the flats in Oswald Court. Whenever I visit her she's always going on about the old days and the people who used to live here. I have to admit that she isn't always very charitable in her judgements. Still, she must have lived in the area all her life.

On a good day she could be very helpful.'

Perhaps Kate should have wondered what she was like on a bad day, but she copied down the name and address into the notebook she always carried with her.

'Thanks. Anything else?'

'Mrs Watts enjoys talking about something she calls "the vaccies".'

'Evacuees,' said Kate knowledgeably.

'Yes, that would be it.'

'I suppose you had quite a few of them in an area like this where there was very little bombing.'

'Do you think Christopher was an evacuee?'

'He could have been. I wonder if Mrs Watts remembers anything about airmen and women soldiers, too?' asked Kate hopefully. 'I'm not sure how keen my agent would be on a story all about children and mothers with young babies. She longs for romance.'

'I thought agents were hard-headed people who cared only about their ten per cent.'

'Estelle's certainly hard-headed. She doesn't want the romance for herself, she just wants to sell it.'

'It's just possible Violet Watts might know about romance,' said Elspeth doubtfully. 'She'll certainly enjoy telling you anything she knows. It takes me an hour to escape sometimes.'

'Sounds promising.'

'I'm enjoying this,' said Elspeth. 'I'd have liked to be a writer myself.'

'I shouldn't think so,' said Kate. 'You'd be amazed at how much of a slog most of it is. This is the interesting part, picking other people's brains and making plans.'

'Sitting at a battered old typewriter, feeding in pristine sheets of paper and watching the words flow down the page. My hands poised over the keyboard, then, with a flash of inspiration, rattling off reams of fluent, captivating prose. Or do you write longhand?'

'Only my notes. When I begin to write the first draft I sit at a computer in my office and watch the words inch their way slowly down the screen. *Very* slowly, usually. Sometimes they stagger to a halt and stay that way for hours on end. Then I go back and delete half of them and start again.'

'I think my way sounds more fun,' Elspeth said. 'I'll have a go at it when I've got the time.'

'Hmm,' said Kate, trying not to sound too sceptical. As long as Elspeth didn't tell her that, after all, everyone had a book inside them.

'Everyone has a book inside them. Isn't that what they say?' said Elspeth.

'Any more contacts for me to look up?' asked Kate brightly, ignoring the last remark.

'You could try the school. It's a remote chance, but it might be worth trying.'

'School?'

'St Mark's C. of E. Primary. It's in Bridgman Street.'

'Thanks,' said Kate as she wrote down the name and address.

She needn't go rushing into Oxford after all. She might be able to do all her research within a stone's throw of Cavendish Road.

'I don't suppose you've been getting around much on your own since it happened,' said Elspeth, as though reading her mind. 'Must be difficult for you, facing up to your fears.'

'I haven't been out much, no.'

'I'm going into central Oxford this afternoon. Why don't you come with me?'

Kate couldn't think of an excuse on the spur of the moment. 'Thanks. That would be wonderful,' she said. Elspeth probably knew she was telling a lie.

'I'll call round for you at George's place at two o'clock,' she said.

Now that Elspeth had specified the time so precisely, Kate knew that she wouldn't be able to wriggle out of the expedition. But then, vicars probably had a fair bit of practice at understanding people and persuading them to do what they wanted. She thinks it'll be good for me, thought Kate gloomily.

4

It felt good to be indoors again, away from the glare of the sun. Away from the watching eyes.

She had time for a quick sandwich before Elspeth came calling for her, and she opened the fridge door to see what was available. At least, she would have time for a sandwich if the phone didn't insist on ringing.

'Hello?'

'It's Roz here. You sound a bit perkier than you did last time we spoke.'

'I've been out,' said Kate proudly. 'I got as far as the churchyard on my own, and then I met the vicar.'

'Watch it,' said Roz. 'Remember your strange attraction for the species.'

'Oh, if you're talking about Tim Widdows, it was just a mild crush and he's forgotten about me ages ago,' said Kate breezily, hoping it was true. She didn't like to think of the pink face above the clerical collar growing wan if he was still pining for her. 'And anyway, this one is female. Her name is Elspeth.' For a moment she paused. Could there be any truth in her mother's suggestion? There had been no sign of a man at the vicarage, and Elspeth had invited herself round in an hour or so to take her into Oxford. No, she had known all about George.

'I've been thinking about your story.'

'Yes?'

'Land girls. Wrens. ATS. There were lots of women in uniform. You could have a glamorous young woman driving lorries, or a staff car.'

'Weren't Wrens something to do with the Navy?'

'Possibly.'

'It's just that we're a long way from the sea.'

'You're quibbling.'

'I'm grateful for the suggestions, really I am. That's lots of things for me to look into.'

'I should put the idea of children out of your head,' said Roz cheerfully. 'No one wants to read about kids, do they?'

'Estelle doesn't. And I don't suppose my editor does either. Land girls. ATS. Uniforms. GIs. You're right.'

She managed to ring off eventually. Roz had been rambling on about her new neighbours, but she couldn't have anything to grumble about with a quiet, retired couple, could she? Roz was just getting fussy in her old age.

She had time for her sandwich, but none left over for checking on the biscuit tin from the loft. It would have to wait until the evening, or even until the next morning. And, anyway, Roz was right again. She must concentrate on grown-ups and forget about children. She told herself this quite sternly, for in fact she was halfway up the stairs to fetch the biscuit tin when Elspeth rang the front doorbell.

'Yes,' she said, 'I'm ready. I'll just pick up my handbag and notebook.'

Walking down the road was easier now that she had a companion. The two women caught a bus into town and the journey passed quickly with someone to chat to. Elspeth left her at the door to the Central Library.

'I'll be about two hours,' she said, not specifying what she was going to do. Kate managed to curb her curiosity just for once. She might need a travelling companion again, after all.

'I'll be up in the Centre for Oxfordshire Studies,' said Kate. 'Drag me away from there when you want to get the bus home.'

She went up the stairs, past the main reading room. Other people were being whisked up to the top floor in a lift, but she didn't fancy being closed into such a small space with one or even more strangers. She should have stopped off at the general collection on the first floor to see what books she could find on the Second World War. She had plenty of homework to do before she could start making notes on her new book. But upstairs they would have old newspapers and material specific to this area. On the way out she could select a book or two – nothing too intellectual, she wasn't feeling up to it – and take them home with her. She walked confidently through to the desk and signed the visitors' book.

The assistant looked at the name she had written and her area of study. 'Oh, are you the one who writes the—'

'Yes,' said Kate. It was better than being the one who'd nearly been murdered in the cathedral. 'And can I look at the local papers for 1945?'

'You'll have to book a reader.'

'Then I'll do that.'

The woman relented. 'There's one coming free in about ten minutes. That will be a pound for three hours.'

Kate paid, then took a key for a locker where she could put away her jacket and handbag. She'd given up the small, polite one and reverted to her usual capacious model. Removing her notebook and biro, she sat down at the reader when it came free a few minutes later. She placed the film in the machine, switched on the power, and was immediately transported back more than half a century.

The pages sloped away from her and were slightly ragged at the edges as though they had been well-fingered before being put on film. She leaned forward to read the first front page. It was a mess of headlines and crowded paragraphs. Paper rationing, she realised. And each issue was only four pages. Since it looked so dull – so *worthy* – she was really quite glad that it was so short.

You'd hardly know this was a local paper, she concluded after studying the articles. It was all news of the war, abroad and at home. And the brief accounts of bombs dropping, of murders, or magistrates' courts, came from all over southern England, as though issued from some central news service. On the inside pages there were two or three letters printed each day, always covering the same trivial subjects. The paper's correspondents seemed obsessed with the price of cinema tickets. Why did it cost 3s.6d in Oxford compared to 2s.6d in Reading?

She found herself yawning; it was an effort to read on. Then she spotted an item about a Miss Marlyn, who'd been fined £5 by the magistrates for misuse of petrol. Just a minute! Was this one of the sainted Marlyns, respectable citizens of Oxford? Tsk, tsk. Pity they didn't give more details of her name and address so that she could be sure.

She passed on to the daily recipe, which seemed to involve a lot of cabbage and a certain amount of hot water. No wonder most of the advertisements were for cures for acidity, or for sleeplessness. 'Wake up your bile ducts!' one of them admonished her. The whole Oxford population was probably lying awake at night with bilious attacks, imagining a decent meal that involved not a single shred of raw cabbage.

An article on road accidents to young children caught her eye. 'Caused by their carelessness,' an unimaginative journalist had written. For a moment, Kate saw the convoys of khaki-painted trucks rattling through the narrow village streets of the county, and the small children who failed to jump out of their way in time. *Careless!* Not a word of criticism for the drivers, she noticed. Children were regarded in a manner that seemed foreign to the twenty-first century.

'I blame the parents,' said a predictable letter. 'Children shouldn't be roaming the streets like that.'

She passed on to another issue, skimming through the indigestible news on the front page, shuddering at the even more indigestible daily recipe. This time, they called it 'Spring Salad' and, in addition to the cabbage, it consisted of shredded raw swede and turnip, surrounded with piles of grated carrot and beetroot and decorated with radishes and parsley. Just for fun, the author of this disaster had dressed it with vinegar. No wonder people were all slim in those days, thought Kate.

She turned to the letters on the opposite page.

Ah! At last an adult who didn't blame child victims of road accidents for their injuries, but suggested that you couldn't expect youngsters to be completely responsible on the roads. It was up to the driver to notice them and be sufficiently in control of his vehicle to be able to stop. Doubtless this correspondent was seen as irredeemably indulgent by the majority of the paper's readers.

And then she took another look at the photograph at the top of the page. A dark picture of fourteen children in a dim hospital ward. These were the road accident victims, she read. The caption gave their first names and their ages. One of them was Christopher, aged ten.

Kate checked the date. She had reached 17th February, 1945. But which one was Christopher? All she could see were fourteen pale blobs for faces with dark smudges for eyes. One child was lying on his back, taking no interest in the press photographer. Her head told her that the child was very ill, possibly sedated or unconscious, but her imagination refused to leave it at that. His hair was cut as short as a convict's and emphasised the prominent cheekbones, the shadows round the eyes. He had a look of . . . what, exactly? Fear? Vulnerability? Defiance, even. Defeat. Any or all of these could she read in the child's face if she put her mind to it. And all it amounted to, in reality, was a pale smudge in a dark photo. Was it even *her* Christopher? Christopher Douglas Barnes?

She was making too many assumptions. The date might fit, but maybe her Christopher had died of whooping cough or diphtheria, or blood poisoning after being bitten by a dog. And why was she so fascinated by this unknown child anyway?

Eyes that follow you round the room. The cliché was all too true in this case. Oh, stop it, Kate told herself. You'll be saying that *you can run but you can't hide* in a minute.

She read the story underneath, which was as impersonal as all the others in the paper. Then she saw it. One of the children had died since the photo was taken, and this time it *did* give his name: Christopher Donald Branes, aged eleven. Not quite her Christopher, but it had to be the same boy. How often did a reporter get a name right? And the age was only one year out.

All the other vehicles involved in the accidents with children were military ones, the article said. Just this one child, Christopher Barnes – ah! he'd got the name right this time – was involved with a civilian vehicle. A delivery van, she read. The child had dashed into the road, following his sister, apparently. The driver had no chance. The girl, Susan, received a glancing blow, but the boy suffered fatal injuries.

I blame the parents too, this time, thought Kate, not to mention the van driver, and she hoped that the court would, too.

Kate wondered what had happened to Susan. Did the rabbit (or possibly teddy bear) belong to her rather than to her brother? The address – High Corner, Armitage Road – came into her head. She must walk down Armitage Road and find the house.

Oh yes? And then what will you do, Kate Ivory? Knock on the door, I suppose, and ask for a little girl called Susan Barnes. Or Branes. Or perhaps she's married and changed her surname. And you don't know what her married name is, just that she's called Susan. It's more than possible that a lot of little girls were named Susan in 1945. Like millions of them.

She had made a few pages of notes in her new notebook and now she drew a curly line underneath them while she thought about the Barnes children. She added a bunch of flowers and some sprays of leaves, then surrounded the whole lot with five-pointed stars. She shaded some of them in.

'Still busy, I see!' said a voice behind her.

Kate snapped her notebook shut and turned in her chair.

'Elspeth. Yes, I've had quite a productive afternoon. I've found a newspaper account of how Christopher Barnes died – he was hit by a van and died later in hospital.'

'Poor little kid. That's it, then.'

'Not exactly. Why did he leave his belongings in our house?'

'Is it important?'

'Possibly not.'

'But?'

'It's the photograph in the paper. He looks so desperate, somehow. White face, hollow eyes. Just lying there. But trying to tell me something.'

'You weren't even born,' said Elspeth sensibly.

'I really want to find out more about him. The report was so stark – there must be more to it.'

'That's the voice of the novelist speaking,' said Elspeth.

The voice of the novelist desperate for a story, thought Kate. 'How was your afternoon?'

'Oh, fine.' Elspeth had a way of closing a conversation. Why was she being so secretive? Perhaps she'd been visiting her lover. Vicars would need to be discreet about that sort of thing, of course.

Kate rewound the microfilm and returned it to its black box. She collected her jacket, slung her bag over her shoulder and she and Elspeth went down the stairs.

'Just a moment,' said Kate, making a detour into the main library. History section – over there on the left. She grabbed a couple of easy-reading volumes and found her library ticket. Two minutes later she and Elspeth walked out of the building together. Kate hardly noticed the crowds in George Street as she dodged through buses and bicycles, she was so busy wondering how to track down the two Barnes children.

'You got some good ideas for your new book, then?' asked Elspeth as they settled themselves into the Headington bus.

'New book?' Kate replied vaguely. 'Oh, *that*. Yes, I have, thanks. Lots of interesting material.' And she'd have to convince Estelle, too, that she'd started work on something racy and exciting. She hoped her agent wouldn't ring her. It would ruin her evening. Oh well, at least George would be lovely to her, the way George always was.

Elspeth left her outside George's house, but Kate watched her walk away – scarlet Capri pants and an emerald-and-white striped baggy sweatshirt. Instead of going indoors, Kate turned the corner and started to stroll down Armitage Road.

Armitage Road, she discovered, was quite ordinary and really rather like Cavendish Road. She walked the length of the even numbers and peered at gates, down paths and drives, looking for house names. There were plenty of the kind you might expect, but nothing remotely like 'High Corner'. She tried the opposite side, the odd numbers, but found only enough tree names for a moderate-sized copse, and one called 'Puevigi' which she had to nearly stand on her head to understand.

House names, she realised, were things of fickle fashion, and 'High Corner' probably sounded élitist in the twenty-first century. Too elevated, too competitive. It could be any of the self-contained red brick establishments that stretched down the road.

In the old days – before the attack – she might have knocked on a door or two and charmed some little old lady into telling her which house was High Corner, and where she might find people who had known Chris Barnes, but those days were over. All she could do now was to return to George's place and try to think of a plan that wouldn't involve her in talking to strangers, or even in leaving the house.

She let herself back into number 74, trying to convince herself that she had had a full and courageous day so far. As a matter of fact, she *had*, now she came to consider it.

'Well done,' said Roz, when she phoned a little later. 'You'll soon be back to normal.'

Kate didn't like to think of herself as ever being anything but normal, but she conceded that to an unbiased observer she had been a little timid for the past few months.

'And how's life in Agatha Street?' she asked. For a moment she had a twinge of something she could only describe as nostalgia. Was she really missing the place?

'Your lovely new neighbours invited me in for a drink yesterday evening,' said Roz.

'That was kind of them.'

'Very kind.'

'You don't sound enthusiastic about them.'

'I'm sure they're lovely people, really. Laura and Edward Foster. They were very generous with the red wine.'

Kate listened to the spaces between the words. 'I'm not going to like them, am I?'

'You might start to miss dear Jason and even dearer Tracey, possibly even dearest little Toadface, I'm afraid.'

'Oh, they can't be that bad!'

Perhaps it was just as well that she and George were getting on so well. Really there was no reason for her to return to Agatha Street, ever, she told herself.

'I'm glad you're feeling better,' said George, that evening.

In Kate's experience, this kind of remark usually meant that someone was about to ask her to do something she didn't wish to do.

'Yes?' she queried cautiously.

'I think it's time we got together with Sam and Emma for a jolly evening out,' said George.

Sam, George's elder brother. Emma, his wife and an old – but usually disapproving – friend of Kate's. Somehow, when Kate was around, things started to crumble in Emma's life, and Emma blamed Kate, even on the rare occasions when it wasn't her fault.

'What a good idea,' said Kate, still cautiously.

'I know you're not really up to laying on a dinner party,' said George. 'Not that you couldn't do it,' he added hastily, 'but it might be a better evening for all of us if we went out.'

Kate waited for a few seconds just to allow him to wonder whether he'd put his foot in it and hurt her feelings, before saying mildly, 'Where would you like to go?'

George mentioned the name of a new restaurant in North Oxford.

'The one in the Woodstock Road? It looks interesting. I'd wondered what it was like,' said Kate. It had looked interesting from the distance and safety of her mother's car, anyway. 'And throbbing with customers – that's got to be a good sign. Yes, I'd like to try eating there.' Kate was perfectly aware that she was storing up Brownie points for her co-operation, even if George hadn't quite realised it. He had the faintly bemused look of a man who is being manipulated by a woman but can't quite see where it's leading. Kate carried on smiling in a friendly way, which confused him even further since he had been expecting an argument.

It was most unfair of Emma to blame Kate for the difficult patches in her life. On the contrary, it was Kate's troubles that were all down to Emma. It was, after all, Emma's mother who had gone missing, and Emma who had bullied Kate into searching for her. And although it had been Kate who had tracked her down, and Kate who was nearly killed, in Emma's mind all the fuss that ensued was entirely due to her friend's habit of attracting trouble. Gratitude had not come into it. And the small fee they had agreed on was only paid after Kate had pointedly submitted an invoice and Emma had just as pointedly examined the receipts for Kate's expenses.

And yet they remained friends. Emma, with her raft of children and messy house, fighting to keep a toehold in the labour market on top of everything else, was a reminder to Kate of what her own life might have been if she had opted for marriage, domesticity and motherhood in her twenties. Emma looked at Kate's cream silk trousers with envy, but Kate's emotions when she saw one of Emma's children make sticky fingerprints on their mother's jeans (fastened with a large safety pin because Emma hadn't yet managed to take off the pounds she had gained with her last baby) and demand a bedtime story, were roughly identical.

Mind you, thought Kate, I'm still only in my thirties. Her biological clock was ticking, but the sand wasn't all in the bottom half of the hourglass quite yet. She frowned at the mixing of metaphors and thought about rephrasing the thought.

'You're sure that will be all right?' George had noticed the frown and misread its cause. 'Would you like me to ring Emma for you?'

'Of course not,' said Kate brightly. 'Emma and I are old friends. I'll do it straight away.'

'Make it clear that I'll be paying for all of us,' said George. 'Emma gets a bit fraught if you suggest she and Sam spend money on inessentials.'

Kate took the cordless phone into the kitchen. She didn't like George to hear her when she was acting a part. He might get the impression – erroneous, of course – that she was sometimes less than frank with him, too.

'Emma? Kate here. George and I were hoping that you and Sam could join us for a meal one evening next week.'

'At George's house?' asked Emma suspiciously. Kate suppressed a sigh.

'Not at our place,' she said firmly. She knew that Emma considered that she played fast and loose with men's affections, and was waiting for her to walk out on George and leave him heartbroken. 'Have you noticed that bright new restaurant in the Woodstock Road?'

'No,' said Emma.

'Believe me, it's there,' said Kate.

'Oh, very well.' Emma sounded as though she was doing Kate a big favour. 'The weekend would be better for us, rather than next week,' she said, giving in a little and sounding friendlier. 'Friday or Saturday.'

'Friday or Saturday?' Kate popped her head round the sitting-room door.

'Friday,' said George, without looking up from the paper he was reading.

'This Friday,' repeated Kate into the telephone receiver.

'Is it very expensive, do you think?' asked Emma, the suspicion back in her voice.

'I don't know, but George is paying,' said Kate.

'Oh.' Emma sounded relieved, but couldn't quite bring herself to thank Kate and George. 'I suppose we'd better dress up,' she said doubtfully.

'Posh frocks,' agreed Kate, hoping that Emma owned such a thing and that if she did she could still get into it and close the zip. A gaping zip closed with an extra-large safety-pin reduced the elegance of one's *tenue de soirée*, she had always found.

'And you will behave, won't you, Kate?'

'Of course.' What on earth could Emma mean? 'I won't use my knife for my peas, I promise,' she said.

'Oh, *you* know what I mean,' said Emma.

'Don't worry. I won't let down the good name of the Dolbys.'

'Our name means something in this town,' said Emma severely.

It meant respectability and conventional behaviour and standing as a Councillor – yes, Kate did know. 'I wasn't planning on throwing bread rolls across the table. And I won't wear that dress you disapprove of with the rather low back–'

'– and front,' put in Emma, who obviously knew the one she was referring to.

'I'm getting the hang of this family thing, really I am,' said Kate.

'I do hope so. But I can't stand here chatting all evening, Kate dear. I have too much to do.'

Meaning I haven't, thought Kate as she rang off.

'I hadn't realised how difficult families were,' she remarked as she sat down next to George.

'Difficult? Oh, I don't think we're difficult,' he said.

'It's the way you have to negotiate with each other, and navigate through everyone's sensitivities.'

'Don't all families do that?' His attention was still on his paper.

'Probably. But I've never had to. I only have Roz, and she's hardly ever there.'

'I had loads of practice. The Dolbys produced one offspring in every generation who went in for childbearing in a big way.'

'Sam and Emma.'

'Exactly. They make up for me, and our parents made up for a couple of unmarried aunts of ours. But I've always had loads of relations.'

And family property, and family pride, thought Kate.

'I suppose your father died over twenty years ago,' said George.

'Well over. And he was an only child, and so was Roz. So I have no cousins, nor aunts and uncles.'

'No one from the previous generation, either?'

'I don't think so. I've never met any of them, anyway. Maybe there was a big argument and a feud,' she said hopefully. 'Or a shameful secret that no one ever talks about.'

'Or maybe they all died, or were never born.'

'My version's more exciting, don't you think?'

'And probably a fiction.'

'That's what I'm good at.'

There was a short pause while they both wondered how to

avoid the subject of Kate's creative block.

'I'll get back to it. I'm full of ideas,' she said eventually. They both knew what she was talking about. 'And tomorrow I'll start following up the leads that Elspeth's given me.'

'Elspeth?'

'The vicar with the nose-stud.'

'Maybe we should invite her and her husband to join us for dinner on Friday.'

'And tease Emma?'

George smiled. Maybe he, too, got tired of navigating the tricky waters of his family relationships.

'I'm not sure whether she's married or not,' said Kate.

'But knowing you, you'll soon find out.'

'I'm not really all that nosy, am I?'

'Yes,' said George. 'I think you probably are.'

5

It was the next morning and George had left the house for Brookes.

Kate had no excuse for ignoring her own work. She had washed their breakfast mugs and tidied the kitchen. She had rearranged the cushions on the sofa and straightened the duvet on the bed. She had even put a small load of washing into the machine and could hear it chugging away in the background.

Now she had made herself a fresh cup of coffee, resisting the idea of a chocolate Hob-Nob to eat with it, and was looking at the rather sparse notes she had made so far.

Violet Watts. Oswald Court. The words stood alone in the middle of a page.

Oswald Court was a short, brisk walk away. The sort of walk that a fit woman in her thirties could manage with no problem on a breezy, sunny morning.

There was no escaping it, Kate concluded, and she went to put on the sort of clothes she thought suitable for visiting an elderly lady. Reading Elspeth's hints, Violet Watts might even be an awkward old bat.

Should she telephone first? There was little point. The residents of Oswald Court weren't likely to be out on the town or enjoying a game of tennis in the park. She could prepare herself for a row of chairs in front of daytime television, and a shouted conversation with a defective hearing-aid plugged into a wrinkled old ear.

She changed into a skirt that came below her knees and a linen jacket, made sure she had a couple of biros in her bag as well as her notebook, and then opened the front door.

It wasn't quite so bad this time. Maybe with practice she could even learn to enjoy walking down the road again. She managed to say, 'Hello,' to the woman weeding her front garden at number 8, to smile at the milkman as he sat in his float counting small change. She gave the fierce dog at number 14 a wide berth, and was feeling quite jaunty ten minutes later as she reached the long, low building that was Oswald Court.

It had been built in the sixties by the look of it, and its liver-coloured bricks needed repointing. The windows were large and all curtained in the same dreary shade of mid-blue. They gave the impression of inviting the passers-by to stare in at the residents rather than providing a view on to the outside world for them. The interior seemed a world apart – a place of high-backed chairs and women with scanty white hair sitting with their backs to the road. Whatever their lives were, they didn't seem interested in what the rest of the neighbourhood was doing.

Kate had to shout her name into an entryphone before someone would let her in. She found this reassuring. Presumably they checked before allowing in axe-murderers or women wielding vicious knives. She hoped so.

'I've come to see Violet Watts,' she told the girl in the blue overall who let her in.

'Is she expecting you?'

'No. Does that matter?'

'I shouldn't think so.'

They walked down a corridor painted a cheerful shade of yellow and decorated with jolly figurative paintings of easily-recognisable scenes. The place seemed clean, and smelled of antiseptic which didn't quite mask a background whiff of incontinence and leg ulcers.

They stopped by a door wide enough to admit a wheelchair and the girl showed Kate into the sort of room she'd been expecting. The windows had the same regulation blue curtains and the floor was covered in some sort of vinyl that was presumably easy to keep clean. Not very cosy. There were three or four elderly women dozing in brown-covered chairs in front of a television set. The sound was turned down so as not to disturb their nap. In a corner, as far from the television as it was possible to get, sat another woman, knitting something in a violent shade of magenta, as though protesting at the forcible brain-washing by chat show and the bland, institutional colour scheme.

'Mrs Watts,' said the girl who had shown Kate in, 'I have a visitor for you,' and she disappeared.

Kate looked for a hearing-aid but failed to see one. And, actually, now she was close to her, she could see that Violet Watts was old, but not excessively so, and didn't look the least decrepit. In her mid-eighties, perhaps. Not much more. Kate tried an ingratiating smile.

'What are you grinning at?' snapped Violet Watts.

Kate removed the smile, which had apparently failed to ingratiate.

'Mrs Watts? My name's Kate Ivory and I'm a writer,' she began, moving an empty chair so that she could sit opposite the older woman.

'What do you write?'

'Novels. Historical novels.'

'Never heard of you. What name do you use?'

'Kate Ivory,' said Kate with resignation.

'You look a bit like the one who nearly got herself killed in the cathedral.'

'Yes, that was me.'

Violet Watts looked more cheerful at this and opened her mouth to ask intrusive questions.

No, thought Kate, I am not going to discuss my operation or show you my scar. 'I'm about to write another book,' she put in quickly, 'and I was hoping that you could help me.'

'And what's this one about, then? Sex and violence, I suppose.'

'Not—'

'That's all you young people ever think about,' Violet Watts interrupted. 'Think you invented it, don't you?'

'No—'

'But you're wrong. I could tell you stories that would make your hair curl.'

'That's what I was hoping,' Kate told her, timing her interruption for the moment when the old lady drew breath. 'You see, I'm setting this story during the Second World War and I was looking for background material.'

'You want to hear my stories?' Mrs Watts looked so surprised by this that Kate could only imagine that no one had ever willingly done so before.

'Yes, I do,' she said firmly. 'But first, I wonder if you could tell me where I can find the house called High Corner, in Armitage Road. I've looked all along both sides and I can't find it.'

'It's the corner one,' said Violet Watts immediately.

'Then it's not called High Corner any more.' Of course, now she thought about it, it made sense that it would be on a corner with a name like that. 'I don't suppose you remember which particular corner it was?'

'Of course I do. Do you think I'm daft just because I'm old?'

'Certainly not,' said Kate smartly.

'It was the corner of Armitage Road with Cavendish Road. The council changed the numbers for some reason best known to themselves. The end house in Armitage Road became the last one in Cavendish Road. It would have been one or two Armitage Road, but it must have been one of the high numbers in Cavendish Road, seventy-something I should think. An even number, anyway. They're even numbers on that side.'

Kate worked it out. A high, even number in Cavendish Road, on the corner of Armitage Road.

'Seventy-four?' asked Kate. 'Seventy-four Cavendish Road?'

'That would be it, I should say. Something like that.' The old lady sounded impatient. She wanted to get on with her account of life in the old days. 'Why, don't you believe me?'

'Yes, yes. Of course. It's just that that's where I'm living at the moment.'

'Well, it's the corner house on that side I'm talking about. And if that's where you're living, you're living at High Corner. John Marlyn, the man who built it, he fancied himself and his family's position. That's why he gave it a stuck-up name like that. You say it's not called that any more? Well, I'm not surprised. It was Elinor Marlyn's house. She left it to that funny niece of hers.'

So it *was* the same house. Kate rapidly flicked through mental notes. 'Her niece Sadie?'

'Stupid name to give her. Yes, that was it, Sadie. She was away all through the war with one of the women's services. She was the sort of girl who liked wearing uniform,' she said, leaning close to Kate so that the mingled smell of peppermints and, perhaps, sweet sherry gusted over her.

'Oh?' said Kate, trying not to jump to conclusions.

'Those Marlyns bred strong-minded women in every genera-tion. There was Elinor's Aunt Margaret before her. She wasn't the marrying kind, either.' More meaning looks at the phrase 'not the marrying kind'. But then, Mrs Watts would hardly use the term 'gay'.

'You knew them all well?'

'Knew them? I worked for them! You can't help knowing people better than you want to when you work in their houses.'

'So you worked in High Corner?'

'She liked the place kept clean.'

'What about during the war? I thought people had to give up their –' she was about to say 'servants' but thought better of it '– give up employing people to look after them,' she finished lamely.

'You wanted to say "servants",' said Violet Watts. 'And that's what we were, Arthur and me. We were her servants. At least we knew our place,' she added darkly.

'You mean there were those who didn't?'

'I'm not saying anything against Arthur's brother Danny. Especially since the boy isn't here to defend himself.'

The boy must be eighty or so by now, thought Kate.

'It's a pity Danny wasn't called up for the Army, he might have had a better time of it, but the Wattses all have weak chests, and he maintained he was working on the land.'

'What happened to him?' asked Kate, forgetting for the moment what she was really here to learn.

'All the money he was earning did him no good,' said Violet Watts crossly. 'Took him into bad company, and the boy had never learned to swim.'

'No?' She wasn't following this story very well. Perhaps the old lady was senile after all.

'He fell off his bike by the bridge over Wheatley way. He'd have been all right if the river hadn't flooded and he might have saved himself if he'd been sober.'

'So he drowned? That's terrible! He can't have been very old.'

'He had such plans for the future. But the accident with the child upset him. He had a soft heart, that boy, and he never really got over it, though I told him it couldn't be helped. He was going to be a millionaire before he was thirty, young Danny reckoned. And where is he now?'

'It's a very lovely churchyard,' said Kate, knowing her remark was inadequate. She hurried on: 'Do you remember any children living in the house during the war?'

'Vaccies, do you mean?'

'Evacuees, yes.'

'Vaccies – children down from London. First of all they came as soon as war was declared, with their mothers, and they were all home before Christmas. Then a few months later they were back again, running from the Blitz. Most of 'em went home again just a few months after that. Couldn't take the country life, they said. Couldn't stand the soap and water and the decent food and respectable folks, *we* all said. Then in the summer of forty-four they flooded in again. Running from the doodlebugs this time.'

'Doodlebugs?' Kate realised she had a lot of work to do on this period of history.

'Flying bombs. V1s and V2s. Came out of the blue, just when we were thinking the war was going to end. It was all over for that Hitler, he didn't have a chance once the Yanks joined in, but still he sent his wicked bombs. They fell over the south-east, and London of course. I don't think they got much further north or west than that. Yes, we had vaccies all right.

103

She wanted me and Arthur to have them at our place, but Arthur stood up to her for once. He said we only had the two bedrooms, and Danny was already using the little one at the back, and she had that big place to herself, rattling round in it like a dried-up old pea in a pod. "I'm saving my spare rooms to take in air-raid victims," she said in that plummy voice of hers. "There haven't been any," my Arthur told her, "and it's about time you did your bit."

'She'd have told him what for if they'd been on their own, but the Billeting Officer, young Naomi King, she was standing there listening to it all, and Miss Marlyn had to bite her tongue and look as though she was pleased to be doing her share of war work after all. "I'll take a girl," she told Naomi, as though she was ordering a pound of best Cheddar from Grimbly Hughes. "You'll have to take two," said Naomi, standing up to her in her turn. "We don't like to separate children from the same family, especially when they've been through so much back in London." That was telling her! "Two girls," says Miss Marlyn. "Two *children*," says Miss King in her turn. And she had her way.'

'So High Corner took in two evacuees?'

'A girl and a boy. She didn't like it, Miss Marlyn, but she did it. They weren't bad children, I'll say that for them. They weren't slum kids or anything. We had no lice or fleas and they knew what a proper lavatory was. You heard dreadful stories about some of the children people took in. And they'd had a rotten time back in London, what with their dad dying and their mother being so ill. White faces, black smudges for eyes, and they looked as though they hadn't had a decent night's sleep for months. Just stood there, with him holding on to her hand as though he'd never let go. She was dressed neatly enough, but you could see where the tears had streaked the dirt on her face, and she needed a clean handkerchief. It was a long journey for them, with the train stopping every mile or two, then the bus trip to the community hall and the walk out to Armitage Road. Proper little refugees, they looked.'

'Christopher Barnes and his sister.'

'Chris and little Susie. How did you know that?'

'I've been doing a fair bit of research,' said Kate smugly.

'That's what you call it when you sit and listen to gossip, is it?'

'I've been reading newspapers, too,' said Kate defensively.

'They tell lies. I shouldn't believe what you read in them.'

'The *Oxford Mail* said that Christopher Barnes was hit by a delivery van and died a few days later in hospital,' said Kate.

There was a silence which lasted until Kate wondered whether Violet Watts had dozed off. But the blue eyes were still blazing at her.

'Isn't that true?' she prompted.

'Yes, it's true.'

'Can you tell me any more about it?'

'I can tell you it was our Danny driving and our Danny who got blamed for the death. But what can you do when these kids just come running out into the road without looking? There was nothing he could do about it, was there? It was only his skill with driving that stopped the little girl, little Susan, from being killed too.'

Violet Watts came to a halt.

'I'm sorry,' said Kate. 'I didn't mean to upset you.'

'I'm not upset!' Violet shouted at her.

No, she could see from the expression on her face that it was anger the old woman felt.

'Everything all right?' It was the girl in the blue overall, drawn no doubt by the raised voices. Probably afraid

I'm a granny-basher, thought Kate.

'We're fine,' she said. 'Just reminiscing about the good old days.'

'There wasn't anything very good about them,' grumbled Violet Watts when the girl had left the room. 'They say in London there was this great spirit of co-operation and brotherly love, everybody pulling together to defeat Jerry. But it wasn't much like that out here. We were just spectators, really, of a war that was going on somewhere else. Oh yes, the planes filled the skies and Beaverbrook had the Morris works mending them every time they got damaged. And we had the Yanks and the convoys going through every day. And a whole lot of civil servants and boffins down from Whitehall crowding into the colleges. But we weren't in any real danger out here. Hitler wanted it for himself when he won the war, they say. Well, he was welcome to it, as far as I'm concerned.'

'Why's that?'

'The likes of Elinor Marlyn bossed us around before the war and they were still in charge here afterwards. We lived in her gardener's cottage and we had to mind what we said and what we did or we'd be out. That's not what we fought a war for, is it?'

'Probably not,' said Kate, who came from a generation that hadn't known war on its own territory and couldn't imagine what it might feel like. Apart from her agent, she didn't have to worry about who had power over her life, either. Her mother's generation had gone on protest marches for what it believed in (had Roz? she wondered), but her generation hadn't even done that. The politically apathetic, that's what they were. Too absorbed in their personal development, in making money and having a good time.

'Not that she lived long into peacetime,' continued Violet Watts, cutting into Kate's train of thought.

'She didn't?' Kate felt a brief pang of guilt at encouraging Mrs Watts to gossip about members of George's family, but suppressed it quickly. How else was she to discover what had happened? And anyway, she was interested in George and all that affected him. 'Tell me about it,' she encouraged.

'She killed herself!'

'What!'

'That's right. One day in late autumn, it was, when the nights were lengthening and the dew was coming down heavy in the mornings. Lovely time of year, I always think, with the smell of bonfires on the air and the long evenings in front of a good coal fire to look forward to. Though there was a fuel shortage that winter, now I come to think about it. Everything froze. Puddles, pipes, window panes. I had terrible chilblains.'

'And Miss Marlyn?'

'What? Oh yes. She kept a little van in her garage. Didn't take it out much because they'd caught her using it for her own amusement and fined her five pounds. We had petrol rationing in those days. I don't suppose you knew that, did you?'

'Yes, I had heard,' said Kate.

'Well, she went out to her garage late one evening it must have been. She got into the cab, turned over the motor, and asphyxiated herself with the exhaust fumes. She must have sat there in the dark and died in the stink of petrol fumes,' she added lugubriously.

'But why?'

'She knew the accident was as much her fault as Danny's. She'd encouraged him to have silly ideas about himself, pushed him on to be ambitious. But Danny didn't have the brains to succeed at anything, not without her behind him. You can bet they were off on one of their barmy adventures in the van that day.'

'You're telling me that Elinor Marlyn and Danny were involved in shady schemes together?'

'You don't believe me. Well, there's plenty of unusual things happening in this world that people like you don't know about.'

'It's just that it sounds unlikely,' said Kate lamely.

'Why ask me questions if you're not going to believe the answers I give you? What's your interest in the Marlyns anyway?'

'It's nothing personal,' said Kate defensively.

'Let me see, now. Elinor Marlyn left the house to her niece, Sadie, like I said. And Sadie wasn't a Marlyn, she was a Dolby – another family that likes to think well of itself. They were well-suited, Sarah Marlyn and Robert Dolby.'

'I'm losing the thread a bit,' confessed Kate.

'Elinor Marlyn's sister, Sarah, married Robert Dolby. He was Mayor one year – back in the thirties, before the war, that must have been – and then he was something big in the Chamber of Commerce. They fancied themselves, those two. Didn't seem to be any worse off after the war. People like that always do well, don't you find? Their son bought himself a big house just off Headington Hill.' Sam and Emma's place, thought Kate. It belonged to Sam's father before him. 'And they had a daughter called Sadie, who joined the ATS and went off up North. When Elinor died, Sadie inherited, and she came back from Manchester or wherever it was, bringing her schoolteacher friend with her.'

'I thought you said she wasn't the marrying kind.'

'She wasn't. This was a *lady* schoolteacher,' said Violet Watts, pulling her lips into a prim line.

So what? thought Kate. But presumably it had caused a bit of a stir in respectable Armitage Road in the 1940s. And in the respectable Dolby family, too. George had mentioned none of this.

'Mind you, she had her comeuppance in the long run.' Mrs Watts was well into her stride by now, her pale blue eyes alive and sparkling in their pink, hairless rims.

'How was that?' prompted Kate obligingly.

'The other woman was expecting to inherit the house, you can be sure of that. She'd lived there with Sadie for over thirty years and must have thought she had her feet firmly under the table. But Sadie died quite suddenly.'

'An accident again?' put in Kate.

'It was her heart, they said. You can never trust those women with a high colour like hers to make old bones, I always think.' Mrs Watts sounded as though she'd have liked it to be something more sinister. 'But there was this young woman –' fifty-five or sixty, calculated Kate '– suddenly out on the streets. It must have come as a bit of a surprise, I can tell you.'

'Poor thing,' said Kate.

'Serves her right for her godless ways,' said Mrs Watts severely. 'And she'd have had her pension. She'd worked all her life, after all. It was just that she didn't get her hands on the Dolbys' property. No one's likely to do that. You just remember that, young woman.' An arthritic finger poked Kate's knee to emphasise the point. 'You make your own way. Keep writing those books of yours. Don't go relying on Dolby property. They never leave it outside the family, whatever silliness they're led into by their romantic fancies.'

'I'll remember that,' said Kate, who had never thought of herself as a romantic fancy before. (She saw it as small and circular, covered with milk chocolate and decorated with a crystallised pink rose.)

'Can you remember the name of Sadie's friend, or where she went after Sadie's death?'

'She was a Meg or a Madge, perhaps a Marjorie. I never

gave her the time of day, myself. And I think she went back up North. Maybe her own family took her in.' Mrs Watts sniffed to show that if she'd been part of that family she'd have done no such weak-willed thing. 'She'd be dead by now,' she said. 'I shouldn't go wasting your time looking for her.'

'No. I won't.' Kate could see that Meg, Madge or Marjorie would probably know very little about Christopher Barnes and his sister Susan. Time to steer Mrs Watts back on to the track.

'And I can't see that any of this is going to be any use to you in your book.'

'Oh, it's all wonderfully rich background material,' said Kate.

'I thought you were just being nosy about your young man's family.'

'Well, tell me more about the young Barnes children, then. If you can remember anything,' she added, throwing out a challenge she thought Violet Watts would find hard to resist.

'I'm getting tired,' the old woman said. 'It must be time for my nap.'

'Elspeth Fry told me you could talk for hours,' said Kate unsympathetically. The old could sleep any time of night or day if they wanted to, surely?

'That vicar's got a sharp tongue in her head. And I don't hold with lady vicars, anyway.'

'I shouldn't tell *her* that. I reckon she could be quite fierce if she tried.'

'You're laughing at me now. I know what you young people are like.' Violet sounded quite huffy.

'Who would know about Christopher Barnes?' asked Kate quickly.

'You could try the school. St Mark's C. of E. All the children went there. They rebuilt it some years back, but it's only the buildings that changed. Lots of people in this neighbourhood never moved away from where they were brought up. It's still like a village round here, see, in spite of all the incomers. There should be young people in their sixties who'd remember him.'

'Thanks a lot,' said Kate. 'I'd better be going now and leave you in peace. Would you like me to bring you a copy of the book when it's published?'

'Don't bother, dear. I like real-life stories myself. True crimes. Adventures that happen to actual people.' She fumbled in her knitting bag and drew out a paperback. 'I've finished with this one. You can have it if you like.'

Kate took it from her. The cover showed a spacecraft like a saucepan lid with acrials. Weird green figures swarmed out of the open doors. *Aliens Have Landed*, she read. *They're Living with Us Now! Read the Facts!*

'You don't want to go bothering with all that made-up stuff,' said Violet Watts. 'You want the real thing, like me. Do you watch *The X-Files* on TV?'

'I can't say I have,' said Kate, handing back the book. 'But I mustn't take this away from you, I'll have to get my own copy.' She rose to her feet. 'Thanks for talking to me. It's been fascinating. I'll say goodbye now, Mrs Watts.'

'Goodbye, dear.'

And then, as Kate opened the door to leave, the old lady added, 'What did you say your name was?'

Aliens, thought Kate. How much could you believe of her story when she was obviously off her head? Though as she said goodbye to the girl in blue on her way out, she did wonder whether there weren't one or two Living With Us Now.

As she walked back towards Cavendish Road she thought over all she'd heard. She should really have brought a tape-recorder with her so that she could play the conversation over

111

again. But she'd been so enthralled with the gossip about the Dolbys that she hadn't even taken many notes. She'd scribbled down 'St Mark's C. of E. School'. That was the school Elspeth had mentioned, too. It was only round the corner from St Mark's Church and she could call in there before going home. It didn't occur to her, in her childfree state, that it was still the school summer holidays. She didn't think, either, of looking all around her and checking on the presence of a woman with a knife. She had forgotten about being frightened by every shadow in the street as she concentrated on following up her story.

Luckily, although the school was empty of children, there were a couple of people in the office, catching up with administrative chores. The building, Kate realised, must have been rebuilt at about the same time as Oswald Court and resembled it quite closely. Only the smell was different: less antiseptic and more unwashed socks. She rang the bell and shouted her identity into a similar entryphone. Then she knocked on the door marked *Office* and walked in.

A woman with neatly groomed hair and carefully applied make-up sat at a desk behind a name-card reading *Janice Carlton – School Secretary*. She wore a professional smile and a pair of large spectacles that might well terrify any small child bent on wrongdoing.

'How can I help you?' she asked.

Kate went into her well-rehearsed spiel. 'My name is Kate Ivory,' she began.

'The writer?'

'Yes.' That made it easier. 'And I'm trying to find out background information for a book I'm writing set in the Second World War.'

'And how do you think we can help you with that at St Mark's?'

'There were evacuees billeted in this part of Oxford, and the children who were at school here in the nineteen-forties must have memories of them, and of what it was like to live here, in the war,' she finished lamely.

'And you'd like me to find you their names and addresses?'

'Yes. That would be wonderful.'

'I expect it would, but I really can't do that.'

'Why not?' It was frustrating to have hope held out like that and then immediately whisked away.

'We don't give out names and addresses held in our files,' Janice said. Kate could tell it was no use trying to trick her into revealing a single one. The School Secretary had long experience of being conned by small children and their parents, and was quite capable of dealing with anything Kate could dream up on the spur of the moment.

'Is there any way you can suggest of finding these people?' she asked, without much hope of receiving a helpful reply.

'Former pupils are more likely to keep in touch with their secondary school than with a primary school like ours,' Janice said. 'In those days the children from St Mark's would have moved on to Berry Road Secondary School, or to the girls' or boys' grammar school. Both of them will have an Old Pupils' Association.'

'And they won't cough up names and addresses, either,' said Kate.

'If you have access to the Internet, you could try their web pages,' suggested Janice. 'You'll find contact names and addresses there, and you can post your enquiry there, too, I think you'll find.'

'Excellent! Thank you very much.'

'There is one other thing.'

'Yes?' Kate was picking up her bag and preparing to depart.

'I believe that when the London schoolchildren were evacuated, entire schools moved into the area, complete with their teachers.'

'Yes?' Where was this leading?

'One or two of the teachers stayed on at the end of the war. They liked it here, or they had settled down with a husband or wife. And some evacuees came back to live here when they were old enough to be independent.'

'And you can give me a name?'

'She was well-known to all the children,' conceded Janice Carlton. 'Her name is Miss Arbuthnot.'

Kate made a note of the name. She looked an enquiry.

'No,' said Janice. 'Don't even ask. I don't believe she even possesses such a thing as a first name.'

'And where can I find her?'

'She still lives in the same small flat she's lived in for over fifty years. And she attends Sunday morning service at St Mark's Church, as she's done every week since she came here.'

And, as Janice Carlton was nowhere near old enough to have observed this fact for herself, Kate inferred that Miss Arbuthnot was a local institution.

'She wears a plain black coat and a grey hat the shape of a large pancake,' added Janice. 'You can't miss her.'

On her way back to Cavendish Road, Kate reflected that she might well persuade Elspeth Fry to be less particular about the provisions of the Data Protection Act than Janice Carlton had been. She didn't feel like waiting until Sunday morning to track down the redoubtable Miss Arbuthnot and with a little coaxing, Elspeth might well disgorge her address. It was all a question of approach, she had found.

On the other hand, it was possible that Elspeth was just as discreet as Janice Carlton. Life was always ready with another little disappointment.

There was a phone call from Estelle soon after Kate arrived home.

'I'm not pushing you, Kate,' she said briskly, 'but I'd like a little progress report on the new book. I don't want you falling behind any further.'

'Don't tell me, you're doing this for my own good.'

'Of course I am. Now, what have you been doing?'

'I've been down to the library and I've been looking up the newspapers for the war years.' Only a little exaggeration there, after all.

'Good. It's important to get a feel of the times. It makes for a rich texture in a historical novel.'

'And I've made contact with a source of oral history,' said Kate. 'I've had a very rewarding session already and I've been given more names to follow up the stories.'

'Excellent. This will be first-hand narrative on the life of the typical young, passionate woman in the services, will it?'

Kate remembered Violet Watts and her magenta knitting, disapproving of anything that could possibly be labelled 'passionate'. 'I'm getting there,' she said.

'Good. Well, keep me posted. We don't want you to disappear from view, do we?'

No, we don't, said Kate, after she had rung off. But she had to admit that the reality of her research was a long way from what she had suggested to Estelle. All she had found out was the local gossip about her partner's family – probably highly inaccurate and biased – and the beginnings of a story about two unfortunate London children evacuated to Headington in the last year of the war. Estelle wouldn't be at all pleased with her if she found out. Kate filed the phrase 'rich texture' away for future use, though. It could come in useful when fobbing off her agent. *I'm working on the texture, Estelle.* Yes, that should keep her sweet for a day or two before she started to wonder where she had heard it before.

Maybe she could read a serious book. There was quite likely to be something suitable on one of the many crowded book-shelves in this house. These books were not only those collected by George over the years but had also come from previous genera-tions living in the house. She could tell by the faded cloth covers of the hardbacks and the brittle brown pages of the paperbacks that they'd been waiting to be read for a great many years.

Unfortunately for the progress of her novel, they merely reminded her, for some reason, of the biscuit tin that Christopher Barnes had used to store his treasures in.

She went to the room she was using as a study intending to check her e-mail. She would make herself a cup of tea and then indulge herself with an hour's study of the contents of the biscuit tin before George got home from work. She wouldn't want him to think she was nosing into the recent history of his house and family.

But there was only one e-mail waiting for her, and that was from Estelle: 'Why aren't you working on your novel?' it demanded. Oh, very well. She e-mailed back, 'I am! I am!' then thought perhaps she'd better do what she said. She could sketch out one or two likely characters. Write a page or two of notes. Forget all about Christopher Douglas Barnes. Resolutely, she shoved the tin back into the bottom drawer of the desk.

She managed half an hour's work before remembering that she'd promised herself a cup of tea.

6

After drinking a cup of tea, Kate forced herself to concentrate on her novel again. She jotted down a few likely names for her characters then realised that she needed to find out about Army and Air Force ranks. She didn't want to get that sort of thing wrong. And her mind kept slipping back to Christopher and Susan. Where had they come from? 'London' was too vague and Barnes too common a surname. Did they have family? Just as she was working out how to approach Elspeth Fry and extract from her the information she needed about Miss Arbuthnot, so that she could follow up that lead, there was a ring at her front doorbell.

'Hello, Kate. I have some goodies for you.'

'Come in, Elspeth.'

Some days, everything went right for you.

'Shall I make tea or coffee or something?'

'Not for me, thanks. Vicars are awash with tea after visiting parishioners.' She indicated the large package she was holding in her arms. 'Where would you like me to put this?'

'This' was dusty as well as large, so Kate took Elspeth through to the kitchen and Elspeth placed it on the table. 'It' consisted of several cardboard boxes of assorted sizes.

'What is it?' asked Kate.

'Treasure,' said Elspeth.

'Where from?' tried Kate.

'One of my predecessors at St Mark's, the Reverend Aidan

Gloster.' Elspeth was enjoying being mysterious. Kate touched the top of one of the boxes. She traced a K in the dust and waited.

'Oh well, I'll tell you what they are. Aidan is a great one for tradition, and for listening to the older generation who embody the wisdom of the years. Aidan actually talks like this, you understand. So he started up this one-man project for getting people to talk into a tape-recorder about their lives, their thoughts, their dreams.'

Kate lifted the lid off the box she had marked with a K. Inside, sure enough, were stacks of audio cassettes.

'Hundreds of them,' she said. 'Hundreds of hours of reminiscence.' Weeks of work, maybe even months. But she didn't say it aloud.

'I expect that some of them have deteriorated,' Elspeth warned her. 'The old boy didn't think about conservation. He got people to talk into his magic machine, but he wasn't much of a techno-whizz.'

'Right. A few hours' chat. In fragments.'

'I expect the more recent ones are in working order. Have you got a cassette recorder? We can try one and find out.'

'And we can sort out the years we need,' said Kate, cheering up. 'He's labelled them quite methodically with the name of the contributor and the year and place of the memory.'

'Some of them even have a subject. *Country Fairs*, *Visiting the Dentist*, *The Coming of Electricity*. Sounds positively messianic, don't you think? Good old Aidan. Such neat handwriting, too,' said Elspeth, who appeared just as keen as Kate to bury herself in the past. 'He's only marginally dotty. I'm sure these will be really useful.'

'And he's never heard of the Data Protection Act,' said Kate quietly.

'What?'

'Nothing. Just as thought.' You never knew about vicars: they could suddenly go all ethical on you and it was probably best to keep them in the dark.

Now that she'd milked Violet Watts's memory and drawn a blank at St Mark's School, Kate realised that her best hope might lie with these dusty boxes. After all, they could well provide her with the sort of material that Estelle was hoping for. They were quite unlikely to tell her anything more about Christopher and Susan Barnes, or the Dolby and Marlyn families. And that was really a very good thing, she persuaded herself. Estelle would be livid with her if she wasted any more time. And if she didn't get on with some proper work she could kiss goodbye to her career as a writer. Young women in uniform, young men in fighter planes, plenty of passion. That's what she was looking for.

She rinsed the dust off her hands at the kitchen sink then started to sort through the tapes.

'Oh, look,' she exclaimed. 'Here's one marked *Sexual Activity.*'

'I rather fancy listening to the one about *Visiting the Dentist*,' said Elspeth. 'Where's your cassette player?'

And so Kate sat and listened to a reedy old voice telling her that the dentist used to come to the school once a term in a horse-drawn cart. 'The boys and girls would line up and he would see each of them in turn. He had a drill operated by a foot-treadle and a brawny nurse who held you down in an ordinary school chair while the dentist—'

But Kate managed to blank out the rest and let her imagination range freely over the possible contents of the *Sexual Activities* tape. The blissful expression on Elspeth's face as she listened to accounts of dentistry, unaided by anaesthesia, made her wonder whether her new friend had distressing tendencies towards sado-masochism.

The tape eventually reached its end.

'Fascinating stuff,' Elspeth sighed.

'Isn't it just,' said Kate and hoped she sounded convincing. 'It's really very kind of you to go to all this trouble for me.'

'Not at all,' said Elspeth breezily. 'I shall be writing my own book one of these days, and I consider this my apprenticeship. I shall watch you at work and then go away and do it myself.'

'And you think this method of learning the craft of novel-writing will be successful?' asked Kate faintly.

'I shall introduce a few of my own improvements,' said Elspeth.

'Yes.' Like actually getting down to some work, thought Kate. That would be a great improvement on her own haphazard method.

'There's just one more thing you could help me with,' she said.

'What's that?'

'Do you know Miss Arbuthnot?'

'Black coat, hat like a cowpat, knows the words to all the hymns and disapproves of women priests,' said Elspeth succinctly. 'Everybody knows Old Ma Arbuthnot. Terrifying woman.'

'Do you know where she lives?'

'She's got a ground-floor flat in that rather nice block at the side of the park. She's lived there for years, apparently. Why do you want to know?'

'She was a teacher at a London school and was evacuated here with all her children. She never went back.'

'A secret romance. A soldier dying heroically in action. A broken heart,' surmised Elspeth.

'I'll have to introduce you to Estelle,' Kate said drily. 'The two of you would get on famously.'

'Would you like me to come with you when you visit Miss Arbuthnot?' Elspeth offered. 'I could sit very quietly and take notes.'

'No,' said Kate. Then, remembering her manners, she added, 'Thank you, but I think I'd learn more if I were on my own. Two of us might be too intimidating for an elderly woman.'

Elspeth laughed in what Kate considered was a vulgar way for a vicar. 'I think you're the one who'll be intimidated! Well, don't say I didn't warn you. You'll wish you'd brought reinforcements when you meet the old dear.'

When Elspeth had left, Kate went back to her study and logged on to her favourite search engine. Then she gave it the name of one of the secondary schools that Janice Carlton had told her about. After a few seconds she saw that the woman was right: there was a web page. It was a dreadful dried-blood colour with yellow icons and text, and quite difficult to navigate. But after a short while Kate managed to find a couple of contact names and e-mail addresses. She printed out the page for future reference and then fed in the next school on her list. No luck this time.

She sent a friendly and only mildly inaccurate message to the contact address at the first school. Soon she could be communicating electronically with people who had actually known Christopher Barnes.

She wondered for a moment what would come up if she searched for members of the Dolby family. No, she'd only find some distant cousin who'd moved to Arizona in the 1920s and now wanted to get in touch with her roots. She resisted the temptation. She would be prying into George's family for no

121

good reason, impelled only by idle curiosity. And anyway, she thought, she could always do it tomorrow.

She went back to the kitchen and dusted all the boxes of tapes then removed them, too, to her study. Then she went and fetched the tape deck. She could sit here in solitary comfort and listen to the tapes, she thought. But she found herself unwilling to do so, feeling that here she might actually find the material that Estelle wanted her to work on. There would be stories of young pilots taking pretty land girls out to the dance at the local hall. They would dance to Reg Crowhurst and his Rhythmic Serenaders at the Holyoake Hall. Then they would wander home, hand in hand in the moonlight. On Sunday afternoon they would skate on a frozen Port Meadow as the sun sank into the misty horizon.

Kate was sure the tapes would be full of stories like this and, in spite of Estelle's nagging, she just couldn't feel enthusiastic about them. And you had to feel enthusiastic before sitting down to write eighty thousand words on a subject, she had found, or you tended to slow down and then come to a halt before you'd even reached the quarter mark.

No, what was tugging at her interest all the time were those little evacuees. Children separated from home, and family and everything that was familiar, to be dumped in a strange countryside while they worried about what was happening at home. Their stories, too, might be there in the tapes, but if they were, she didn't want to listen to them while George was around. She had a relationship of sorts with these evacuee children and she didn't want anyone else moving in on it and sharing it with her: not George, and not Elspeth, either. They were hers. Her private property.

And then, of course, she wasn't interested in evacuees in general but in two in particular. Christopher and Susan Barnes.

They had lived in this house, they had run up and down these stairs, had sat in the same kitchen and eaten their meals in the room she was now using as a study. Would Elinor Marlyn allow the children to eat in the dining room? she wondered. Or would they sit at the table in the kitchen? Probably, she thought, they had used the same plain pine table that was still there and where she would peel the vegetables for George's dinner.

Whatever had happened to those children had its roots in this house. Christopher had left his box of drawings and notebook behind as though wanting someone to find them. He wanted her to interpret his story and find out what had really happened. Now you're being fanciful, she told herself. But there was a grain of truth in it. You didn't make drawings or write pages of a notebook unless you wanted, at some stage, someone else to look at them. As a writer, she knew this to be true. She wondered for a moment whether Christopher had written anything else, some diary or letter that he *hadn't* wanted anyone to find. Children were always hiding their treasures in secret places, weren't they? In which case, she told herself, she was unlikely to find it after all this time. The biscuit tin had lain undisturbed under the floorboards. Where else would he have hidden anything?

And whatever had happened to those children, it was down to George's family. She knew that, too. Her own shadowy great-aunts and uncles had no significance for her. They had bequeathed her nothing but their various genes. But the Dolbys, and the Marlyns before them, were rooted in this place. The idea of 'family' meant something tangible to them. She and Roz might gossip for twenty minutes a day on the telephone, but this was something recent, something transient. When Roz moved on – and Kate knew that she would some day – then her only family would be gone, to exist in her memory and not in reality for another few years. George and Sam also talked on the phone nearly every day, Kate knew. And Emma rang to chat to George, too. And there were other family members with old, raspy voices who phoned and asked for young George. A whole network of Dolbys who knew that they had a place in this town and a history they regarded with pride.

Maybe she was exaggerating, she conceded. Maybe she only looked at them in this light because she had no family of her own. Maybe all families, except hers, worked this way.

She went back to the kitchen to use it for its proper purpose – preparing something lovely for George's supper when he returned from a hard day's work at the Department.

There was something satisfying about living a conventional female life, she decided. She must talk to Roz about it some time. They could compare notes.

Much later that evening, when she checked her e-mail again (nothing more from Estelle, thank goodness!) she found a message from someone called Brenda Boston who was willing to talk to her about her years at Berry Street Secondary School during the late 1940s. Brenda Boston lived only a few streets away. For a moment, Kate visualised their messages winging their way back and forth, like fireflies in a tropical night, through the light years of cyberspace, only to come to rest in the same square mile of Oxford.

She made a note of the poetic image – she didn't believe in wasting any phrase that might come in useful in one of her books – then replied to Brenda Boston's message, suggesting a time when she might call on her. Since she was not known for her patience, the date she suggested was the next day.

Brenda Boston was a well-dressed, well-preserved woman with

short, wavy grey hair. She wore a navy-blue jersey dress with a matching jacket and the touches of white recommended by high-class women's magazines of the 1960s. That's the sort of outfit that had to be immaculate, thought Kate, quickly tucking her scuffed handbag under her arm. Behind Mrs Boston the window panes sparkled and the open door breathed out the synthetic lemon smell of furniture polish spray.

'Hello,' said Kate pleasantly. 'We've exchanged e-mails. I'm Kate Ivory, a writer, and I'm doing research into the lives of children who were evacuated from London to Oxfordshire during the war.'

'The Reception Area,' said Mrs Boston bleakly. 'That's what they called it. It gives you the flavour of the bureaucracy that was to rule our lives, don't you think?'

'I suppose it does.'

'I've been mulling over what you said in your message,' said Mrs Boston, still firmly barring the entrance to her house.

As far as Kate could remember, the message was innocuous to the point of blandness. Nothing there to terrify anyone. And yet Mrs Boston *was* frightened. Surely not of a simple writer of novels, though?

'I just wanted a chat about the old days,' said Kate soothingly. 'A few reminiscences about your schooldays.'

'You were going to say "the good old days", weren't you?'

'Not necessarily. I can understand that they mightn't have been much fun if you were separated from your family.'

Mrs Boston stood looking at her without stepping aside to allow her to enter the house, but Kate could tell that she was wavering. At any moment she would ask her to come in. It was really nothing personal, just that Mrs Boston had been brought up to have very good manners. Kate concentrated on a calm, non-threatening expression. Interested, and yet not investigative.

'I suppose you'd better come in, since you've taken so much trouble. Even if it's only to hear why I don't want to talk to you.' It had worked.

Mrs Boston's sitting room was just as Kate was expecting. The smell of air-freshener and furniture polish was stronger in here and she was invited to sit on a sofa that looked as though it had only just left the showroom and which held four neat, square cushions each balanced on a corner and placed with exact symmetry. She hated to dent a cushion or spoil their arrangement and so she perched uncomfortably on the edge of the sofa.

'I've just made coffee for myself. Would you like some?'

'Yes, please.'

Maybe Mrs Boston was defrosting slightly. She brought in a brass-topped cafetière and poured coffee into dark blue porcelain coffee cups ringed in unchipped gold.

The coffee was good.

'Were you evacuated here from London?' asked Kate when the silence had stretched a little too far for comfort.

'I don't know what to say to you,' the woman replied, looking distressed.

'There's no hurry, Mrs Boston,' said Kate, careful to put her cup back in its saucer without spilling any coffee.

'You'd better call me Brenda.' It was said, Kate thought, less as an automatic response than as a decision consciously taken. The conversation that followed might be more informal than Kate had feared. 'Yes. My two sisters and I all came to Oxford in 1940, during the Blitz. They were younger than me and they went back in the spring of 1945. I was settled into my school and I stayed with my foster parents until I was fifteen.'

'That's a long time to be away from your family!' exclaimed Kate, trying to imagine how it would feel. Worse than going away to boarding school – which she had never experienced anyway. Worse than your mother leaving when you were seventeen – which she had.

'I'm sure my mother missed us, and she used to visit every couple of months or so, but she must have grown used to a life with no children around, don't you think? She had a nice job – something she hadn't had before the war – and money in her pocket that belonged just to her. She didn't have to account for it to her husband.' She corrected herself: 'My father.'

'You didn't get on with him?'

'We didn't know him. Well, you don't, not after all those years away, do you? We thought of him as her husband, not our father. Not that we ever talked about it. You didn't, not then. It's only recently it's all started to come back into my head and worry me. Funny how we never talked.'

'Funny, too, how we don't understand children,' said Kate. 'You'd think we would. We've all been children, after all.'

'It's as though there was a grand conspiracy that kept us all silent. You'd have thought sisters would confide in each other, but we never did. And if you can't talk about it, it doesn't really exist, does it? It wasn't much of a childhood back in those days. The children these days have it much easier.'

Brenda paused for a moment, reflecting. Then: 'Things change with the years,' she said. 'At least, I don't suppose the events themselves change – it's more the way we look at them.'

Kate thought about her notebook, sitting in the depths of her bag, but rejected the idea of bringing it out. Its presence would only put Brenda Boston off.

'Or maybe,' Brenda continued, 'it's only with the passage of years that we grow strong enough to look at difficult things. For years now I've been in charge of the Berry Road Secondary School Association. That sounds grand, doesn't it? But it wasn't a very grand school at all, just the place you went to if you weren't bright enough to pass for the grammar school. I think now that plenty of us *were* just as bright as the grammar children, but our minds were too preoccupied to concentrate on schoolwork.'

She leaned forward and picked up her cup, drank the remains of the coffee, and replaced the cup as precisely as before. She adjusted the sugar spoon so that it was placed just so. Punctuation marks, thought Kate, and waited for her to continue.

'I sometimes wonder whether I took on the job as Association Secretary just so that I could control it,' she said. 'Not that I wanted power over people,' she added. 'It was more that I wanted to be sure that I knew first what they were saying.'

Kate wanted to ask about Christopher Barnes, who could well have been a contemporary of this woman's, but realised she was going to have to listen to Brenda's experiences before they got to anyone else.

'Not that it was all bad,' said Brenda. 'The countryside was pretty and I learned about wild flowers and animals.'

'Of course,' said Kate, beginning to go into automatic listening mode. The room was stuffy and she'd find herself nodding off if she wasn't careful. She sat up straighter to keep herself alert.

'A lot of the host families just treated us like servants, dusting and polishing all day, with never a moment to get our homework done. No wonder they only wanted girls – you can't see a boy putting up with that, can you? And my poor little sister Betty, she couldn't help wetting the bed. They needn't have put her out in the back garden, out there in the dog's kennel, and the dog sleeping on Betty's cot every time she gave them a wet sheet. I broke a cup once, while I was drying it after doing the washing-up, and the woman hit me for that – right across the knuckles with a wooden hairbrush. I can still remember how it stung. After the nights in the dog kennel they did move us to a new billet, I'll give them that,' Brenda was saying. 'We got on all right there. And we never mentioned the first place, not even among the three of us. We just pretended it had never happened.'

'And your new billet was better?' Kate was learning the language.

'We had Naomi King to thank for that. She was the Billeting Officer. Cycling round Headington on that heavy old black bike of hers, she looked such a drippy girl with her mousey hair and thick glasses, and her tweed skirts flapping about her legs and getting caught in the chain. But she did her best for us. I don't suppose she had much experience of life before the war. "A steep learning curve" – isn't that how they describe it nowadays? That's what Naomi had to go through.'

'You didn't tell your parents about the first billet?'

'No. When Mum came to visit, she just wanted to hear the good news, you could see that on her face. "Of course we're fine, Mum," we said. "We love it here in the country with all the wild flowers and the little lambs and that." We knew what the adults wanted to hear and we didn't disappoint them. And our foster parents were poor, too, I realise that now. Life must have been hard for them. They didn't know how to be soft with kids. We learned not to ask for too much. That was the secret of life in those days.'

'I'm surprised you settled here later.'

'London was like a foreign country when I went back in 1948. You could still see the bombsites, though they'd started to rebuild by then. But nothing looked the same and I felt like a stranger. Yes, I came back to Oxford as soon as I'd done my shorthand-typing course – found myself digs and a job. I'd lost the habit of living in my family, I suppose. And this place was familiar.'

You did all right for yourself, thought Kate, looking round at the polished furniture, the pleated pelmets over the heavy curtains, the bright colours of the rugs on the floor.

'What happened to Naomi King?' she asked.

'I saw her around for years. She went on riding that bike for a while, then she got herself a little car. She must have found a decent job, maybe even got married. I expect she still lives somewhere in the neighbourhood. I didn't keep in touch with her, I'm afraid. I wanted to forget all about the war, forget it ever happened.'

'I could try the phone book,' said Kate. 'It's a good place to start.'

'I expect you're good at finding out things, writing those books of yours. I looked at one of them in the library. They don't say much about the hard parts of life, do they?'

'They tend to concentrate on the lighter aspects,' agreed Kate. 'But that's not to say that this new one will be like that.'

'I should stick with the romance, if I were you,' said Brenda. 'It's what people want to read. No one wants to hear about little Betty being stuck outside in the dog kennel on a cold night.'

It was time to move on, Kate could see.

'I don't suppose you remember Christopher Barnes or his sister – Susan, wasn't it?'

'He's the one who died.' Brenda's voice was flat.

'That's right.'

'He was a bit younger than me. Only a year or so, but it makes a difference at that age, especially when it's the boy who's younger.'

'But you do remember him,' insisted Kate.

'Yes. I was quite envious to begin with.'

130

'Really?'

'He lived in that big house in Armitage Road. High Corner, it was called. You could imagine the warmth and the brilliant electric light from the outside. I was passing the house as he went in. The door opened and the light blazed out – more light than I can ever remember seeing before, except at the cinema. I thought it must have been like Hollywood inside that house. It just shows how naïve we were. We were all sure they sat down to sumptuous meals every afternoon. That house belonged to Miss Marlyn, and the Marlyns were substantial people. Still are, or so I've heard – though they're not called Marlyn any more.'

Kate managed not to say that they were now called 'Dolby'. She wasn't sure how popular she'd be if she revealed her relationship to George.

'But I don't know that Chris and Susie were any happier than my sisters and I were. Don't get me wrong, Miss Ivory – most children here were fine. They enjoyed themselves once they'd got over their homesickness. We all worried about our mothers, left behind in London with the bombs, but from day to day, kids were happy enough with their lives and the new freedom they had to explore the countryside. We only had lessons for half the day; we had to share the school with the local children. For the rest of the time, we roamed wild. At seven-twenty someone from St Mark's Church came out into the street and rang a bell. It was the old-fashioned sort with a wooden handle and a metal clapper. When we heard that, we knew it was time to go back to our billets. We three girls had our chores to do, but we had free time, too. If I'm honest, it wasn't all bad.'

She seemed more cheerful as she came to this conclusion.

'And I don't suppose Miss Marlyn was really a wicked

person, either,' Brenda continued. 'She wasn't married and she'd not had much to do with children. It can't have been easy, having a couple of strangers in her house. But she was a martinet, that I do know. I heard her laying into those two once, and she had a voice that could strip paint.'

She looked surprised for a moment, as though not used to using such colourful language.

'Of course,' she added thoughtfully, 'there were stories going round about her.'

'Really?'

'But I'd better not talk about that. It would just be gossip.'

'I've always enjoyed a good gossip,' said Kate.

'But it wouldn't be right.'

Kate gave up, at least for the moment. 'And do you remember the younger girl, Susan?'

'She was a pale little thing, without much to say for herself, though she did seem happier than her brother. Chris was always very protective of his sister, that I do know, and he was a bit of a worrier. Of course, I only knew them for a term or two, before I moved up to the secondary school. I daresay I only remember them at all because of what happened.'

'He was run over,' suggested Kate.

'Yes. It wasn't uncommon at that time. So much traffic on the roads and none of the drivers looking out for children. Convoys, mostly. I used to think Oxfordshire was just one great convoy in those days, rumbling through the streets night and day. Driving much too fast. A child didn't stand a chance.'

'But it wasn't a military vehicle that killed Chris Barnes, was it?'

'No, it was a delivery van, driven by the Watts lad. He was never up to any good, that one.'

'You knew him?'

'I wasn't allowed to speak to him. But everybody knew Danny. They all said he was just a little spiv.'

More gossip, thought Kate. How much of it could she trust? Probably very little.

'What happened to Susan? After Chris's accident, I mean.'

'Why are you so interested in the Barnes children?'

'It's just that I saw the plaque with Christopher's name and age on it in St Mark's churchyard, and somehow it's stayed with me. I'd like to know more about him.'

'Don't put those children in your book,' said Brenda. 'You don't want sad things like that spoiling the story.'

'Did you know Susan? Did she go home to her mother?'

'I forget now. I think there was some reason why they stayed here even after so many others had returned. A sick mother. A missing father. I can't remember now, but I think it was something like that.'

'So they had no parents, effectively.'

'There was someone. Some man who'd been invalided out of the services. Let it go. It's all a long time ago.'

Brenda Boston rose to her feet and smoothed her blue skirt over her hips to get rid of the faint creases. She picked up their coffee cups and took them to the door.

'I'm afraid that I have things to get on with now,' she said over her shoulder.

'I'd better be going,' said Kate obediently.

Brenda came back into the room.

'You've been very generous with your time,' Kate said. 'Thank you.'

'I suppose these days people would say that I ought to talk about it. Talk about all the dreadful things that happened at that first billet – I haven't told you the half of it. But I'm not from your generation. We endured things. We waited for them to be over so that we could get on with the rest of our lives. We didn't think it would do any good, dwelling on things. And I'm not so sure that your generation has it right. Maybe it was better to leave things buried after all.'

Kate didn't know how to answer this, and so she stayed silent.

'I can see you're curious about Chris Barnes and his sister. Maybe there's a story there – maybe there's even some mystery. But it's not going to do them any good to dig it all up, and I don't see how it can do you any good, either. Let it go. Leave him there in the graveyard with his small, plain plaque. Just his name and his age. That's all he's due, isn't it?'

But as Kate left the house and stood for a moment on the pavement outside, she thought, No, it isn't! Christopher Barnes was due a life and it was taken away. And I don't believe I know the truth of his story yet, either.

Brenda had mentioned Naomi King, just as Violet Watts had, so maybe it was time she looked her up. A Billeting Officer must surely have had the right to enter houses and see what the conditions were like; she would speak to the children and find out what was on their minds. That's what I'd have done, if I'd been a Billeting Officer, Kate told herself.

She couldn't imagine Naomi King, in her old tweed skirt and thick spectacles, skating by moonlight on the frozen expanse of Port Meadow, in the company of a dashing Captain of Guards, though. No, Naomi wasn't the kind of romantic heroine that Estelle would be interested in.

7

'Hello. Is that you, Elspeth?'

No. It was an answering machine. And much as Kate liked to use one on her own phone, she hated to be greeted by one when she made a call herself. She always had the suspicion that there was someone in the room at the other end, listening to the stilted message – someone who had decided that they didn't want to talk to Kate Ivory. And was Elspeth the sort of person who listened to her messages and dealt with them straight away, or did she go away and forget all about them? One tended to think the best of vicars, but one could never tell. She gave her message after the beep, anyway.

'I was wondering whether you'd come across a woman called Naomi King. She was the local Billeting Officer during the war, and stayed in the area afterwards. She might have married, of course, and changed her name – in which case she'd be Naomi something else. But she wore thick spectacles and thicker tweed skirts and I don't suppose they've changed much over the years, even if her name has. Anyway, ring me back if you can help. Or if you can't. I'd like to know that you got my message.'

Kate had already tried the phone book, but there were so many Kings – even with the initial N, and who was to say whether or not N was Naomi's first initial – that she hadn't liked to phone and ask whether they were the one she was looking for. She would just have to wait for Elspeth to phone back.

135

The house was empty. George was out and wouldn't be back until the early evening. This might be a good time to settle down with Christopher's belongings. She went back to her study and closed the door behind her. Then she spread the notebooks and papers out over the desk.

First, the horrid drawing of planes dropping bombs on High Corner. What did that mean? Was it simply the sort of thing that a ten-year-old boy drew? Or was there something more sinister behind it? Was he making a comment on the house and on Elinor Marlyn? Was it a deep-seated resentment or an hour-long tantrum? Emma would know about the typical behaviour of children, but she didn't fancy ringing her to ask. Emma would ask sharp questions about why Kate would possibly want to know, and then she would make derogatory remarks about Kate's brand of fiction, and be cross because Kate was trying to pump her about George's family behind his back.

No, she couldn't face one of Emma's outbursts. But for a moment she wondered what, in fact, her motives *were*. Were the Dolbys, *en masse*, a little too pleased with themselves, and did they need to be taken down a peg or two? Not, she told herself, that George was at all like that. George was no more pleased with himself than any other man who had prospered in his chosen career, lived in a large house in a good part of town, had a woman as lovely as Kate Ivory living with him, and no problems that couldn't be sorted out in a day or two. But, she asked herself with unusual honesty, if she didn't want to find something to belittle the Dolbys, then why was she raking up this mystery from their past?

Oh Kate, it's not a mystery, she told herself. Just a story. A story you could weave into your romantic novel. One to draw a tear to the eye. Think of it as sub-plot. Really? She couldn't even manage to convince herself, so she'd have no chance of convincing Emma.

She continued to turn over the things on the table.

There were a few photographs that she hadn't looked at before. George had been so dismissive of the tin's contents that she'd only had the most cursory of searches through it. It couldn't be that he'd been trying to dissuade her from looking at the contents, could it? Not very likely, she told herself, since he didn't know what they were.

All except one of the photos were just old snapshots in black and white, not particularly in focus, nor particularly interesting unless you were obsessed with the story of a particular ten-year-old boy.

A woman, thin, with prominent bones in her face and long, dark hair falling on to her shoulders. She was trying to smile into the camera, but the smile turned her face into a death's head. She was wearing a summer dress with short, bunched sleeves, from which her arms stuck out like two fleshless bones, the hands like claws.

Kate shivered. She turned the photo over. The careful writing said *Mum at Southend*. Another photo of the same woman, not quite so ill, perhaps taken a year or so before the previous one. She was holding a plump toddler, a little girl, whose hair had been coaxed into corkscrew curls tied with a narrow ribbon. The child stared solemnly at the camera while the woman smiled more naturally this time. She looked quite pretty, or at least she would have done if she'd been just a stone or so fatter. *Mum and Susie in the garden at Reckitt Street*, this one said on the back. Christopher used purple, indelible pencil, so that no one could contradict the words on his captions, or erase them.

No photo of Christopher himself. But then, if this was his collection of treasures, there wouldn't be. Kate certainly hadn't kept photos of herself when she was ten, and she didn't suppose that Christopher had, either.

The next photo showed a man in soldier's uniform. If Kate had only been more knowledgeable she would have recognised which regiment he belonged to, but she didn't have a clue. He smiled a jaunty smile at the camera – this one was taken in some photographer's studio by the look of the fake stone pillar and painted backcloth – but there was something about the thinness and vulnerability of his neck that gave away his age. Well under thirty, thought Kate. It was difficult to tell what sort of man he was behind the smile. The uniform took away any individuality, and his youth and the photographer's practised technique made him look like every other young man about to embark for war. *Dad* was the only word written on the back of the photo.

The last picture showed a group of three people, two men and a woman. Whoever took the photo wasn't very good at focusing the lens, and the faces in particular were fuzzy. Kate turned it over and read *Mum, Dad and Uncle Alan*. The two young men were alike enough for her to deduce that they were brothers. They were both fairer than the woman and with faces that were the same long, bony shape with ears that stuck out. Their hair shone with some oil that plastered it to the scalp. One looked a few years older than the other, and she thought this was probably Uncle Alan. Alan Barnes. Could she find him if he was still alive? Such an ordinary name, though. You'd find one in every town or suburb you visited.

She left the photos spread out across the top of her desk where she could see them and turned to the notebook. She leafed through a page or two and read:

Christopher Douglas Barnes, 26 Reckitt Street, Peckham, London SE15, England, Europe, The World, The Universe.

Of course. She could remember writing her name and

address in just that form when she was a child. Many years later someone pointed out to her that it was an example of children thinking in sets. Maybe, she thought, Harley from Agatha Street would have told her it was a Venn diagram. It was a pity she no longer lived next door to Harley. He would have been a great help in understanding the psychology of a ten-year-old boy who was separated from his home and parents. He would have made sure she kept away from mawkish sentiment, too.

There were a few letters written by Christopher himself. Were they never sent? She read the careful, purple writing. Christopher was still using his indelible pencil.

Dear Mum,

I hope you are well. Susie and I are very happy staying here at High Corner. We are going to the school near here and I hold Susie's hand the way you told me to . . .

Boring. Dutiful.

She turned over a few more. All the same stuff. Perhaps they handed out pattern letters at school for the children to copy out for their parents. Bland phrases. Reassuring stuff.

The only honest note came in the last paragraph of one of them.

Are you sure you're alright in Reckitt Street? We've been hearing about the doodlebugs in your part of London and every night I imagine it's our house that's been hit. Are you *sure* you're still alright? You could live here with us where it's safe. There's lots of room here. (And then, as though in an afterthought): And there's room for Uncle Alan too, of course.

The notebook was in the form of a rough diary, interspersed with more of the childish drawings. 'Miss Arbuthnot' figured as a caricature of a strict schoolmistress. Kate closed the notebook and tidied it away in the drawer with the drawings. She had hoped to understand more about Christopher Barnes, but there was nothing here of any interest to her. In fact, she was close to admitting to herself that he was as boring as any other boy of his age. And yet there had to be more to him than appeared here.

As she went to close the drawer, a thought struck her and she took another look at his London address. She copied it into her own notebook just in case it should ever come in handy.

Did anyone at 26 Reckitt Street still remember Christopher? Maybe there were members of his family still living there. Dad. Uncle Alan. She looked again at the photo of his mother. She couldn't believe that Mrs Barnes had lived for long after it was taken. Antibiotics were only just coming into use, she seemed to remember, and people died of diseases that a few years later could be cured. And what about his father? Did he come back from the war, looking for his son and daughter? And Susan, the sister. She'd only be in her early sixties now.

Should she go looking for them in the streets of Peckham? She could take a bus into Oxford, get on a train, then travel across to Waterloo or Charing Cross or wherever it was that one found a train for south-east London. Sit on another train . . . No, she couldn't do it. It was asking too much of herself. She wasn't well enough yet. She could think about it again in a month or two. But not now. Not this week. And anyway, would the Barnes family – even if she could find them – welcome a stranger who wanted to talk to them about events that must still be very painful, even if they did happen a long time ago? She would concentrate on speaking to Miss Arbuthnot and Naomi King.

She pulled out a sheet of paper and a pen. She should make a list of things to do.

Speak to Miss Arbuthnot, find Naomi King, read Christopher's notebook all the way through instead of just dipping in and out of it. She must listen to the cassette tapes that Elspeth had brought her. Trace any surviving members of the Barnes family. Think of a plot. Write a book.

Since her illness, Kate had found it difficult to concentrate on anything for any length of time. She would start to do something, then push it aside. Her mind went blank and refused to work. Apart from all the things on her list, she had a couple of books from the library she should be reading. She needed to learn a lot more about the period she wanted to write about, she told herself severely.

Outside, the sun was shining. Birds cheep-cheeped in the background. It was warm, and a gentle breeze was moving the trees around. Someone had left a reclining chair out next to the wooden table. Not only was the chair a welcoming sight, it was irresistible. Kate sat down in the chair, put her book on the table, open at Chapter One, and then leaned back and closed her eyes.

Obviously, she needed to rest. She'd been overdoing it recently. She pushed the chair back a few notches so that it was nearly horizontal and very comfortable. She'd get round to all the things on the list in due time. When she'd dozed for a few minutes, she'd sit up and read all through Chapter One of the serious book on the Second World War, without stopping. She'd take notes, she'd commit facts to memory, she'd force herself back into the habit of disciplined work, of concentration.

* * *

Kate opened her eyes to find that a large cloud had blocked out the sun and the temperature had dropped several degrees. She sat up, wondering for a moment where she was and what she was doing. Some time after lunch, in the garden at High Corner, she concluded. No, not High Corner, but George's house – 74 Cavendish Road. She closed the serious book before large raindrops fell on its open pages and then she folded up the chair and put it back in the shed. How long had she dozed? she wondered. It must have been at least fifteen minutes.

Her watch told her it was nearer two hours.

She'd better start to prepare the supper. She went back indoors and threw cold water over her face to wake herself up and reflected sadly that the long sleep had done nothing for her alertness and concentration. She felt at least as fuzzy as when she'd first closed her eyes.

Her face buried in a towel, she realised that the phone was ringing.

'Hello,' she said.

'Hello? Kate? You sound different. Are you all right?'

Kate removed the towel. 'Yes, I'm fine – is that better? Who is it?' Which showed that sleep had done little to help coherent speech, either.

'It's Elspeth. You left a message on my machine.'

'So I did.' Kate did her best to remember which of her lines of thought she had confided to Elspeth. 'Was it about Naomi King?'

'Yes. You said she'd been a Billeting Officer, though I'm not sure they have many of those in Headington these days.'

'That's right, Naomi King,' said Kate, remembering at last. 'Do you know her?'

'I'm not sure.'

That was a great help.

'The thing is,' Elspeth continued, 'I conducted a funeral for someone called Naomi King, last week some time.'

'Do you think it was the same one?' With her luck, Kate was sure that it must be, but she might as well try.

'Female. About seventy-eight or nine. Tall for a woman. Lived alone in a small flat in one of those roads off the High Street. Not a block of flats, but a house that had been divided up thirty or forty years ago.'

'It sounds depressingly like my Naomi King,' Kate admitted. Sure enough, she was just a couple of weeks too late to talk to her. 'Can you give me any more details?'

'I can give you the address, and the name and address of the woman who organised the funeral.'

Kate wrote them down as Elspeth read them out.

As Elspeth had said, Naomi King's flat had been in one of the small streets off the High Street. The woman who had organised the funeral – sister, cousin, niece? – came from a village near Northampton and her name was Mrs Joan Angers.

'Thanks a lot, Elspeth,' said Kate. Then in a rush of generosity, 'We must have a creative writing session one of these days. I'll give you a few pointers about writing a novel.'

'I look forward to it,' said Elspeth. But Kate was left with the faint suspicion that she had been smiling as she said it.

She looked at the clock. Still plenty of time before George was due back. If she simplified her ideas about their meal she could get it ready in fifteen minutes. That meant she could pop round to Naomi King's flat right now. There could well be no one there, but on the other hand, if the funeral was only a matter of days ago, there could just as easily be someone there, clearing up. It was a good time of day to catch people at home, she had always found.

What do you hope to find? she asked herself. I don't

know, came the answers, but there might be *something*. It was better than chopping vegetables or reading that dreary book, anyway.

Joan Angers had been a teenager when Christian Dior introduced his New Look. And she must have been at her peak then. This much was obvious to Kate as soon as Mrs Angers opened the door and stood framed, like an outsize hourglass, against a hall heaped with bulging black binliners. Someone nearby had been burning rubbish by the smell of smoke that lingered in the background.

'Yes?' An officious voice with accurate vowels and well-defined consonants. She's been an efficient secretary, thought Kate, summing her up in the way a novelist would.

'Mrs Angers?'

The pencilled black eyebrows raised their assent.

'Kate Ivory. I'm a writer. I was expecting to see Miss King and find out from her some background material about the 1940s, but then I heard of her unfortunate death . . .'

The eyebrows drew together at the word 'death' and Kate wondered whether perhaps she should have used the word 'passing' instead. No, it wasn't in her vocabulary. Mrs Angers would have to get used to the Ivory approach.

'I don't know what you think *I* can do for you,' said Mrs Angers. 'I was a child during the war – a *small* child,' she added, in case Kate's arithmetic was too good. 'I know nothing about it.'

Behind her, one of the black bin bags toppled over and spilled its contents on to the floor in a sad tangle of old lady's petticoats and vests.

'Can I give you a hand with those?' asked Kate sympathetically. Actually, she wasn't sure what she was after, either, but she wasn't going to leave until she'd found out everything she could.

'I'm sorting out her belongings,' said Mrs Angers unnecessarily. 'Most of her clothes will have to go to the tip, but there are just one or two nice things that Oxfam might like. Her books are very old-fashioned and all of them well-read. It's such a sad business, isn't it, getting rid of an old person's life like this?'

Kate made sympathetic and affirmative noises, picked up the plastic bag, stuffed the contents back in and tied the top in a knot.

'Did you know my aunt well?' Mrs Angers asked, possibly touched by Kate's helpfulness. 'I don't remember seeing you at the funeral. But then, there were barely ten people there.'

'I'm afraid I didn't hear about it in time, otherwise I'd have been there,' said Kate truthfully. The fact that she'd never met Naomi King in her lifetime wouldn't have kept her away. 'But I'm sure Elspeth conducted the whole ceremony beautifully.' Probably wearing a lilac cassock and a jet bead instead of the diamond in her nose.

'I don't believe in lady vicars,' said Mrs Angers primly.

Kate didn't say you *had* to believe in them since they existed, though you might doubt their validity, but she was tempted.

'What sort of material was it that Aunt Naomi was going to give you?' asked Mrs Angers, walking back into what must have been the sitting room and allowing Kate to follow her.

'Um,' said Kate, thinking fast. 'Notebooks? Photographs? Diaries?'

'There was very little of that in the flat. And I've burned it all now. You don't want that sort of personal stuff lying around for people to read, do you?'

'No,' said Kate, but she meant, 'Yes.' It was her day for

being just a little too late for everything.

She looked round the room. Signs of Naomi King were disappearing fast, but there was an old grey cardigan over the back of one chair that she couldn't imagine belonging to Mrs Angers.

'I haven't had the heart to throw it out yet,' said her niece, noticing what Kate was looking at. 'She was always wearing it whenever I saw her. That and her coat.'

The coat, hanging behind the door, as Kate might have expected, was grey tweed and had belonged to a tall woman. There was a smell in the room that she associated with old ladies. It must have been stronger while Naomi King was alive, and by the time Mrs Angers had got rid of all her belongings, it would hardly notice at all. Old dust and mould, antiseptic mouthwash, talcum powder and an undercurrent of toffee, as though her last act on earth was to stir a pan of boiling sugar so that she could be ready with home-made sweets for any visiting children. Mrs Angers's voice interrupted her analysis.

'I don't suppose this will be of any use to you,' she said. She was standing by the oak drop-leaf table and holding up a bundle of papers. 'I was on my way out to put it on the fire when you rang the doorbell. It's just a few sheets of notes, but it's dated 1945, and apart from all the romantic nonsense she scribbled down, it seems to be about evacuees. That's what you were interested in, was it?'

'Oh, yes,' said Kate, forgetting about mouthwash and toffees on the instant.

'I expect Aunt Naomi had put it out ready for you.'

'How kind of her, and how typically thoughtful.' Even though Naomi King couldn't have left it out for her unless she'd been a mind-reader in the last days of her life.

Kate extracted the first page and skimmed down it. Lovely,

neat, legible handwriting in washable blue ink on lined paper. Sentimental drivel perhaps, but there might be a nugget of useful information hidden within it. She put the bundle of notes away in her bag before the other woman could change her mind.

'Such a sad life,' said Mrs Angers. 'I've thrown away all the other photographs, but I was still wondering what to do with this one.' The photograph she held out to Kate had been standing on the mantelpiece. The plain silver frame held the picture of a young man with dark hair and a direct gaze. He was wearing what even Kate recognised as the uniform of a naval officer. He looked young and optimistic and really rather attractive.

'He died, of course,' said Joan Angers.

'I'm so sorry.' It seemed inadequate. She would have liked to have offered to take the photograph away with her but couldn't think of a reason why she should do such a thing.

'Was he her young man?'

'Her fiancé. They had decided to wait until the war was over before they married. I think she realised afterwards that they should have been impulsive for once in their lives. Mooning over a photograph's all very well, but you need more than that. They should have grabbed their chance while they could. At least my aunt would have had those memories to see her through the empty years.'

'Were they really empty?'

'I suppose it's my generation, but I think that years spent without a man are empty, yes,' Mrs Angers said. She bent down to pick something up from the floor underneath the table. 'I don't suppose it's of any interest to you?'

It was a snapshot of the kind Kate was growing used to: black-and-white, not very well focused, slightly muddy. But it showed a tall young woman, not graceful or pretty even then, when she must have been in her early twenties. Her hair was light-coloured, very curly, and worn in no particular style. At least she wasn't wearing her hallmark spectacles. Gathered around her were a number of children, the youngest about six, the oldest not more than twelve. One of the little girls, head encased in a woollen pixie hood, could have been Susie Barnes. One of the boys had moved just as the photo was taken and his head was a blur. But Kate thought he might be Christopher. *Her* Christopher.

'Do you know who they are?' she asked.

'The young woman is Naomi, of course, but I have no idea who the children are.'

Kate turned the photo over. Someone had written in very careful handwriting. *'My' children. Brenda, Trevor, Shawn, Shirley, Ricky, Christopher, Graham, Susan, Bobby.*

'May I take this, too?'

'I can't think what you want it for, but I was only going to throw it away.'

Clues, thought Kate. Maybe I can track down some of the children in this photo, though without surnames it might be tricky.

'They weren't really her children,' said Mrs Angers unnecessarily, as she led the way back to the front door.

'I know very little of her personal life,' said Kate, hoping she could get away without too much more chat. Mrs Angers wasn't really her type and she was obviously not going to learn anything more of interest. She was longing to read the pages of notes and find out whether Naomi had mentioned Christopher and Susan. 'And perhaps it was her choice to be alone,' she said, hoping to bring the conversation to an end.

Mrs Angers didn't bother to reply to that. 'If Philip hadn't

148

been killed in the war like that, things might have been so very different for her.'

It was only after the front door had closed and Kate stood on the pavement that she thought about what Joan Angers had said. She was so intent on her pursuit of Christopher and his sister that she had allowed an opportunity to go by. Could Naomi's have been the story of lost romance that she had been looking for? She had forgotten that an old lady in tweed skirts and hand-knitted cardigans might once have been young and attractive. And even if she was as plain as Naomi King appeared in the snapshot, she had still had a love life. But then, she wasn't interested in romance at the moment. It could wait until later. And if she remembered what had happened to Naomi and her fiancé when they thought they had all the time in the world, she decided it didn't apply to her.

She hurried back to Cavendish Road. If she could persuade George to eat a Chinese takeaway from the place down the road, then instead of doing all that preparation of fresh food, she'd have time to read Naomi's notes before dinner.

She was nearly twenty pages into it before she reached the interesting part.

8

. . . know some people dread the approach of autumn with its lengthening nights and hints of winter to come, but I love it. I love the whiff of woodsmoke in the evenings, the mist that floats like the breath of angels in the valley in the early mornings. I love the dew that dapples the windowpanes and drips off the eaves, and most of all I love the feeling that this is the serious time of year, the time of beginnings, of hope.

Traditionally, I suppose that other people think of spring this way. But spring is different. Spring brings with it the possibility, even the inevitability, of failure. Spring forces us to measure ourselves against the bright, the beautiful, the successful. Spring finds us wanting. Spring makes me fearful, lets me know how I have failed to live up to my expectations of myself.

Is it just my imagination, or has this war been one of hot, rich summers with cloudless skies and soaring temperatures, while the winters have been harder and colder than usual? I don't know. Perhaps it's because our senses are sharper, as though we knew that this summer, this hot, cloudless day of humming bees and vapour trails stammering across an azure sky, might be our last.

Not my last day, but yours, Philip.

'Now you're just being melodramatic, Naomi.' That's what you'd say – what you'd have said if you'd still been here with me.

You'll say I'm going mad, but I often talk to you, Philip, as I go about my days. I ask your advice sometimes, and I only wish that you were here to answer me in reality, because the answers are beyond my reach.

I am trying to shape my life to have some meaning without you. I don't understand why I'm still here while you're lying dead on the bottom of an unknown sea. All I can do is to undertake my work to the best of my ability. Does that sound formal and forced? It probably is.

It isn't always easy. Oh, sometimes it works. Sometimes I put ordinary children into ordinary families and they all get on, they adapt to fit. They even learn to love each other. But this is the last year of the war. We all know that. We all know that it really won't go on for much longer, and yet the bombs are still dropping on London and along the south-eastern corridor. So the trails of small children, and mothers pushing pramloads of sad belongings, come in from the eastern corner of our town.

I do my best. Really, Philip, you have to believe that I do my best. But sometimes it goes wrong in spite of my best endeavours. The working classes are tough. They can be hard on their children – especially on those who don't belong to them. Their own children contribute to the household and so they expect these little visitors to do the same. And the London children just aren't used to our way of life. They expect to run free in the streets at all hours of the night and day, to eat their 'piece' while they're on the move. They don't know about the family meal, or the regular bedtime of the children out here in the country.

Why am I telling you all this? Those, anyway, are minor problems. A question of adaptation which will come about eventually.

I'm talking about Christopher and Susan Barnes. You know that, don't you?

I should never have placed them there in High Corner. I

know that now: hindsight is a wonderful thing. But what was I to do? I couldn't ignore the big, middle-class houses that had refused all these years to take in evacuees. I couldn't keep asking the same poorer families to make the sacrifice over and over again while the well-off were seen to get away with it every time.

'They're finding it hard to adapt to middle-class ways,' she said in that arrogant voice of hers. But they came from quite a nice home, I could tell. Oh, they weren't rich like the Marlyns, but they were clean and they were used to behaving properly. I listened to her complaints but I wouldn't place them with another family.

I could see that Elinor Marlyn was difficult, but I didn't know she could be cruel. And, of course, it was the little girl who got the worst of it, and the boy who tried to protect her. I feel bad about the child because I couldn't help disliking her. There, I've written it down. She had a dreadful whining accent that I could hardly understand and whenever I saw her she'd clutch my hand with her damp, sticky one and wouldn't let me go. She was missing her mother, of course – but all the children missed their mothers and their homes – and that was no excuse for *clinging* so. And she had ears that stuck out and a runny nose and could never find her handkerchief. Christopher would take out his – ink-blotched, mud-stained, ragged, but still a handkerchief – and wipe her nose for her. She rewarded him with a soggy smile. He loved her. Poor boy, he must have known his mother was dying and his father would never return home. All he had left were the shadowy uncle and his little sister. So he looked after her. I gave them some of my own sweet ration, to try to make up for the bleakness of their lives. It wasn't much, but they enjoyed my toffees.

And then came the accident. He was only trying to save her

life. You do see that, don't you? I read the account in the newspaper and they seemed to blame him. They blamed the child for being careless. Susan ran into the road and Chris dashed after her to stop her from going under a lorry. But he was hit instead. Danny Watts will have to go to court, of course, but I doubt he'll get more than a £2 fine. That's the value they put on a child's life these days. And now Christopher is dead, and Susan's lying there in hospital with her poor, damaged leg and that blank expression on her face all the time. And I feel as though the whole thing is *my fault*.

I know I must be missing something. It wasn't a case simply of two different cultures coming into conflict. I can only describe what I felt in that house as *evil*.

'You're just being melodramatic, old girl,' that's what you'd say, isn't it?

And perhaps I really *am* being melodramatic, Philip. I don't even know what I mean myself, so how can I expect to explain it to another person? No one would listen to me.

I've never trusted Danny Watts. And I don't much like Violet and Arthur, if I'm honest.

'You know you can tell me the truth, old girl.'

Yes, Philip. Well, Danny was a spiv. Oh, nothing very great, but he was always on the lookout for a bargain. I called round at their cottage once – it was Miss Marlyn's gardener's cottage – and they invited me into the kitchen. Danny was there, and Arthur, sitting on a kitchen chair, while Violet was cutting his hair. He has such thick, wavy, black hair. It reminds me of an animal's – some wild creature that you'd meet in the depths of a dark forest. It grows far too long for a respectable man, and once a month Violet cuts it all off for him.

'Don't just stand there gawping,' Violet said to Danny. 'Go and fetch the dustpan and brush and sweep it up.'

She orders those men around. I don't really want to know for sure what they're up to, but I'm sure that Violet knows. There was something in the air that day. I could feel it in the atmosphere in that kitchen. They couldn't wait for me to leave, I know that. I forget now what I'd gone there for – to collect empty jam jars or some such thing. But they weren't comfortable with me there. Violet put down her scissors, found the jam jars and showed me out again, all inside five minutes.

The trouble is that I was responsible for those two children, and now one of them is dead. I expect it's the guilt and the feeling of helplessness that are giving me all these wild ideas. That's what keeps me awake at night, longing for the autumn and a new beginning in a world where the war will be only a memory.

When the war is over.

How often we said those words, you and I, and now they mean something so different to me, facing a life without you.

I visited the hospital before Christopher died. I wanted to tell him that it was all right, that I'd look after Susan for him. But I couldn't speak to him. He was lying there with his face pillow-white and his eyes sunk in dark hollows. His head was bandaged, but I couldn't see what other injuries he had. He was heavily sedated, and already slipping away from this life and into the next.

What am I supposed to do with Susan when she comes out of hospital? I can't send her back to live with Miss Marlyn. I can see that she's afraid that's what I'll do.

'Don't worry, old girl. You'll think of something when the time comes. You'll do the right thing. You always do.'

I wish you were right, Philip. And yet it's hardly possible to send her back to London. It's not just the bombs, it's the awful situation with her . . .

* * *

The last page ended there.

Kate wondered what Naomi King had eventually decided to do about Susan when she came out of hospital. The welfare services weren't as well-organised as they became later, and Susan's future would have been in the hands of well-meaning amateurs like Naomi King.

She probably disappeared into a suitable house with a fresh set of foster parents, but whether in Oxford or in London, there was no telling.

9

It was just as well that the phone rang when it did next morning. Kate was sitting slumped on the sofa in a welter of indecision. She had just drunk her third large mug of strong coffee and was watching her hand shake as she tried to write a list of things to do that day. She was concentrating on adding only those items to her list which she knew she could achieve, but had got no further than 'Stand up' and 'Walk away from sofa'. Both actions were beyond her. Luckily the phone was only inches from her hand.

'Kate? It's Roz.'

And Roz in one of her brisk moods was what Kate needed at this moment.

'I'm just ringing to check that it's all right to use your computer downstairs in the study at Agatha Street.'

'Yes, fine. I've got my notebook with me.'

'Notebook computer? Oh, good.'

'What are you using the other one for?' asked Kate.

'It's connected to the Internet.'

'And you're spending your days surfing?'

'I've found some very rewarding websites,' said Roz, sounding smug. 'I don't suppose you've ever really explored the full potential of that machine of yours.'

'You've discovered cyberdating?'

'Certainly not. I've never believed in having a virtual love life. I've always gone in for the real thing.'

'So what is it you're looking for on the web?'

'You're sounding very waspish today, Kate. But I can do research just as well as you can,' said Roz. 'And the Internet is merely the latest tool for research.'

'Speaking of which,' said Kate, who recognised her mother in stonewall mode, 'I'm not doing very well with mine.'

'What seems to be the matter?' Roz sounded relieved that they were no longer speaking about her own doings.

'Lethargy.'

'I thought you were getting on so well? Leaving the house, speaking to strangers, even going into a church.'

'I was. And now I seem to be suffering some sort of reaction. My mind says, "Leave me alone. I've done enough. I want to sleep." '

'And you don't fancy listening to it.'

'I've rested. I've slept. And now I'm bored, but I can't seem to get going on anything.'

'Low energy levels? Lack of interest in the outside world? Failure to concentrate? No appetite for sex?'

'Yes, yes, yes, no, in that order.'

'All right. But I still think you're suffering from depression.'

'Thank you, Dr Ivory.'

'Mock your mother if you will, but I'm coming straight over.'

Well, at least it would get her mother away from whatever she was exploring on the Internet. Knowing Roz, Kate was afraid that it involved something nefarious, or disreputable, or possibly even pornographic.

Fifteen minutes later the front doorbell rang with an insistence that could only herald Roz Ivory. Kate opened the door.

'Fruit juice,' said Roz, walking straight through to the kitchen with her bulging plastic bags. 'I could tell by your voice that you'd been drinking far too much coffee. And berries. Raspberries, red currants, blueberries, small red grapes, blackcurrants. Just rinse them through, take off the stalks and place them in a deep glass bowl. Very invigorating. Just what you need. And fish steaks for brushing with olive oil and placing under the grill for our lunch. A green salad to go with them.'

She was unpacking as she spoke and Kate couldn't get a word in, even if she had wanted to say anything.

'Exercise video,' said Roz, handing it across. 'Something gentle for the older woman. I thought it would be appropriate for your current state of mind.'

'I don't want to exercise,' said Kate.

'I know you don't, or I'd have brought you your running shoes. But you can watch this and join in when you feel up to it.' She spoke so sympathetically that Kate immediately determined to do twice as many repetitions as recommended for the elderly. Then she realised that this was what her mother had intended all along.

'I'll think about it,' she said.

'But you're feeling more cheerful already. Admit it.'

'All right. I admit it.'

'Well, pour us each a glass of the cranberry and whatever and we'll move back into the sitting room.'

'Would you like a slug of vodka in yours?'

'Not when I'm driving,' said Roz piously. 'I'll have a drink this evening when I'm safely home again.'

'You are being horribly improving today. I find it rather disconcerting. Do you think you could revert to your usual irresponsible self?'

'Not until I've got you back on the rails,' said Roz firmly.

'And how do you propose to do that?'

'Let's have some lunch, and while we're eating it you can tell me about the new book and how and why you can't write it.'

They munched their way through grilled fish and green salad, then spooned up assorted berries. Roz allowed Kate to sprinkle hers with a little sugar. She looked at her afterwards as though expecting to see an improvement already. Kate hated to disappoint her.

'Shall we go into my study?' she said. 'I can show you what I've been doing.'

'What about this collection of cassettes?' asked Roz when everything was out on the desk.

'I've only listened to one of them so far,' confessed Kate, 'and I didn't even get all the way through that. I could have picked up on Naomi King's sad story if I'd been willing to listen to her niece, but all I could think about was getting home so that I could read what she'd written about the evacuees.'

'That's the answer,' said Roz.

'What is?'

'You're not going to be able to write a romantic novel for Estelle until you've solved the mystery of the two children in the attic.'

'Did they live in the attic?'

'I've no idea. I was speaking figuratively.'

'I see.'

'Give yourself a time limit – a week or two, say – to find out everything you can, then put it away and think about land girls or whatever it is you're going to write about.'

'Land girls are quite a good idea, but hasn't somebody got there before me?'

'Don't ask me. I never read that sort of book.'

'I'm dithering again, aren't I? You're right. I must concentrate on one thing, and then it will be finished and I can move on.'

There was something wonderful about allowing her mother to take charge, like lying back in a hot bath and letting the bubbles settle all over you. Roz might have her scatty moments – years, even – but she was really quite competent.

'Well, what have you got here? Christopher's treasures?' asked Roz.

'There's nothing very special about them, I'm afraid. He gives nothing away. Except for this rather vicious drawing.'

'Mm. It does seem even more violent than one would expect.'

'But I can't find anything else.'

'Let me look.'

Roz sat and looked at the photos, then went carefully through the notebook and the letters. 'These must be drafts,' she said, putting aside the letters. 'Or written to be read by some adult censor.'

'Naomi King?'

'It's more likely to be Elinor Marlyn, I should have thought. She wouldn't want the children writing nasty things about her.'

'Perhaps she had a dark secret and was making sure they didn't give it away in their letters.' Kate spoke flippantly, but then thought a moment. 'Maybe *that's* what was wrong. That's the "evil" that Naomi King wrote about.'

'And maybe you're letting your imagination run away with you again. But carry on, Kate. It's good to know that you even have an imagination these days.'

'No, really – it's here in Naomi's notes.' She passed across the few pages and waited while Roz read through them.

'How sad. The poor girl is getting ready for a life of loneliness and service to others, by the sound of it. It's such a pity that her fiancé died. I do hope she escaped.'

'Not from what I learned. And I heard from her niece how empty a woman's life must be without a man to fill it.' Roz made an explosive sound. 'But look, there's the bit where she talks about evil.'

'It's very general, isn't it? And isn't she writing with hindsight, after the accident?'

'I think there was something nasty going on.'

'Let me finish looking through this.' Roz had turned back to Christopher's notebook.

'I see what you mean about giving nothing away,' she said after a few minutes. 'This child did not lead an exciting life. "Got up. Went to school. Sausages for dinner. Susie and I had one each and shared the third one between us for seconds." Riveting stuff. The child seems obsessed by food and what he ate.'

She continued turning the pages in silence.

'What's this?' She read aloud: ' "She's given Susie some soap, just a little piece but it smells like pink flowers. I've told Susie I'll hide it away for her with the other things." ' She looked up at Kate. 'What "other things"?'

'These treasures were hidden under the floorboards in this old biscuit tin. The electricians found them. He must have meant he'd keep it there for her.'

'But there's no soap here,' said Roz, turning the box upside down in case they'd missed something. She sniffed at the inside, but could smell no pink flowers. 'Fancy living in a world so dull and grey that you could be thrilled by a bar of soap.'

'Not even a whole bar, from what her brother says. That was wartime for you. But where is it?'

'I expect she used it up.'

'I bet he hid some other things – his real treasures – somewhere else.'

'In his bedroom,' said Kate. 'I used to hide things under the floorboards.'

162

'I know,' said Roz. 'I think most children do.'

'But we've already found the biscuit tin.'

'The child was a squirrel. There must be biscuit tins under floorboards all over this house.'

'Hm. That's unlikely with Miss Marlyn's beady eye upon him.'

'I wonder which his room was?'

'Probably the one where the electricians were working.'

'Or he could have hidden them in the attic.'

'We have the whole afternoon ahead of us,' said Kate, forgetting that an hour before she had felt too tired to do anything.

The two women wandered through the house, considering the possibilities.

'He wouldn't have hidden them on the ground floor. The rooms must have been in constant use,' said Kate.

'I think we should start by making no assumptions.'

'But we have to start somewhere. Let's look upstairs. It's lucky there are no tenants in at the moment,' said Kate as they started to look through the upper rooms in their own half of the house. 'We can poke around in all the rooms. Then we can go up to the tenants' flat.'

'Unfortunately, there is one major problem.'

'Only one?'

'I was thinking of the problem involving carpet.'

'Fitted carpet,' agreed Kate.

'Makes it a bit tricky to get at the floorboards.'

'We could pull it up and look underneath.'

'All of it? If Christopher's treasures are still here, they're bound to be in the last room we look in. Sod's Law.'

They both stared at the carpet which lay, smooth and bland, on the floor of every room.

'Up to the tenants' rooms.'

But the rooms were relatively empty, with no clutter to hide any children's hidden treasure.

'I think the electricians would have found anything in these rooms,' said Kate.

'The attic,' said Roz, conceding defeat.

'More of a loft,' said Kate, leading the way.

So they climbed the ladder and crawled around under the roof space.

'I'm filthy,' said Roz. 'Don't you ever clean up here?'

'Certainly not. I've never been quite *that* bored.'

'These cupboards have been put in since the house was built,' said Roz, pointing at the row of sliding wooden doors that cut off the roof slope as it approached the floor.

'We need a torch. I know there's one round here somewhere.'

'Here it is,' said Roz, and shone it into the dark, triangular space.

'Dead spiders. Mouse droppings. Ends of carpet rolls,' said Kate, exploring.

'Fifteen copies of the *Radio Times* for 1952. Why on earth would anyone want to keep them?'

'Put them over here. I'll leave them out on Monday for recycling.'

'And a box, probably made at school in woodwork class, suitable for keeping treasures in,' said Roz.

'Eureka, to coin a phrase,' said Kate, blowing away dust.

'He's fitted it with a padlock,' said Roz, surprised. 'You could be right that this contains his real treasures. Or someone's. We don't know that it belonged to Christopher. There were loads of Dolby children, after all.'

'But this house has always belonged to the maiden ladies of the family. Children, apart from the evacuees, were occasional visitors. They didn't live here. It has to be Christopher's.'

'You don't want to accept everything you've been told about people's families. Everyone embroiders the tale a little. Or a lot, sometimes. Families develop a common myth and everyone sticks to it.'

'What's the Ivory myth?'

'We don't have one. Or rather, it's that we're all wild, free, gypsy-like characters, too original to settle down to suburban life.'

'I'll try to remember it to hand on to my grandchildren.'

Roz made a noise that sounded like *hmph*.

'We need to open the box. That will settle the argument.'

'Where do you keep your smallest screwdriver?' asked Roz.

'Downstairs in the kitchen drawer.'

And Roz was scrambling down the ladder then racing down the stairs towards the kitchen while Kate replaced the torch, switched off lights and followed her down.

'It's not fair,' she muttered. 'It's *my* mystery.'

Roz was already attacking the wooden box when Kate arrived in the kitchen. 'I can't get the screws out,' she grumbled.

'I'll get the 3-in-1 if you promise not to drip it all over George's table,' said Kate.

They coaxed oil around rusty screws and Kate made Roz wait while it soaked in and got to work.

'Calm down and have a cup of tea,' Kate suggested. 'Or is tea not allowed on this healthy diet of yours?'

'I'll put the kettle on,' said Roz.

Five minutes later they tried the screws again and this time were able to remove the simple lock that Christopher had fixed to the box. If it *was* Christopher's.

'Told you so!' said Roz, opening the lid.

'I always wanted a penknife like that when I was a kid,' said Kate.

'Soap?' was all Roz said.

They couldn't see any. But when they both sniffed at the contents of the box they could smell carnations, very faintly.

'Evidence of the presence of soap, some time in the past,' Roz declared.

'What's this?' Kate picked up a tangle of thin white metal tape.

'The bombers used to drop it to confuse the radar, I think,' said Roz. 'He must have picked it up in London. I don't suppose they dropped much of it round here.'

'And this?'

'A cap badge. Maybe it was his father's. Didn't Naomi mention that he'd died?'

' "He'd never return home". I suppose she meant he was dead. Poor little kids.'

'A folded paper, as found in all the best mysteries,' said Roz, unfolding and reading it. 'Something nasty about his school-mistress – correctly spelled, by the way. He's put the correct number of t's in "bitch". These days, the kids wouldn't write it down on paper. They'd just spray-paint it on the woman's front door.'

'Is there anything else in there?'

'A letter,' said Roz.

'Not written by Christopher.' No indelible pencil, but a scratchy steel pen nib and permanent blue-black ink on lined blue paper.

'It's from his mother. "Hope you're well. Hope you're being good. Hope you're looking after your sister. We're both well and miss you." '

'She must have been referring to the shadowy Uncle Alan.'

'Perhaps. Or she could have been living with a sister, or a friend, or another man, or her own mother – anyone. Really, Kate, you know very little about these people. You're just making up the bits between the lines.'

'That's what I'm good at, remember?'

'As long as you don't confuse it with the truth.'

'You can see how ill she is,' said Kate. 'Look at her handwriting. It's shaky, like a very old woman's.'

'She looked ill in the photographs, certainly.'

'I think she's dying. Brenda Boston thought their mother was sick. Otherwise she'd have taken the children back to London, wouldn't she? Everyone knew the war was nearly over, all the books say so.'

'What books?'

'The one I've been looking at. Stop being so logical. It's not your style.'

'I find your argument quite convincing.'

'I wish we could find the uncle, but I don't fancy wandering the streets of South London looking for him. Actually, I'm not keen on wandering any streets anywhere at the moment.'

'You could write.'

'What?'

'To number twenty-six Reckitt Street, SE15.'

'But that was fifty-five years ago!'

'It's worth a try. You could mark the envelope *Please Forward*. You never know, it might work.'

'It's a daft idea, but I might just do it. Yes. I'll write a simple letter saying I wish to contact Alan Barnes. I won't even say why.'

'Do it now,' said Roz.

So Kate did, sitting at the computer and composing a very short letter.

'How about the envelope?' she asked Roz. 'Printed or handwritten?'

'Handwritten. It looks less like junk mail, more like a long-lost relative.'

'OK.'

'I'll put it in the post for you on my way home.'

'You're not going yet?'

'Not quite. We still have to sample some of those tapes of yours. They may be full of gems of information.'

'They may be full of reedy old voices telling me about the village maypole dance.'

'That's the old, negative you speaking,' said Roz bracingly. 'Surely that grilled fish and bowl of berries has started to work by now.'

'If you say so.'

'And who's this Miss Arbuthnot you have on your list? Didn't Christopher mention her?'

' "Miss Arbuthnot is an evil old bitch" ', quoted Kate. 'She must have been his schoolteacher. I can't wait to meet her! She's stayed in the area for all these years and Elspeth has given me her address so that I can contact her. Vicars have their uses.'

'We still have time to listen to a tape or two before you need to start preparing George's supper,' said Roz.

'You and Estelle appear to be competing for Nag of the Year.' But Kate plugged in the cassette recorder and slipped a tape into the compartment.

What have we got?' asked Roz.

'*Village life*,' said Kate and pressed the play button.

A reedy old voice came out at them in waves, as though the speaker had been rocking in his chair and approached and then receded from the microphone.

'The privy was in a shed at the bottom of the garden,' the speaker began. 'Ours was very nice. My dad had planted flowering bushes around it so's you had a bit of privacy. Mind you, there was a hole bored in the door at eye-height so's Mum could make sure everything was well if you spent too much time out there. And no toilet paper the way people have now, just squares of cut newspaper hung on a nail on the door. And our privy grew the largest spiders in the village, I used to believe.'

'Do we have to listen to this?' asked Kate.

'Try fast-forwarding it a bit.'

The voice gabbled and squeaked, then carried on: '. . . kept a pig, of course. Half of it belonged to the Ministry, and they sent a man round the day Dad was going to slaughter it, just to make sure they got their half.'

This time it was Roz who hit the Fast Forward.

'. . . Mrs Clack kept her false teeth in a dish of water by the front door. It was a pretty dish with a blue willow pattern. She kept them there so that she could put them in before opening the door.'

'Mustn't frighten visiting tradesmen,' said Roz, hitting the Off button. 'Look, here's one marked *Evacuees*. That might have something useful on it.'

'Where? I must have missed that one.'

'It'll be *full* of stories of outside privies!'

'Just put it on. I want to hear it.'

The voice this time wasn't quite as old. A woman in middle-age, guessed Kate – about the age Roz was now, though 'middle-aged' was not a term one used in her hearing. 'We found it very dull in the country after London. There wasn't much life, not what we were used to. And they made us do housework the way our Mum never did. We got our own back, though. She told us to take the toddler for a walk every afternoon, and we'd teach him words they never heard out there in the country. That bucked 'em up a bit, I can tell you.' She ended with a loud laugh.

'Move it on,' said Roz.

'I quite like her,' said Kate, but did as her mother said.

It was a man's voice this time. 'People think of the black market as being a city thing, especially a London thing,' he was saying. 'You think of men in sharp suits and hats at a raffish angle, talking out the side of their mouth in Cockney accents. But it was rife out here in the sticks, too. These country people might look stupid, but they knew where to get what they needed, even if it wasn't available in the shops. By the time it got towards the end of the war, everyone was at it. Petrol, car tyres, nylons, chocolate, pork chops and sausages, bottles of whisky. Oxfordshire was full of aerodromes, Yanks many of them, and there was always someone at a back gate could get you what you wanted.'

'Maybe that's what Miss Marlyn's great secret was,' suggested Roz.

'A black marketeer? I can't imagine it, can you? The stiff and starchy Marlyns getting their hands dirty? I'm sure they were the upright sort who never cheated on their rations, or points, or whatever the things were called.'

'When you're rich, even in wartime, you're cushioned to a certain extent from the hardship,' said Roz. 'Apart from anything else, she probably had a house full of useful objects, from bath towels to saucepans, and a larder full of preserves going back to the thirties. It's not the same as being poor and always being in need of something that's unavailable.'

'I wonder how they made their money.'

'Trade,' said Roz. 'Grocery shops, I should think. Or

something old-fashioned, like drapery.'

'I've never been sure what that was, but I imagine male assistants pulling out bales of cloth and unrolling them with panache the length of the counter, showing off to ladies in large, feathery hats.'

'I expect it means knickers, really,' said Roz.

'Whatever it was, they were certainly good at it.'

'Not short of a bob or two, your Marlyns and Dolbys.'

'Have we heard enough of these tapes yet?'

'No, but we could put them away for another time. We've achieved quite a bit for one day.'

Kate never trusted her mother when she substituted 'we' for 'you'. It meant that she was about to embark with great enthusiasm on one of Kate's pet projects.

'Time to get back to my own work,' said Roz. 'And I won't forget to post the letter to Alan Barnes on my way home.'

Kate was able to put everything away tidily in her desk before George came home and found her busily preparing his evening meal.

'By the way,' said George later that evening, in the tone of voice men use when they've done something they want you to go along with even though they haven't consulted you about it beforehand, 'I've invited the Forrests to come out to dinner with us on Friday.'

'Your friends Nick and Megan?'

'Yes. They already know Sam and Emma. You get on with them all right, don't you?'

There was always a slight doubt, thought Kate, about introducing one's friends to one's lover. It was probably just as tricky as meeting your in-laws for the first time – not that she and George were planning to get married, she told herself quickly, and not that George had any living parents, anyway.

'Of course I like them,' she said. 'At least, Nick's very amusing, though I haven't met Megan yet. She and I will probably find lots of girly things to talk about.' As a matter of fact, it would dilute the Dolbys a little. Emma was definitely a member of her husband's family and it would have been Kate versus three. Now it had evened up a bit.

'I'll wear that green dress you like,' she said. 'I'm really looking forward to tomorrow evening.'

'Me too,' said George.

10

On Friday afternoon Emma phoned Kate.

'Kate? What are you wearing this evening?'

'Hello, Emma, nice to hear from you. How are you?'

'What?'

Emma could be single-minded enough to ignore all the minor social conventions. Kate said, 'I thought I'd wear the pale green dress. I'm not sure you've seen it.'

'What's it like?' Emma sounded like someone's Victorian maiden aunt.

'Boat neck, sleeveless, knee-length, has a matching long jacket. The green is that of freshly-opened willow leaves.'

A short pause while Emma digested this, or perhaps racked her memory for leaves, willow, youthful.

'I shall wear a pair of pale, simple pumps to go with this outfit,' Kate continued, quite aware that she was winding Emma up. 'My make-up will be both cheekily naïve and subtly sophisticated.'

'All right,' said Emma. 'No need to go on. I get the picture. And anyway, you're talking nonsense.' Trust Emma to see through her.

'And I shall worry about my hair, which hasn't been cut recently and is just starting to fall out of shape,' said Kate. Actually, it was also starting to show a couple of centimetres of her original hair colour, which was something she usually managed to be vague about. When she was feeling really strong she'd make an appointment with her hairdresser. Perhaps next week.

'Did you want to ask me anything in particular, Emma?'

'I've got nothing to wear!' wailed Emma, getting to the point of the phone call.

'Do you want me to accompany you into Oxford to buy something new?' asked Kate, hoping that Emma would say no. 'Or do you want me to come round and rifle through your wardrobe and find a suitable outfit that has somehow escaped your attention?'

'Could you come round?' There seemed to be a higher level of desperation than usual in Emma's voice.

'I'll be there in ten minutes,' said Kate, mentally rearranging her afternoon and hoping she could sort Emma out and still leave herself time for a relaxing bath. 'Who's babysitting for you?'

'Jane, the teenager from next door. The children like her. She might even manage to get them all to bed before we return at midnight.'

'Well, give her a ring and ask if she can come an hour or two early. You don't want children hanging on to your posh frock and decorating it with creamed spinach while you're trying to dress.'

'It'll cost more money.'

'I'll pay. Let it be my treat.' Was Emma really always hard up, or was it just an act? Kate always found herself paying for the coffee and cakes when she met Emma in town and felt that her friend added up the price of everything she was wearing and then disapproved of Kate's extravagance. Emma considered anything extravagant that didn't relate directly to one of her children.

Kate decided to drive to Emma's, in spite of her voluntary one-week ban, and found the babysitter arriving at the same moment.

'Just keep the little darlings out of our hair for a couple of hours,' she said, passing over a ten-pound note, not entirely sure how much one paid babysitters, but hoping it was enough. 'Emma will give you your usual evening rate.'

The door was opened by one of Emma's middle-sized children, who smiled at Jane and stared at Kate.

'You have seen me before,' said Kate, returning the stare. It paid to be firm with Dolby children.

'I'm upstairs!' called Emma, and Kate sidled past the suspicious child and went up.

Emma's wardrobe was just the kind of tip you would imagine, she thought, frowning at the jumble of clothes. They didn't even smell very fresh and they certainly weren't hung in any sort of order – those that actually were on hangers. Many of them were just heaped in a jumble on the floor with Emma's shoes. Kate started at one end of the rail and went through them. Emma stood watching her, apparently incapable of making any decisions. Is this what childbearing did for you? wondered Kate.

'Throw this out, the colour's hideous,' she said, passing over a pea-green and yellow dress. 'And this one's got a ragged hem.' She'd soon have the wardrobe in some sort of order at this rate.

'But we're not organising my clothes, just trying to find something to wear,' objected Emma.

'I can't see what you've got until I've weeded out the total dross.' And she handed a couple of faded skirts over and pointed at the discard pile.

Fifteen ruthless minutes later, Kate looked at the clothes that were left on the rail.

'Goodness,' said Emma. 'Maybe you should come and sort out the rest of my house.'

'Bin those,' said Kate, indicating the pile of cast-offs on the floor and inwardly shuddering at the thought of this large house, with its numerous cupboards overflowing with junk.

'I usually take them to the charity shop.'

'No, Emma, Oxfam would not be grateful if you took your old clothes there. They have standards, you know.'

'It seems such a waste!'

'No, it's not. Your clothes have lived long and useful lives which are now over. Now, to get to this evening's outfit.'

'My clothes do look more promising now you've sorted them out a bit.'

'This slate blue's a good colour for you,' said Kate. 'Can you still get into it?'

'Yes, but it's too long. It's supposed to be a tunic to wear over my good black trousers. And they're too tight round the waist. And hips.'

'Try them on. I don't think you're that much fatter than normal. We'll see what can be done.' Kate had no time to be diplomatic and coaxing.

'Not bad,' she said. 'The tunic hides the tight bits of the trousers – no, Emma, I will not allow you to use a safety-pin – though it needs a stitch here and there. Where do you keep your pins? Needle and cotton? And a damp cloth, some cleaning fluid and the iron and ironing board. And you can choose a pair of shoes and polish them,' she added bossily.

Emma, the hope of dressing elegantly for once spurring her on, found all that was needed and she and Kate set to work.

As Kate sewed, she asked, 'Just what is the matter, Emma? You don't usually get this het up about a family evening out. It's not a competition, as far as I know.'

'I'm not het up,' said Emma, in a very tight voice.

'Come off it, you're furious about something.' Kate snipped cotton and threaded a needle.

'It's Sam,' said Emma. 'He's being horrible to me.'

'Sam?' Emma's husband reminded Kate of a large and particularly hairy teddy-bear. His normal expression was a friendly smile.

'I was just saying to him that Jack has got to the age when he really should have a little sister or brother,' said Emma.

'And all his big brothers and sisters don't count?'

'Of course not. It's not the same thing at all.'

'I suppose you need to keep producing infants to write stories for.' Emma wrote wholesome books for children that were published by a respectable publishing house but never did anything as vulgar as reaching a bestseller list.

'It's not like that at all! The two things are quite separate. But Sam said all the things you've just said, and then he finished by telling me that we had enough children and really should stop.'

'And you don't agree?' said Kate, trying not to take sides but realising that she had probably already indicated agreement with Sam's point of view.

'I think Jack needs a little brother or sister. And I'm well short of forty,' she added.

'Won't you need a bigger house, and a whole fleet of motor cars to ferry them around?'

'Stop exaggerating. Why do you always exaggerate?'

'It's a habit. And you can stop polishing those shoes now, by the way. You've given them a quite terrifying shine. Try this tunic on instead, but go gently with it.'

Emma's head disappeared beneath the blue tunic, still grumbling about Sam's attitude to having another child.

'The hem won't last for long, I was too quick with it,' said

Kate. 'You'll have to have another go at it tomorrow, before you put it away, and before you forget.' She knew, somehow, that Emma wouldn't get round to it. And that next time she wanted to wear the tunic, its hem would be hanging down on one side. Well, at least it looked clean now, and the trousers were pressed. They smelled both musty and chemical, but that might wear off before they got to the restaurant.

'I shan't forgive him,' said Emma.

'Who?'

'Sam. Jack really wants that baby brother or sister, you know.'

'Ah.'

Emma was still wearing the tunic, but her face looked quite pink above it.

'I'll help you out of it,' said Kate, afraid that her good work would be ripped apart. 'And I hope you have some better underwear than that.'

'I don't bother with flashy new underwear.'

'I can tell.'

'I'll try to find a clean bra,' conceded Emma.

'I have to go now,' said Kate, slipping Emma's tunic and trousers over a hanger on the rail. 'I'll see you at the restaurant. And try to calm down a bit.'

'That was really kind of you to sort out my clothes,' said Emma awkwardly. She wasn't good at being grateful.

'Use the rest of the extra babysitting time to have a shower and wash your hair. Maybe Jane could help you to pin it up.'

'Yes, yes, I will.'

'And try to forget about your difference of opinion with Sam. It doesn't make for a happy evening out to row with one's partner just before leaving home. Trust me, I know from experience. I'm sure you'll work out a compromise between you.'

'Compromise? What sort of compromise could there be? He'll just expect me to give in, the way I always do.'

Kate would like to suggest that Emma see a psychiatrist, or a counsellor, or whatever was the latest fashion in people who sorted your head out for you. Why should Emma be so dependent for her happiness on having a baby around? Kate managed to be reasonably cheerful with none at all. She thought Sam had been quite easygoing enough with Emma. Soon the whole of Headington would be populated with their offspring if they went along with Emma's wishes.

On the other hand, she felt she had done a good job on winning Emma over to her side for the forthcoming evening. I've never heard Emma so happy with me, she thought as she drove back to Cavendish Road. Emma was one of those people who remembered every little mistake you'd ever made, and brought them all out at the dinner table, one after the other. But not this evening, thought Kate smugly. This evening was going to be perfect. With Emma's help she would impress George's friends and his brother and sister-in-law with her sparkling personality and social know-how. She would be welcomed into the Dolby family as a bona fide member. She was sure that by the time Emma left her house she would have retrieved her usual good humour with Sam. They weren't one of those couples that rowed in public, after all.

They met for pre-dinner drinks in the bar of the restaurant, which was heaving with the local twenty-somethings, most of whom were smoking. Emma coughed ostentatiously and waved her hand about a bit, but no one took any notice. I do believe she had enough time over after I left her to knock back a glass or two, thought Kate. That's not blusher on her cheeks, it's the effects of strong drink taken. Emma was being sparkling and animated, waving her hands around more than usual. It was Sam who looked a bit quiet.

Nick and George were catching up on news of their respective work, and hadn't noticed Emma's unusual state. Emma had got into a conversation with Megan that involved babies and children, so maybe drink wasn't really affecting her in any potentially embarrassing way. In fact, at the moment it looked as though it might develop into a really conventional evening. Not even interesting enough to use as a scene for one of her novels, and none of the characters at the table would be of any use to liven up a chapter, either.

She was grateful when they moved through to their table, and even more pleased when the wine they'd ordered turned up and was poured out by the waiter so that she could start catching up with Emma.

Emma, too, seemed to be knocking back the wine at quite a rate, she noticed. It was as though, once away from her children and domestic cares, she was making up for years of lost time. They ordered food, Emma asking noisily for an explanation of every dish, then Megan set about being friendly to George's girlfriend.

'George told me you're a writer, like Emma,' she began. 'Should I have heard of you?'

How the hell did you answer that one?

'Probably not,' she said. 'And I don't really write like Emma. She writes for children and I aim at the adult market.' Oh dear, that had come out wrong. It sounded as though she wrote erotica for bored housewives, which was very far from the truth. 'What sort of books do you read?' she added quickly.

'Novels, certainly,' said Megan. 'Fay Weldon, Anne Tyler, Jennifer Johnston, people like that.'

'Yes, I like them, too. But the novels I write are quite different. I've been writing historical romances—'

'Light on history, strong on romance,' put in Emma, waving her hands around and sending a glass of water flying. A waiter turned up with a cloth and mopped the table in her vicinity.

'I didn't think you'd ever read one of my books, Emma,' said Kate, aware that she was sounding unpleasantly sharp.

'Well, perhaps not, but—'

'I don't think you should comment on books you haven't read,' said Megan. 'What period of history do you set them in, Kate?'

'Various periods,' said Kate vaguely. 'But my agent wants me to write something modern, so I'm working on the nineteen-forties at the moment. The Second World War,' she explained, in case Megan's knowledge of history was worse than her own.

'And I suppose you're reading as much primary material as you can find?' said Megan.

Kate translated for her own benefit. 'Oh yes. I have diaries and notebooks, and quite a number of tapes. Oral history is so important, I find.' She saw Megan preparing to ask her another question to which she wouldn't know the answer, so she added quickly, 'And I've come across some very interesting material in George's house.'

'What's that?' asked George, catching the final sentence.

'She's unearthing the family skeletons, by the sound of it,' put in Sam.

'Oh, but I'm sure there aren't any!' exclaimed Emma with deep sarcasm. She had already emptied her glass a couple of times and was starting on a third, helping herself from a bottle that had been left within her reach. Sam stretched across and moved it a couple of feet to the left. 'How could the Dolbys possibly have any scandals in their background?' She added a merry laugh that made Kate's toes curl. Oh Emma, where are you taking this conversation?

Kate, counting, reckoned Emma had had a gin in the bar beforehand and had been at the drinks tray before leaving the house, followed by the three glasses of wine at the table. Her own head would be spinning after that lot, and this was Emma, who kept herself pure and alcohol-free for her children. The evening promised to get a lot livelier.

At this moment their starters arrived and once the waiters sorted out who was having what, Kate watched Emma as her fork swayed over her assembly of wild mushrooms in a puff pastry case. Her face was growing pinker and shinier by the minute, and she certainly hadn't remembered who had hemmed that rather attractive slate-blue tunic for her a little earlier in the day. She attempted to spear a mushroom and missed. Oh dear, thought Kate. Mushroom juice didn't improve the white tablecloth.

'No skeletons in the Dolby family cupboard!' cried Emma, unable to leave the subject alone. Frustrated by mushrooms, she was giving herself to witty dinner-party conversation instead. 'Their cupboards are too full of the family silver to have any room left for skeletons. They've always been *so-o-o* proper, you just wouldn't believe it. Do you know, Megan and Kate, when Sam and I went away for just a tiny little weekend, a few months before our wedding, well . . .'

'Shut up, Emma,' said Sam good-humouredly. It was no good, he'd need a gag to stop her now, thought Kate. Perhaps he could use one of the table napkins. She might offer to hold Emma down while he inserted it in his wife's open mouth.

'Of course,' Emma continued, managing to fill her mouth with mushrooms at last, but speaking through them quite audibly, 'they are all frightfully well-off, too. Not like my family. Not like yours, either, Kate, I don't suppose. No, we're not loaded, like the Dolbys. They like women like us, though.

Did you know that? They can use their money to keep us in our place. They let us scrimp and save while they salt their money away in stocks and shares and property. And then, when we ask them for one small thing, the sort of thing any woman would want, and any man, too, if he had any family feeling at all, then he just . . .' But Emma had lost her train of thought and sat staring at her empty fork in a puzzled way.

'Have you finished with this?' asked the waiter, attempting to remove Emma's plate. She held on to the other side of it.

'No. I have several mushrooms left.'

The waiter, perhaps reading the situation, continued to clear the others' plates. The clatter while he did so covered Emma's comments for the moment.

As soon as the table was cleared, she started up again.

Sam and George were carrying on a loud conversation about football, Nick was looking nervous and pretending not to hear what she was saying, and George was probably praying that the main course would arrive and shut her up again, but Megan and Kate were still listening avidly to Emma.

'To the Dolbys, money has always equalled virtue,' she was saying in a meaningful tone. 'Or do I mean equated to? You're the words person, Kate, what do you think?'

Kate, who had always been put in her place by Emma on questions of grammar and syntax, let alone semantics, said, 'I hadn't realised what an expert you were on the Dolby family,' ignoring George's warning glance and grabbing her opportunity to learn more about them. 'So I expect you know about the little evacuees who stayed at High Corner during the war?'

'Megan and I are going to Corsica next month,' said Nick, who was a nice man and couldn't bear to see his friend Sam being embarrassed by dear Emma in public. 'Are you and George going away anywhere interesting, Kate?'

'Don't interrupt, darling,' said Megan. 'No one's talking about holidays. Kate's busy with the research for her new book and she won't be going away just yet. What was it you were asking about, Kate?'

'Evacuees.' George was definitely frowning at her now. She should have taken the opportunity Nick had given them to change the subject. She didn't care.

'That's a big house you're living in,' said Megan. 'I suppose they would have filled it with several families from the East End during the Blitz.'

'I don't think there was ever a question of that,' replied George swiftly. 'I believe my Great-aunt Elinor was prepared to have it used as a reception centre for air-raid casualties.'

'And how many air raids did Oxford suffer?'

'Not many,' he conceded. 'There were a few incendiary bombs in a field near Abingdon one night. And there were casualties when a plane crashed into a house in Littlemore.'

'So she wasn't overwhelmed with war work,' said Megan. 'One woman in a house large enough to shelter a dozen homeless people.'

'The house belonged to her,' George objected. 'She could live there alone if she wanted to. And she shared it with her niece before the war, until Sadie was called up for one of the women's services.'

Megan was about to ask another sharp question, but Emma got in first.

'When Kate talks about evacuees, she means those poor little orphans who were murdered by Sam's wicked Aunt Elinor.' She put as much ham into the statement as when she was reading bedtime stories to the children.

'Stop being ridiculous, Emma,' said Sam, abandoning any pretence that he and Nick were really deeply interested in football, and sounding less amused than before.

'There were no orphans in Aunt Elinor's house,' said George firmly. 'And she certainly didn't murder them.'

Work that one out if you can, thought Kate.

'Yes, there were,' insisted Emma. 'Violet Watts told me about them.'

'How do you know Violet?' asked Kate.

'She's an old Dolby retainer. I visited her when she moved out of the gardener's cottage and into Oswald Court, just to make sure she was happy. I was stuck there for an hour or more listening to her stories.'

'She's a bad-tempered old gossip,' said George. 'You shouldn't pay any attention to her.'

'Why don't you finish your starter, Emma? You're keeping us all waiting,' said Sam.

Kate could have told him that this was not the way to handle Emma, especially after she had had too much to drink. And Emma *had* obviously had too much to drink for someone who hadn't eaten since her very light lunch and who wasn't, in any case, used to drinking.

'I have finished now,' she said, hurt.

'I think we should change the subject,' said Nick, who was looking more nervous by the minute. Megan, on the other hand, appeared amused.

'But this is fascinating,' she said. 'You can't possibly leave the subject there. Family retainers? Murders committed? And of poor innocent *children*?'

'One of them did die, but he wasn't murdered,' said Kate, attempting to save the situation. It didn't come out sounding quite as bland as she'd intended, though. 'He and his sister were hit by a delivery van driven by Danny Watts.'

And now George raised an eyebrow. 'You didn't tell me you

were carrying on your researches into our evacuees.'

'It was just that the same name cropped up so soon after we found the boy's notebook,' she said.

'Not that old box of junk from under the floorboards?' asked Sam.

'I thought we'd got rid of it,' said George, who was less good at deception than the rest of his family.

'So you'd seen it before?' Kate was surprised. She'd somehow received the impression that the contents were as new to George as they were to her.

'Possibly. I'd forgotten all about it.'

'The Dolby family is very good at selective amnesia,' said Emma, anxious to get back to her own grievances.

'*You* remember the old biscuit tin,' said Sam, missing George's silent messages to let the subject drop. 'We found it under the floorboards in one of the first-floor bedrooms. After we'd looked all through it, we put it back again.'

'So you *had* seen it before. Why didn't you say so?' asked Kate accusingly. She might as well join in this Dolby argument if she was going to consider herself as one of the family.

'I suppose Sardinia might be just as beautiful,' said Nick desperately. 'What do you think, Megan?'

'Who was Danny Watts?' asked Megan.

'I wonder what's happened to our main courses?' asked Sam.

'I've caught the waiter's eye. I think they'll be here in a moment,' replied George.

'Danny's brother and sister-in-law worked for Elinor Marlyn, and he did odd jobs for people and drove a delivery van,' explained Kate.

'Who ordered the swordfish?' asked Sam.

'I believe that's mine,' said Nick. 'What was yours, Megan?'

'Guinea-fowl. What did you say, Emma? I missed it.'

'Danny Watts may have been driving,' repeated Emma. 'But he and Elinor were like *that*.' She crossed her fingers and squinted at them to indicate the closeness of the relationship.

'Not that there can possibly have been anything wrong between them,' she insisted. 'After all, she was Sam and George's great-aunt, and therefore of *the very highest character*. It was all just nasty gossip.' She sounded as though she personally was quite prepared to believe every word of the gossip, the more scurrilous the better.

Kate silently ran through what she'd learned. Danny's sister-in-law Violet Watts was a servant at High Corner, while his brother Arthur looked after the garden. Great-Aunt Elinor was carrying on with a member of the lower orders who was around twenty years her junior! Scandal in the family. Mind you, you'd have to believe a drunken Emma, and Kate wasn't sure she did.

'I don't understand what anyone's motive would be,' said Kate steadily, 'for murdering a ten-year-old boy.'

'That's a good point,' said Megan. 'But suppose he'd found out something he shouldn't?'

'Even if he'd discovered that Elinor and Danny were having a steamy affair –'

'Kate!' This was George, but she took no notice.

'– it's hardly a reason for murder.'

'Are you having the lamb, madam?' asked the waiter, which broke the conversation up, to Kate's annoyance and George and Sam's evident relief.

'Eat up your dinner,' said Sam to Emma. 'It'll help to blot up some of that alcohol. And I've poured you a glass of water. Drink it up.'

'Shan't,' said Emma and smiled at her husband.

Oh dear, divorce courts are beckoning, thought Kate. And what will they do with all those children, even if anyone could remember just how many they had.

'The other interesting thing,' insisted Emma, ignoring her fast-congealing lamb and swigging Nick's glass of wine since Sam had removed her own, 'is the performance of the Marlyn stocks and shares during the war.' And at this point one had to remember, thought Kate, that Emma was quite a well-read lady, even if one wasn't entirely sure where she was leading.

Nick opened his mouth to say something but Megan was quicker. 'No, I'm not interested in Corfu either, Nick. And neither is Kate.'

'Sorry?' said Kate. 'What's Corfu got to do with it?'

'Could you pass the bread please, Kate?'

Kate passed bread to George without taking her eyes off Emma.

'While everybody else lost money and ended up poor as a church mouse – that's what happened to my grandfather, Kate. It wasn't his fault, you see, it was just that the bottom fell out of it.'

'Really?' Kate wasn't sure she was following Emma's line of thought. She'd have to think about it afterwards when people weren't constantly interrupting with names of Mediterranean islands and demands for bread.

'Anyway,' said Emma, attacking her food at last, 'they tell you how proud they are of their family, but there are dark secrets out there they'd prefer you not to know about.'

'Very amusing, Emma,' said Sam.

'I think the Dolbys and the Marlyns certainly do have a lot to be proud of,' said George. 'It's fashionable to sneer at the middle classes, and at tradesmen, but that's what our forebears were, and they helped to make Oxford the profitable place it is now.' Kate had never imagined that George could sound so pompous.

188

'They contributed more to its reputation than the University did, you think?' asked Megan.

'Members of the University come and go,' said George, ignoring the traditions of the past seven hundred years or so. 'It's families like ours that are the bedrock of this place.'

Emma was starting to yawn, and Kate hadn't much interest in the stock market, or in the solid middle classes, and seeing the desperate expression on George's face, thought she'd better do something to rescue the dinner party, even if a touch belatedly.

'Tell me about *your* work,' she said to Megan. And, 'Eat up your nice vegetables, Emma. They're good for you. They'll make your hair curl.' If she'd been Nick, sitting next to Emma, she'd have cut up her lamb to encourage her to start eating and stop talking, but Nick had apparently never seen Emma in action with her own children and didn't know how these things were done. Emma, after all, was regressing to a behaviour level of around eight years old and should be treated appropriately.

'The broccoli's very good,' Emma said, responding to Kate's approach. 'Much better than I manage at home.'

And Megan said, 'I work for the Health Authority.'

And Kate said, 'How interesting. You must tell me all about what you do.'

And George smiled at her, so she must be doing something right.

When the waiter said to Emma, 'Would madam like more wine?' George and Sam said 'No!' in unison.

Kate listened to a fascinating account of management techniques in a modern, forward-thrusting health service and wished she could unleash Emma again. But she thought that the most she could hope for was that Emma wouldn't keel over and bury her nose in her *petit pot au chocolat*.

* * *

'That was an interesting evening,' she said to George on the way home.

'Yes. But not quite the one I'd planned.'

'Had you really forgotten all about the biscuit tin under the floorboards?'

'Completely. We unearthed it when we were only about ten years old ourselves. We put the thing back where we'd found it and I never thought about it again.'

Kate was going to say, 'Not even when I asked you about Christopher Barnes?' But she thought better of it. There had been quite enough dissension in the Dolby family for one evening.

'Are Sam and Emma all right, do you think?' she asked.

'Of course they are. Those two are solid,' said George.

Well, you'd have to be solid if you had that many children and a house that would take about five years to sort out, thought Kate.

11

It was Saturday morning, and Kate woke up knowing that she needed to drink a pint or two of water before doing anything else. George was still asleep, sprawled across most of the bed, so she quietly picked up a set of clean clothes and crept out of the room.

A pint of cold water, a shower, and two mugs of coffee later she was feeling a lot better. It was past nine o'clock but George still hadn't appeared. He probably needed plenty of sleep to erase the effects of the previous evening.

The phone rang and she caught it on the first loud peal. Men who were forced to wake up before they wished to do so were not lovable creatures, in her experience.

'Kate? That was quick.'

'And with good reason. How are you, Roz?'

'I'm fine. Bursting with energy. How about you?'

'Improving by the minute. Why the early phone call?'

'I wanted to buy you a little treat, and I wondered what you'd like?'

'Why? What's happened?' Roz was not the sort of mother who rang her daughter with messages such as this. Not usually, anyhow. Perhaps the whole world was going mad, with Emma getting drunk and attacking her precious Dolbys, and now Roz wanting to 'buy her a little treat'.

'Do I need a reason?' Roz was saying. 'Look, if you must know, I've made a little money recently and I thought I'd like to spend some of it on my daughter.'

'How did you make the money?' asked Kate suspiciously. 'You haven't been betting on the horses again, have you? Or playing poker with the Frightful Fosters?'

'Nothing like that. Though I think I was doing rather well at the races. But this is all quite seemly and legal. Now, what would you like? I wondered about one of those nice little digital voice recorders so that you can wander round, murmuring into it and recording all your passing thoughts.'

Three figures, calculated Kate. They run to three figures, I'm sure. 'I think I'd be embarrassed to share my thoughts with passing strangers. I'm more of a words on paper person.'

'Or what about a new notebook computer? Isn't yours out of date by now?'

Four figures. 'No, really. I've had it little more than a year.'

'Clothes? Shoes?'

She'll suggest a trip to New York in a minute.

'I could pop over to New York and get them for you, if you like. I know that a flight like that would be out of the question for you at the moment and I wouldn't ask you to consider it.'

'You've robbed a bank.'

'Only figuratively speaking. Now, think about it and let me know what you decide.'

She sounded positively smug, thought Kate, staring at the receiver after her mother had rung off. And how could you rob a bank *figuratively*? She was definitely up to no good.

She could hear sounds of George moving from bedroom to bathroom, however, so she put worrying thoughts of Roz out of her head and turned her mind to producing toast and marmalade, crispy bacon, and lots more coffee. Her mother's bad habits, even when they resulted in generous sums of money, were not something she could discuss with George.

'How are you feeling this morning?' she asked.

'After last night, do you mean?'

'Last night was perfectly satisfactory, I thought. I was wondering about what came before it.'

'I've never seen Emma drunk before. At least, I've certainly never seen her both drunk and stroppy. What got into her? What did the two of you talk about when you went round there?'

'Her funny mood was nothing to do with me. I just helped her to find something half-decent to wear. She and Sam had apparently had words some time earlier in the day.'

'About what?'

'Emma wants another baby. Sam believes they have enough already.'

'It's six now, isn't it?'

'Something like that. Sometimes it seems like more.' Kate was never entirely sure how many children Emma had and it was long past the point where it would be polite to ask. George sounded as though he was no more sure than she was on the number of his nieces and nephews.

'Poor Sam. He's only just got over his bike accident. What on earth is wrong with Emma?'

'She's making the excuse that Jack needs a little brother or sister, but the child has loads of those already, of all shapes and sizes. There must be something missing in Emma's life if she has to keep filling it up with babies.'

'She has a very full life,' said George. 'Too full, really. Writing, teaching, running the house, looking after Sam.'

'Well, what do you think it's about?'

'She seems to resent the fact that Sam and I come from a good, middle-class family.'

'I know that both those words are insults, these days, but

there seemed to be more to it than that,' said Kate slowly. Emma's resentment wasn't about the Dolbys' virtues or social status, but because she thought they were phoney. Upright people guarding the doors to cupboards bursting with skeletons. She liked the image. She must go and write it down in her notebook.

'How about you?' asked George. 'Do you agree with her? You weren't doing much to head her off the subject last night.'

'I persuaded her to eat up her broccoli. I even sneakily removed her wineglass and pretended it was mine. What more did you expect?'

Both of them knew that she hadn't answered his question.

'You and Emma have been friends for a long time,' said George.

'But we haven't seen eye to eye about everything for all of that time.' Kate realised she was defending herself. How had she got into this position?

'But you've been poking about in that kid's things, haven't you? I sometimes think you use the excuse of your writing just to stir up old scandals. Have you been talking to Emma about it?'

'No, I haven't. And why didn't you tell me you and Sam found the biscuit tin years ago?'

'I told you. I'd forgotten all about it.'

'And did you know the boy had died while he was living here?'

'No.' But he answered so quickly that she thought he must have been expecting the question and had decided on his answer before she asked.

She wondered whether to mention the second box of treasures. Had he and Sam found those, too? If she kept quiet, then she was being deceitful. She tried a different tack.

'And what happened to Elinor Marlyn?'

'What do you mean, "happened"? She lived out her life and died a peaceful death,' said George shortly.

'I thought she died soon after the end of the war. She can't have been so very old.'

'She was ancient,' said George. 'And I'm sure it was years later.'

Well, she really should believe George rather than Violet Watts, who was probably senile. Should she ask whether it was suicide?

The phone rang again, delaying her decision.

'It's Elspeth for you,' said George. At least she could score Brownie points by being pals with the vicar. There was nothing like the C. of E. for propagating respectability. She must check with Roz one of these days to find out if she was ever received into any sort of church as a baby and, if so, which one. She couldn't trust Roz to do the conventional thing, of course. Perhaps she was a Buddhist or a member of some coven of witches.

'It's Saturday. Why aren't you busy marrying people?' asked Kate, taking the phone from George.

'One of my assistants is doing them today, and I have some free time. I think we should listen to some more of the tapes. I don't believe you've been doing your homework properly. I think you should consolidate the progress you've made in the past week. You mustn't slip back into your depressed state.'

'When did you plan to do this?' replied Kate, heart sinking. She didn't like to be taken on as a good cause but Elspeth was difficult to evade. It sounded as though she had all exits covered. 'George and I are quite busy.'

'This afternoon would be a good time.'

'What about tomorrow's sermon?'

'I've already written it. And you sound as though you're trying to escape from something. Have I said something to offend you?'

'See you at three-thirty,' said Kate, recognising that she'd met her match. If she told Elspeth she'd lost interest in everything except tracking down the story of the two evacuees in High Corner, she'd only get another brisk talking-to about concentration, prioritising and focus. Usually she enjoyed the time she spent with George, pottering about the house and garden, sharing the chores. But that had been something approaching a disagreement over breakfast and she hadn't enjoyed it. Perhaps she and George needed an hour or two apart, anyway.

'I'm off to Homebase to buy some paint,' said George. 'I'll see you in an hour or two.'

'Yes.' Which left her to tackle Tesco's all by herself. And he hadn't asked her what colour paint to buy. He was bound to come back with brilliant white gloss. Never mind. Tesco's beckoned, she was a big girl now, and she was getting bolder about the outside world by the day.

Elspeth found Kate slumped on the sofa, drinking mint tea. She had discovered that the back door was normally unlocked when George and Kate were at home, and so she had come straight through to the sitting room.

'What's wrong?' she asked.

'Take no notice,' said Kate. 'I went to Tesco's for the weekly shop, and I'm still recovering.'

'Tesco's? Oh, well done!' said Elspeth, sounding just like the gym mistress at Kate's school who had been just as patronising when Kate achieved something quite simple. 'Is George in?'

'He's in the upstairs flat, doing something with sugar soap. Will you join me in a mint tea? No? I'll just finish mine and then we'll go to my study.' That was crisp enough to stop Elspeth from patronising her. And she kept her waiting for a minute or so, just to show her whose house it was.

In the study, Elspeth went straight to the box of cassettes. Fair enough, thought Kate, she did bring them here in the first place. But she might have asked before making herself quite so much at home in my study!

'*Evacuees*,' said Elspeth, sitting down in Kate's chair and finding the right tape. She handed it to Kate. 'Put it on,' she said. 'I think I might write something about this period, too. I'm getting really interested in the background material.'

'It has a certain texture to it,' said Kate, trying not to resent Elspeth's presence. But then, when she'd done another thirty minutes on the tapes it would be Elspeth's turn to help *her* again.

The voice on the tape was saying, '. . . when the doodlebug fell. There was a great cloud of dust and debris, like a ragged umbrella, then the bricks and planks of wood rained down again. There was a silence, then the sound of running feet. That's what I remember. I was glad to get away from it, out into the country. It wasn't bad out here, you know. There are stories people will tell you, but we had a good times too, out with our toboggans in the snow. It was like a holiday. And I used to enjoy going out collecting salvage from all the big houses round about. Me and my friend Chris –'

Kate started to pay attention.

'– we had an old pram that Auntie Naomi let us have and we'd fill it up with paper and old clothes and take it back to her place. Goodness knows what they used all that old rubbish for, but we got thanked for our good work. Course, my friend Chris was the one who died. It was sad, that. They fined Danny Watts for careless driving, though Miss Marlyn was in the van, too. She didn't do much hand-wringing over Chris's death, just said it couldn't be helped. She was a heartless woman. But you couldn't say anything against the family in that big house. It just wasn't done.'

Yes! It was *her* Christopher. Nothing much new there, but confirmation of what she'd already learned.

'Do we have a name for this speaker?' she asked Elspeth, when the tape came to the end of Side A.

'Brian Edwards,' she said, reading the label on the plastic case.

'Can we find him?'

'Only in the churchyard. No, I tell a lie.'

Kate looked hopeful.

'He was cremated,' said Elspeth.

'Pity. Oh, and that reminds me. Can we have another look at the plot register? I'd like to check on Elinor Marlyn. Mrs Watts said she died at the end of 1945, but someone else thought it was a lot later than that.' No need to mention that it was George and that they were having a mild disagreement at the time.

'I can't see the point. Don't you want to listen to more of these tapes?'

'Why don't you take some of them back home to the vicarage with you.' Kate gathered together half a dozen of the tapes. 'I've finished with these and you could listen to them in comfort at your own place.'

'You want me out of here,' said Elspeth cheerfully. 'I can't blame you. I'm a terror for sitting around in other people's houses, especially when I've found myself a soulmate.'

'I'll get my jacket,' said Kate. 'We can have a look at the plot register.' And then, she thought, she could check with the Centre for Oxfordshire Studies to see whether it was reported in the local newspaper.

'Oh no,' said Elspeth, when Kate mentioned it to her on the walk back to the church. 'They close at one today. You'll just have to wait until Monday.'

Bother.

It wasn't nearly as bad going into the church as it had been the first time, Kate found. And the plot register did tell them that Elinor Marlyn had been buried in December, 1945.

'I thought they didn't let you into the graveyard if you'd committed suicide,' said Kate.

'What makes you think she did?'

'Oh, just something someone said. I expect she got it wrong.'

'You're not talking about Mrs Watts, are you?'

'Possibly.'

'She's a terrible old gossip, and I think her memory's starting to go.'

But Violet Watts was right about the year of Elinor's death, thought Kate.

She said goodbye to Elspeth in the vestry and made her way back through the churchyard. She might as well find where Elinor Marlyn was buried now that she was here. She hadn't noticed her headstone before because it was in a quiet corner under one of the yew trees.

Kate read the inscription. Elinor had been forty-five when she died. No age at all by today's standards, but perhaps it was more common half a century ago.

On the other hand, she saw, wandering back through the headstones, that the Thomasines and Ediths of the neighbourhood seemed to have made it into their eighties and nineties. It was High Corner that was turning out to be the unhealthy address. And, come to that, what had happened to little Susan, the one whose nose was always running?

She walked slowly back to High Corner – no, number 74 Cavendish Road, she must remember. Had George really forgotten when his great-aunt had died? She wouldn't know the date of death of any of her family, apart from her father, but then she wasn't a Dolby. Not yet, she told herself. Possibly never.

Elinor Marlyn had died long before George was born, and left the house to her niece, the one with the female friend who came to live with her. George had known all that, had happily told her the family history. But he hadn't wanted to talk about Christopher and Susan Barnes, nor about the involvement of his great-aunt.

So something funny *had* been going on. But what?

'Definitely something funny going on,' she said to Roz when she rang her a little later. She had taken the cordless phone into her study so that she wouldn't be disturbed.

'I thought you might have decided by now what you wanted me to get you as a little present.'

'I'm still mulling over your offer. And thank you very much for the thought,' she added stiffly.

'Well, don't worry about the cost. You just let me know what it is you really want.'

'Well, at the moment I'm concerned about the odd happenings in this house all those years ago.'

'And you want me to help you find out what it was all about.'

'Any suggestions will be welcomed.'

'I don't suppose you've heard back from Alan Barnes?'

'No. I don't really think I will. Do you?'

'It's early days,' said Roz breezily. 'Now tell me what these funny things of yours are.'

'First of all the evacuee, young Chris Barnes, is hit by a delivery van driven by a friend of Elinor Marlyn's.'

'We don't know they were friends,' objected Roz. 'It was more of a mistress-servant relationship from what we know of the woman.'

'You could be right, but I'm not convinced.' Kate considered commenting on the 'mistress' part of the description, but resisted the temptation. 'And then Elinor Marlyn dies within the year.'

'I expect she was old and ill.'

'She was forty-five.'

'She could still have been ill. She might have had a heart condition, or any of those nasty things that people died of before the arrival of modern medicine. What do *you* think happened to her, anyway?'

'Violet Watts says she committed suicide.'

'Violet Watts sounds like the sort of old bat who enjoys making the worst of any situation. You can probably dismiss what she says as embroidery.'

'Knitting,' said Kate.

'What?'

'Her knees were covered with magenta knitting. She wasn't doing embroidery.'

'And if magenta knitting doesn't indicate a diseased mind I don't know what does,' said Roz.

Kate said goodbye and sighed. Roz was getting sadly frivolous in her middle age.

Before going upstairs to find George and make sure that they were still good friends, Kate started to tidy the cassettes that Elspeth had left in an untidy heap. She was really getting tired of listening to the reminiscences of these elderly people. The Rev. Aidan Gloster didn't have any very interesting friends, after all. No one who had ever kicked over the traces and done anything more exciting than dance round a maypole or go out collecting salvage.

She dumped the carton of cassettes back into the deep drawer and pushed it shut irritably. The drawer stuck. A couple of the cassettes were on end and wouldn't fit inside properly. She pulled the drawer out again and the whole lot suddenly leapt out and on to the floor. Bother. She hauled out the carton and the rest of the drawer's contents spilled out, too. She shovelled them all back in without bothering too much about neatness. Chris Barnes's old wooden box was there, too, lying open on the carpet. She picked up the contents more carefully and went to put them back, then stopped.

You couldn't call it a secret compartment, she thought. It was too crude and obvious for that. In fact, she and Roz really should have spotted it straight away. It was just a thin sheet of balsawood placed underneath the objects they had already seen. And what was hidden beneath it? A very small notebook – the kind you might keep an account of cash payments in, if you were that sort of pernickety person.

A diary, if you weren't.

The writing was smaller than on the other pages written by Chris, but quite easy to read.

He was still concerned with recording every item of food he ate, she saw. But he was also writing much more detailed descriptions of what was going on around him. She forgot about tidying up the cassettes and sat back in her chair to concentrate.

The phone rang. Why hadn't she taken it downstairs after the call to Roz?

It was Emma. It would be. Kate shoved the diary under a book on her desk and prepared for a long session. She would read Chris's diary later, when she wasn't likely to be disturbed.

Emma sounded quite subdued for once.

'Kate? I just rang to thank you for yesterday evening.'

'Would you like to speak to George? He's the one you should thank, not me.' He was the one who had picked up the substantial bill, after all.

'Well, no. I'd like to talk to you, actually.'

Kate waited. She would be interested to hear Emma offer an apology. She'd never apologised for anything, ever, as far as Kate could tell, however deeply in the wrong she was.

'I know this sounds silly, but do you think you could tell me what happened last night?'

'In the restaurant, do you mean?'

'Yes. Only I woke up with a frightful headache this morning, and I'm still not feeling very well, and Sam's in a dreadful mood, so I don't want to ask him.'

'It's all one great blank, is it?'

'It's like finding your way in fog,' said Emma. 'And when I try to peer into the mist, my head hurts even worse.'

Kate wondered how much to tell her. Wasn't it better that she should never know? On the other hand, if Sam was sulking, then Emma had better be given a small clue as to why.

'I think you may have had one or two glasses of wine more than you're used to,' said Kate carefully.

'Look, I knocked back a couple of shots of brandy before we left for the restaurant,' said Emma. 'I do remember being angry with Sam and thinking, What the hell!'

'Yes, I'd say that was your mood for the rest of the evening, too,' said Kate.

'Did I insult anybody?'

'Sam, mostly. Well, just Sam and George, really. The rest of us escaped quite lightly.'

'Oh, my God! Did I get on to the Dolby family and what hypocrites they are?'

'You did, yes.'

'I only do it because it annoys them so much. That's the trouble with knowing people so well. You know exactly what will hurt, so you throw it at them.' Emma sounded mortified.

'So you invented it all?'

'No, not exactly. But I shouldn't go on about it in public. That was awful of me.'

'I have noticed they can be just a tiny bit smug,' said Kate cautiously.

Emma was asking, 'And did I say what a rat Sam is for not letting me have another baby?'

'You touched on the subject.'

'Poor Sam!' Oh well, they'd soon make up their quarrel if she took that guilt-ridden attitude.

'What about Megan and Nick? Did I say anything dreadful to them?'

'No. In fact, I think Megan was quite fascinated by every-thing you said.'

'Poor Nick!'

'Shall I pass on your thanks for the evening to George, and then a mild apology for getting legless?'

'Make that an abject apology.'

'Very well. And, Emma, I shouldn't worry about it too much. It'll blow over, you know.'

'Do you think so?'

'Yes. I do.' And anyway, she thought, I agreed with most of what you were saying, so where does that leave *me*?

As soon as Emma had rung off, Kate took the phone back downstairs. When she came to read Chris's diary, she didn't want to be disturbed by an apologetic Emma, a friendly Elspeth, or even a Roz bearing gifts.

On Monday she would go visiting Miss Arbuthnot to see what she remembered about the Barnes children. With her luck, she'd better get on with that task or she'd find that Miss Arbuthnot, too, had succumbed to old age. And then she could travel into the city centre to see what the *Oxford Mail* had to say about Elinor Marlyn's death. She would remember to book herself a microform reader before setting out. Oh yes, Kate, she thought. You're getting back to your old self. She felt little more than a tremor of excitement when she thought of all that fearless travel on buses.

Of course, if Alan Barnes should reply to her letter, that would be the best result of all. But she couldn't hope for that. Not after fifty-five years. She wondered for a moment how George would react if he knew what she was doing. Oh, George wouldn't mind. Yesterday evening's disagreement at the restaurant had just been an example of a minor family squabble. Nothing serious.

'Hello, George!' she called up the stairs. 'How are you getting on with the painting? Can I come up and look?'

Emma wasn't the only peacemaker in the family.

12

Christopher Barnes: Secret Reports

She stopped me from writing to Mum and telling her everything that's going on.

'You're a wicked boy, Christopher, writing naughty lies like that and I'm going to tear this letter up so that your mother doesn't see it,' she says. 'Now, write me another one, write me something nice. Your mother doesn't want to be hearing any more bad news. Tell her how you went out skating on Port Meadow with your friends. She'd like to hear about that. Have you forgotten how I lent you my old skates?'

She did too and I tied them on with bailer twine and me and Shawn and Graham had a good time on the ice all Sunday afternoon till it got too dark. She told me off afterwards for getting my clothes wet, but I didn't mind that and I don't think she was really cross.

And I've written letters to Mum with good news in them but she can't stop me from writing my Secret Reports as well. I'll write down the truth and she won't even know about it. I'll hide it from the Enemy where she won't find it. And one day when the war's over everyone will know about her and how she's a thief and probably a spy as well.

Last night was the worst yet.
And all because of Betsy.

It happened like this. Miss Marlyn starts picking on Susie at teatime while we're sitting at the table in the kitchen.

'Where's your handkerchief, Susan?' she says, all sharp.

Susie sits there and starts to cry which makes her nose run worse. She has snot running down and she looks awful. I get my hanky out but Miss Marlyn says, 'No, Christopher, your sister has got to learn proper manners.'

She's a bitch. She's worse even than Miss Arbuthnot.

Miss Marlyn is smiling at Susie but not in a nice way.

'Now, Susie,' she says, 'if you can't behave you'll have to leave the table, won't you? We can't have little girls with runny noses sitting here at our table. And then you won't have any stewed apple and custard.'

'Don't want no apple and custard,' says Susie.

I think Miss Marlyn is going to slap Susie then. Our Mum would have slapped her for talking like that but Miss Marlyn likes to think she's too good for slapping children. She just talks in that tight voice and with her nasty smile.

'I don't want *any*, Susan,' she corrects her in that snobby way of hers. 'Well, now, Susan,' she says, 'we can't have you answering me back like that, can we? You'll have to be punished.'

Susie has Betsy with her. Betsy's sitting on her lap but out of sight under the table and we don't think Miss Marlyn's seen her. But she has. She sees everything. She's got eyes everywhere, that old witch.

'Give me the toy,' she says. 'Naughty girls don't have toys to play with.' And she leans over and takes Betsy off Susie's lap and holds it up by one ear and stares at it. She smiles and it's still her nasty smile.

I have my new penknife from Uncle Alan in my pocket. I take it out and open up the biggest blade and I want to stab her until she's dead.

'What have you got there, Christopher?' she says.

'Nothing,' I say.

But she takes my knife away anyhow. And then she cuts Betsy's paw with it so that the stuffing starts to come out. She does it slowly so that we see just what she's doing. She's watching Susie all the time while she's doing it. And Susie stops crying for a minute or so and she's breathing funny so it sounds like hiccups.

'It's only a toy, Susie,' I say. 'Betsy can't feel the pain.'

But I don't think Susie can hear me. Or if she hears me she doesn't believe what I say.

Miss Marlyn closes up the knife and puts it in her pocket. She's wearing her grey jacket and she puts it in the left pocket.

'And now Betsy is going somewhere where you can't have her for a week,' she says to Susie.

A week. It doesn't seem like much, but to Susie it's for ever. She needs that rabbit to go to sleep.

'And you don't need a knife like that, Christopher,' says Miss Marlyn.

'You can't keep it. That's stealing,' I tell her.

'Don't be silly,' she says. And she goes out of the room and she takes our things with her.

But I can hear her. She's going into the dining room. She won't let us in there ever. She says it's out of bounds and that means we're not allowed in. She probably keeps her radio in there so's she can get in touch with Germany where we can't hear her. She's putting our things in there and I'm going to get them back. She is stealing. She's a thief. I wish Dad was here. He'd tell her.

Susie goes to bed when she's told as usual but I can hear her in bed and she's crying. Our light's been off for at least half an hour and I reckon it's safe to go downstairs. I know Danny's down there with her and maybe Mr Watts as well. They're all thieves, all of them and I can hear them laughing and talking down there. I go down the stairs treading very quietly and then when I get to the dining room I see the door's open. They're making lots of noise and I don't think they hear me or notice me. I thought they'd have finished eating by now but they haven't.

They're making so much noise and taking no notice of nobody else so I stop and I look inside and I see that they're sitting at the table and they're eating, Miss Marlyn and Danny Watts. And it's not stuff like we get. Not dry fishpaste sandwiches and stewed apple, but real food. They've got meat and gravy and a heap of potatoes and veg and they've got glasses full of whisky or something. They're sitting there talking with their heads close together. And Miss Marlyn's dressed up in a frock instead of her usual trousers.

That's our rations they're eating. They give us just one sausage between us and then they're eating all our meat. And I bet they eat our sweets too. They've probably got chocolate from the Americans and stuff like that. But they're stealing from us.

I don't know what to do. I creep back to the stairs and I sit there in the dark until they've finished eating. It seems like a long time and I nearly fall asleep but I keep myself awake by thinking about what I want to do to them when I'm grown up and I've got my knife back. But at last I hear their voices coming out of the dining room.

'We'll leave the dishes, Danny,' she says. 'Your Violet can do them in the morning.'

'What's she going to think when she sees two sets of dishes?' says Danny.

'I don't care,' she says. 'I don't give a damn. Your Violet can think what she likes.'

And they go into the sitting room and close the door.

They've turned out all the big lights but they've left one on, on the wall, like a candle only electric. More waste, I think, and how Mum and Uncle Alan would tell us off if we wasted electricity like that. But it means I can see. There's a big polished dresser thing with plates on the shelves, and she's put Betsy up on the top shelf. I pull a chair over very quietly and I climb up and I get Betsy down. Her paw's got a hole in it where she stuck the knife in, but not too much filling's come out yet. Susie won't mind about it too much. I look to see if my knife's there too but it isn't and I bet it's still in the pocket of her jacket. I bet she'd like a knife like that one and she's going to take it for herself.

I take Betsy upstairs and leave her on the landing then I go back down to the kitchen. That's where she'll hang her jacket, on the hook behind the door. I have to go carefully because there's no light down there but I find the jacket all right and my knife's in the left pocket so I take it back. And I think about the food they've left on the plates in the dining room. It's our food and she's stolen it, I'm thinking, and I go back in there.

They've sliced up meat and left it to waste. And there's little bits of bacon that they've grilled till it's crisp. Mum can't stand food left on the plates when she sees it. She'd go spare if she could see all this waste.

So I start to eat it. I eat the crisp squares of bacon and I've never tasted anything so good. And then I stuff the slices of meat in my mouth. And then I think about Susie and how she'd love this too. And she didn't get her proper tea today because Miss Marlyn was cross with her.

I've got my hanky with me in my pocket. It's not clean but it's good enough. So I put the rest of the bacon in my hanky, and some more slices of meat. And I spoon out some pickle to go with it. And she's done roast potatoes the way we like them and I put a couple of those in too. And a few more because they're our favourites cooked like that in the oven.

She's got fruit and nuts in the bowl on the side table. So I help myself to nuts and a couple of apples and a pear. Susie doesn't like pears so I just take one of those. And that's enough for now. I can't really carry any more.

And I'm coming out of the dining room and I've just got to the foot of the stairs when the sitting-room door opens suddenly and I hear her coming. And before I have time to hide or anything she's switched on the light and she's there.

'Well. Christopher,' she says. And I can hear she's surprised.

She looks at the bundle of food I'm carrying and she says, 'What's that you've got there.'

I don't say anything to begin with.

She says, 'You've been stealing. You're nothing but a little thief.'

And I say, 'It's our food. It's our rations and you've stolen it. I'm taking back what's owing to us. I'm not a thief.'

And she laughs.

I can't believe this to begin with. Why is she laughing?

'But you're so wrong, Christopher,' she says. 'This food has nothing to do with your rations. And what you've stolen there has cost me a lot of money. What do you say to that?'

'I still say you're a thief,' I say. 'And you're a spy too, I should think.'

'So you've seen my food and you've stolen some of it,' she says. 'What else have you seen, Christopher?' She's not laughing now. She's looking really angry and I start to feel afraid.

'Well, Christopher?' she says. And she's got hold of my hair in her bony fingers. She's curled her fingers into the hair right

212

on the top of my head and she's pulling it.

'Get off me,' I shout. Then I remember about Susie being asleep and I stop shouting.

'I just want to know what you saw,' she says.

'I saw you and Danny Watts and I heard you too,' I say. 'I know what you've been doing.'

'Do you indeed.' She sounds really nasty. 'And you'll go telling everyone about it, I suppose.'

'I'll tell my Dad,' I say. Then I remember how Dad's not coming back any more. 'I'll tell Uncle Alan,' I say. 'He's been a soldier and he knows how to kill people.'

Danny Watts has heard us rowing and he comes out of the sitting room too.

'What's going on?' he asks.

'I've caught a little thief,' says Miss Marlyn. 'And he says he knows what we've been up to, Danny.'

'He's lying,' says Danny.

'I'm afraid he isn't,' says Miss Marlyn.

'He doesn't understand. He's just a kid,' says Danny.

'Maybe you're right,' says Miss Marlyn.

She's been holding on to my hair all this time but now she lets it go.

'Go back to bed now, Christopher,' she says. 'I'll think what to do to punish you and I'll tell you in the morning.'

I go up to bed like she said, but first I went into Susie's room and gave her some of my food. I'd picked up Betsy from the top of the stairs and I gave her the rabbit as well. She wasn't properly asleep, I think she was too hungry. And she never does go to sleep unless you give her Betsy to cuddle. I've saved the nuts and the apples so's we can eat them today or tomorrow. I expect she's going to starve me for thieving but she doesn't know about the apples and stuff. I've hidden my knife so she can't get it again. I've put it in my secret treasure box under the floorboards where she won't find it. And I keep my Secret Reports there too.

I don't know what she's going to do to me but I know *she's* the one who's a thief. She and Danny Watts have been stealing our rations and eating them all by themselves. That's why she took in us vaccies. It was just the food and the money she gets from Mum that she wants.

13

I don't think I like the sound of you, Miss Marlyn.

Kate had just got to the end of Christopher's *Secret Reports* and she sat frowning at the final page.

What did you do the next morning? You made that boy sweat, didn't you? You may not have hit those kids, although you pulled his hair; you didn't use physical violence, but that was still child abuse. Emotional abuse. And I reckon you enjoyed seeing them suffer, too. You stood there and watched them squirm, didn't you? And you were completely in control.

She replaced the little notebook underneath the sheet of balsawood in Chris's box and pushed it back into the desk drawer.

Stop getting so upset about it, she told herself. There's nothing you can do about it now. And you've only got his side of the story. They were probably irritating little kids. Elinor Marlyn was no more the maternal type than you are, and she was forced to take in two strange children for the duration. They'd already been there for months, probably, and they were all getting on each other's nerves.

She wasn't stealing their food. That was just an idea that Chris got into his head. She wouldn't do a thing like that. She came from a respectable family, from George and Sam's family. And as for thinking she was a spy, well that's just the sort of thing a kid *would* imagine. I bet they all played Spies and Secret Agents on their Sunday afternoons. And finally, why should you take the side of two unknown children rather than the Dolbys?

It's a gut feeling. I can't help it.

The only thing that will make me feel better is if I go upstairs and take a Stanley knife to those family portraits in the loft.

It was Sunday and she couldn't do much except spend the day with George and try to make sure that they both had a good time. She could help with the painting, or scraping or washing down or whatever he was doing in the upstairs flat. She could cook a meal. Or perhaps she could even sit and read the Sunday papers while George cooked a meal – or until he suggested that they should go out to eat at the pub.

And then it would be Monday and she could walk round and see if Miss Arbuthnot was in and prepared to talk to her. It was no good attempting to speak to her on a Sunday. Sunday was when the school mistress turned up for church in a hat like a pancake, and doubtless spent the rest of the day studying her Bible. The Old Testament, guessed Kate. The nasty bits with lots of smiting.

But Elinor Marlyn wouldn't have pulled the wool over Miss Arbuthnot's eyes. She would get a clear picture of George's aunt, and of the Watts family, and a clear picture of young Christopher Barnes, too, if it came to that.

She couldn't think why she hadn't gone flying round to see the schoolteacher as soon as she heard about her.

Kate had conveniently forgotten just how frightened she had been the previous week, and how much of an effort it had taken just to get out of the house and down the road.

If the Dolbys could indulge in selective amnesia, then so could she.

* * *

Monday morning was grey, damp and muggy, but Kate didn't care. She phoned the Centre for Oxfordshire Studies and booked herself a microform reader for later, then she went and inspected herself in the full-length mirror. Linen jacket, simple round-necked top, trousers (not jeans), high-vamped leather shoes, and all in shades of cream and black. She removed the scarlet earrings before Miss Arbuthnot told her they were unsuitable for school and replaced them with the plain pearl studs that Emma and Sam had given her for Christmas. She had thought they were being recklessly generous until she realised that the pearls had come from a chain store.

She considered taking her small, ladylike handbag with her, but decided on her usual one. She had given it a polish the previous evening and it looked quite good again.

Should she ring before turning up on the schoolteacher's doorstep? A phone call would be more polite, but it would give Miss Arbuthnot a chance to turn Kate away before she even got a toe in the door.

Bother. All this Dolby respectability was rubbing off on her. She rang, quickly putting her story in order before she did so.

'Miss Arbuthnot.' The voice was certainly elderly but sounded as though its owner still had all her marbles. Kate wondered whether she actually remembered what her Christian name was and when someone had last used it.

Kate explained that she was a writer, and was doing research into the children and teachers who had come to the district as evacuees during the war.

'I did not think of myself as an evacuee,' said Miss Arbuthnot. 'I was doing my duty by accompanying my pupils and ensuring that their education was not interrupted by the hostilities. I considered that I was engaged in war work just as important as that undertaken by any soldier on a battlefield.'

'Ah, yes, of course.'

'And you're a historian, are you?' enquired Miss Arbuthnot.

'In a manner of speaking.' Please, please don't make me sit the History test now. I failed it in the Upper Fourth and I know I'd fail it again today.

'Could you repeat your name for me, please.'

'It's Kate Ivory.'

'And would I address you as Miss, Mrs or Dr?' She laughed drily. 'Or Professor, perhaps?'

' "Miss" is perfectly acceptable,' said Kate, trying to give the impression that she could have chosen one of the two latter titles.

'And which institution are you attached to?'

'I'm a freelance,' said Kate.

'How very odd. I didn't realise there were such things as freelance historians. And there was I thinking you might be the young lady who writes those very amusing novels that I borrow from the library.'

Bother. Miss Arbuthnot had seen through her before she even started on her fairy tale.

'May I come round to see you, nevertheless?'

'I suppose that would be satisfactory,' said Miss Arbuthnot, sounding as though she would in fact reserve judgement until she had Kate under her beady gaze. 'When did you wish to interview me?'

'This morning,' said Kate.

'That is very short notice.'

'I have a deadline to meet.' Well, she did. Better not to mention that it was for six months' time.

'Very well.'

'Thank you, Miss Arbuthnot. I'll see you shortly.'

It wasn't far to the flat where the retired schoolmistress lived. The big old house, built of the same mellow red brick as High Corner, stood in a pleasant garden shaded by beech trees. The porch contained three bells and Kate rang the one labelled *Arbuthnot.*

The woman who opened the door reminded Kate of the Maths mistress who had terrified her when she had arrived as a new girl at her secondary school. She was about five foot eight, not at all stooped, she had snowy white hair cut as short as a boy's, and the clearest complexion Kate had ever seen. It must have involved a lot of healthy eating, vigorous exercise and virtuous living throughout her long life, thought Kate.

'Come in and sit down,' said Miss Arbuthnot. 'You look like a coffee-drinker to me.'

'Yes, I am, thank you.' What had given her away? The yellow teeth? The manic eyes? The shaking hands?

The room was very much as she would have expected. It was a large room, well-proportioned, and the furniture looked as though none of it had been bought in a shop but instead had been handed down from mother to daughter, aunt to niece. The effect was comfortable, settled.

Kate sat on a small tapestry-covered sofa and looked around at the photographs displayed on the flat surfaces. She might have expected to see pictures of the children Miss Arbuthnot had taught, but instead there were animals. Ponies and horses, cats, kittens, dogs and puppies.

'You're thinking I'm a sad old spinster, no doubt,' said Miss Arbuthnot, placing a cup of coffee as dark as treacle in front of Kate.

'Not at all.'

'I had enough of children and of their parents while I was a teacher. In my own home I like pictures of the animals I've known and frequently loved.'

'So I see.'

Kate tried the coffee. It was extremely strong. If her hands hadn't been shaking and her pulse racing before she arrived here they certainly would be by the time she left.

'Are you going to tape this or do you take notes?' asked Miss Arbuthnot with interest.

'I take notes usually. But not many of them,' said Kate.

'And I gather you've been asking about the two Barnes children.'

Miss Arbuthnot wasn't going to waste her time in wandering around the point, then.

'Did you know them?'

'Of course I did. Christopher and Susan. He was rather a gloomy child with all the cares of the world on his shoulders, and she was an unprepossessing girl who never remembered to use her handkerchief. He was weak in arithmetic but he was an observant boy, quite good at English. I might have made something of them eventually, but I didn't get the chance, unfortunately. It would have taken longer than the two terms or so that I knew them. Their minds were too intent on what was happening back in London. They needed to concentrate on their work and forget all that sort of nonsense. She needed stiffening, that little Susan.'

Poor child, thought Kate. Why couldn't they allow her to go on being soft and lacking in moral fibre, the way the Lord obviously intended?

'And did you know Miss Marlyn?'

'She owned High Corner, where the children were staying. But you know that already, don't you? What exactly do you want to know?'

'I'd quite like an unbiased opinion. I know what her family think about her and I've read what Christopher wrote on the subject –' she thought it better not to mention Naomi King, whose notes might be thought to be private by the likes of Miss Arbuthnot, even after her death '– and I imagine she was neither monster nor saint, but something in between.'

'Oh, I believe she was a monster,' said Miss Arbuthnot. 'She liked to control people and to demonstrate her power. She could dictate to Violet and Arthur Watts because they worked for her and lived in her squalid little cottage. They had to do what she wanted or they'd be out on the streets. And I believe that she corrupted young Danny Watts. He wasn't up to much and I suppose he would have ended up as a petty criminal in any case. He liked to spend money but he didn't like the hard work that went into earning it.'

Kate felt she should say, 'Yes, Miss,' but instead she sat looking attentive and interested. Not that she wasn't, of course, but Miss Arbuthnot's puritanical views on people and life were more than a little intimidating. If she found out that Kate was living with someone to whom she wasn't married, she'd be out on her ear on the pavement, she was sure.

'I believe he was involved in the black market,' said Kate.

'If there was money in it, young Danny involved himself. And by the end of the war, when you really couldn't get hold of so many of the articles you needed, there was a ready sale for all sorts of contraband.'

'What sort of things?' asked Kate who found it difficult to imagine a world in which one didn't simply go down to Tesco's or Homebase and pick up whatever it was one wanted.

'Petrol, for one. They were very strict about coupons and about using an allocation of petrol for any purpose other than that for which it was designated. Then, any kind of article for mending motor cars. Tyres, for example.'

'Anything else?'

'Many women would pay for clothing to which they were not entitled,' said Miss Arbuthnot austerely. 'And then there was food, of course. And alcoholic drinks.'

'Where were they getting the goods from?'

'I'm sure there was a supply network from London through the Midlands. And then there were all those American air bases. I believe that unscrupulous persons could obtain illegal goods for a suitable payment.'

'Danny Watts sounds rather young and simple to get involved in anything this high-powered,' said Kate.

'He was being used.'

'Not by Miss Marlyn, surely?'

'I know that the woman had a great deal of influence over that silly young man.'

'But she was so respectable. She came from such a worthy family.'

'I dare say. But her family was in trade, you know.'

There speaks a vicar's daughter if ever I heard one, thought Kate.

'And all trade corrupts, you believe?'

'Unless one's reputation and respectability are based on sound moral principles, then I believe that the appearance of virtue may become more important than its actual practice,' said Miss Arbuthnot.

'And the Dolbys equated the ownership of money and property to beatitude, if not sanctity,' said Kate, who couldn't quite equal Miss Arbuthnot's ringing prose. And that's what Emma had said at the restaurant on Friday evening. Emma had been drunk, but an inebriated Emma might well tell truths that the sober one preferred to deny.

It was, however, difficult to equate the Elinor Marlyn that Kate had grown to know with a woman who was willing to fiddle her petrol ration and get embroiled with an unsuccessful petty crook like Danny Watts.

'And then there was the manner of her death,' said Miss Arbuthnot.

'In late 1945?'

'Yes, that would have been about the time. Late November or early December, I should have thought.'

Kate wondered how to approach the subject delicately. 'Did she commit suicide, do you think?' she asked.

'That was the opinion in the neighbourhood, although the family denied it, of course. And they prevailed upon the coroner to bring in a verdict of Accidental Death.'

'How did it happen?'

'She was asphyxiated, I believe. In her motor vehicle.'

'That certainly sounds more like suicide than an accident.'

'There were circumstances, I forget exactly what after all these years, that made an accident a possibility.'

Kate had taken out her notebook and was scribbling down details. This was great stuff, though possibly not very useful for the book that Estelle was expecting her to deliver in six months' time.

'You will have to excuse me shortly,' said Miss Arbuthnot.

'I'm sorry. I've been taking up all your morning.'

'I have nothing better to do with my time these days, Miss Ivory. But I fear that after a period of reminiscence like this morning's, I do get very tired.'

Kate had forgotten just how old Miss Arbuthnot must be. She could be over eighty, certainly.

'You're trying to do some mental arithmetic, Miss Ivory. Well, I'll tell you. I'm ninety-one.'

I hope I'm as game an old bird as you are when I reach ninety-one, thought Kate. *If* I reach ninety-one.

'I have one suggestion before you leave, however.'

'Yes?'

'You might look up young Christopher's friend, Shawn Riley.'

'You know where he lives?'

'Of course. Shawn often comes in to see me and to do any little jobs about the flat. He's a kind boy. Not very bright, but kind. And there's a lot to be said for kindness, don't you think?'

'And he and Christopher were friends?'

'I believe that they were best pals during the months they both lived here. Shawn was very upset by Christopher's death. I'm sure he would be willing to talk to you about his friend.'

Miss Arbuthnot rose to her feet from the upright chair where she had been sitting with little visible effort.

'I'll write down his address for you,' she said.

'And then I'll leave you,' said Kate.

'If you would. Here,' and she handed Kate a piece of paper with her neat schoolteacher's writing on it.

'Thank you very much for all your help,' said Kate, as she left.

'Not at all. But I do hope you're not going to write anything too serious this time. I rather enjoy those amusing and delight-fully inaccurate novels you've produced up to now.'

'Don't worry. If my agent has anything to do with it, the next book will be just as frivolous as my previous ones. Goodbye, Miss Arbuthnot.'

Well, there was yet another view of Elinor Marlyn, and one that differed from George's rather more than it did from Christopher's. And even allowing for her puritanical slant on events, Miss Arbuthnot was a canny old bird in Kate's opinion.

She looked at the name and address that the schoolteacher had given her. Not far away. But she'd see whether Shawn Riley was in the phone book. It would be better to ring before calling in person, especially if this was someone brought up by Miss Arbuthnot's demanding standards. She checked her watch. There was an hour to go before she was due at the library. She had time to change into something a little more casual than she had worn for Miss Arbuthnot.

When she reached the house that she always thought of now as High Corner, Kate found there had been a second delivery of post: a letter for her in a handwritten envelope, postmarked South London. It had to be from Alan Barnes!

She took it up to her study to open it.

It was a carefully-written note on lined paper telling her that the current occupant of 26 Reckitt Street had lived there for only the past six months and had never heard of Alan Barnes and was therefore unable to forward Kate's letter to him.

Bother.

She screwed up the note and threw it into her newly-polished and handsome brass bin. It clanged in a satisfying way as it went in.

To cheer herself up she checked Shawn Riley's number in the phone book and rang him up. He would be happy to see her that afternoon, he said.

Down at the library, Kate checked the local paper for any report of Elinor Marlyn's death. She found it, as she had expected, in an issue dated in late November of 1945, but the paragraph was discreet to the point of reticence. 'A much-respected resident. A well-known family. A terrible accident.'

She moved forward another week or so and found the report of the inquest. Apparently, Elinor Marlyn had made the mistake of starting the engine of a small delivery van while it was parked inside the garage adjacent to her house. The garage doors were closed. There was no ventilation. Miss Elinor Marlyn died of carbon-monoxide poisoning. There were no suspicious circumstances and no reason to believe that she intended to take her own life. It was a dark and murky night and no one heard the engine, which must have been running for an hour or two. The body wasn't discovered until the next morning, when Mrs Violet Watts arrived at High Corner, Armitage Road, for her usual morning's work.

The assumption appeared to be that a woman, even as practical and respected a woman as Miss Marlyn, couldn't be trusted with mechanical gadgets.

Don't tell me, thought Kate. They shouldn't worry their pretty little heads with such things, but should stay in the kitchen where they belonged.

Once you removed the hysteria and the gossip, it sounded as though the verdict was a perfectly reasonable one. The question remained: why on earth had she run the van's engine while still inside the garage? But the night was cold and wet and the van wouldn't have had a heater. And perhaps it was true that Miss Marlyn didn't realise how lethal the exhaust fumes from a petrol engine were.

I'm not sure I'm convinced, thought Kate. But I don't see how I can find out any more, at least for the present.

Then she thought, *And that's the garage where I've parked my car.*

14

Shawn Riley lived in a terraced cottage in one of the narrow streets behind the shopping centre.

'Come on in,' he said. 'I'll make us a cup of tea.'

Kate was shown into a small front room crammed with well-polished furniture and ornaments of the kind she associated with seaside holidays. On the walls were framed photographs of children of all ages. On closer inspection they proved to be pictures of the same three children at all stages of their development.

'I've sent the wife over to her sister's,' said Shawn. 'I thought we could talk in peace if she wasn't here.'

'I'm not interrupting your work?'

'I've been retired for a year now, and I'm glad of something to fill the day apart from the list of chores that the wife writes out for me every morning.'

He was a nice, ordinary man in a checked shirt and a blue cardigan. He wore bifocals and a pair of tartan slippers. He was moderately overweight and his hair was receding, and he made an excellent cup of tea. Kate reminded herself that Christopher Barnes, if he had lived, would probably have been a man very similar to this one.

'I was hoping you could tell me about Chris Barnes,' she said, when they had helped themselves to chocolate digestives and sipped at their tea.

'What's to tell? We were just a couple of ordinary lads. There was nothing special about us. The only extraordinary thing was Chris's death. And even that wasn't so unusual in those days. Too many kids round here were hurt in road accidents.'

'I read about his death in the *Oxford Mail*. I was just hoping you could tell me more about it, fill in a bit of the background.'

'I don't understand what your interest is in it,' he said. 'Would you like another chocolate biscuit, by the way?'

'Thanks,' said Kate, who rarely said no to a chocolate biscuit.

'I only know what was said at the time. The two children ran into the road and Danny Watts, who was driving his van down the road, couldn't help hitting them. Susie escaped with a damaged leg and cuts and bruises, but Chris had head injuries and didn't recover.'

'Did you know them in London, before you were evacuated?'

'No, I was born here. I'm a local boy. It was quite unusual for the two of us to be such friends. We didn't mix much as a rule, the vaccies and the locals, but Chris and I were the same age and in the same class at school, and we just got on together. We hit it off. We were mates.'

'Did you ever go to his house?'

'His billet – that's what we called it. High Corner. Big posh place with a dragon of a woman living there. I was never invited in – no one was. But I saw inside it once and it looked like a palace to me. A blaze of lights, I remember, and the smell of real food cooking.

'It must have been the previous autumn because I remember we were collecting empty jam jars. We'd go from house to house, and put these jars on a trolley that we took it in turns to pull along. High Corner was on our route, and I said we should call in there, too. But instead of going round to the kitchen door, Chris dared me, and I went up to the front door, bold as brass.

'She shouldn't have been showing all those lights. She had a chandelier and all. I think it was the first time I'd ever seen one of those. But we still had the blackout then and she shouldn't have been showing any light at all. But she didn't care. I could tell that.'

'And did she give you her jam jars?'

'I don't think she knew what a jam jar looked like. She left all that sort of thing to Violet Watts.'

'And did you know Violet's brother-in-law, Danny?'

'Everyone knew Danny. He was our local wide boy. I saw him around every day. There was a group of them used to have their dinners in the summer sitting outside the pub. One of them would go inside for a jug of beer, and they'd sit on the wall and eat their sandwiches and drink their pints. I wasn't supposed to speak to them. I came from a respectable family, I did.' He laughed.

'Did you see Chris in the hospital? Did he say anything to you?'

'You're keen with the questions, aren't you? Give me a chance to think about it. Well, I saw him once. There wasn't any point in going more than that. He was unconscious.' Shawn sighed. 'Poor kid. I was really upset, too. It was the first time something serious like that had happened to someone I knew as well as I knew Chris.'

'Did he speak?'

'What would he have said? But no, he didn't say anything to anyone as far as I know. I saw Susie there, though.'

'I'd almost forgotten about her.'

'Funny little kid, she was. I think she quite liked it out here in Oxford, so far away from her home. She can't have been very fond of Miss Marlyn, though.'

'And I don't suppose she said anything, either.'

'She never said much. But the odd thing is that when I saw her in the hospital I got the impression she was hiding something, that this time she did have something to say only it was her secret. In an older kid I'd have called it sly, the look she had.'

'How odd. I wonder what it was.'

'It was probably nothing. She was only about seven years old. I don't expect she knew anything really. But you know what kids are. She went straight back to London afterwards and I never spoke to her again, so I can't tell you any more about her.'

'Did she go to her uncle's place?'

'Yes, I think so. Her Mum was ill and her Dad was away. It was his brother, Chris's Uncle Alan, who was looking after their Mum and keeping an eye on the kids.'

'You didn't keep in touch with him?'

'No. There was no reason to. But I know someone who did.' He sounded really pleased that he could help.

'Who's that?'

'The young Billeting Officer, Naomi King. She wanted to know how Susie was getting on. She was the conscientious kind and I'm sure she'd have kept in touch. I think she always felt it was her fault somehow that Chris died. Not that it was, of course. It was just one of those things. But she lives round here somewhere – you should be able to find her.'

'I found where she lived all right,' said Kate. 'But I was too late. She died just a few weeks ago.'

'That's a bugger,' said Shawn sympathetically.

'It certainly is.'

The route from Shawn's house back to High Corner took Kate quite close to Naomi King's house, and on an impulse she

230

took the small diversion that led past the front door. As she approached, an idea suddenly hit her.

Please, let Joan Angers still be there.

There was a silver Ford Fiesta parked outside that looked just like the sort of car Mrs Angers would drive. Kate rang the front doorbell.

Just let me have some luck for once in this affair.

The door opened.

'Oh, hello. It's Miss Ivory, isn't it?'

'Yes. And I was hoping that you'd still have Naomi's address book,' said Kate quickly, and probably less politely than Mrs Angers might have expected, but it was too late now to go through all the 'Good morning, how are you?' routine.

'Her address book? Well, I did have it, of course. I used it to find the addresses of all the people who should be informed of her death. I don't believe yours was in it, though.'

'It wouldn't be. I only live round the corner. Have you still got it?'

Perhaps it was Kate's desperation that got through to her; Joan Angers relented. 'Come in for a moment. I'll have a look.'

Kate stood in the sad little hallway. Many of the bin bags had gone and the place looked more forlorn than ever. If Joan couldn't find the address book she was prepared to search through the bags of rubbish.

'Here it is. What did you want it for?'

'It's just possible that she has a note of the recent address of someone I was hoping to trace.' She was close to grabbing the little brown leather book out of the other woman's hand.

'Have a look through, then. You can see if it's there.'

Kate turned to the B's. Yes. Alan Barnes. First the Peckham address, with a line through it. Then below that, an address in Forest Hill, also in South London. That, too, had been crossed through. And finally, over the page, she found an address in West London, with a telephone number.

She copied them down before Joan Angers could change her mind, and handed her back the little book.

'Thank you so much,' she said, with such enthusiasm that Joan looked quite surprised. 'I have to be off now,' she said, and turned and raced down the road towards High Corner.

She had to get in touch with Alan Barnes before something dreadful happened to him and she was too late.

She phoned Roz from High Corner.

'Good news, bad news,' she said breathlessly.

'Yes?'

'Bad news is that I heard from Reckitt Street and they didn't know anything about Alan Barnes.' That disappointment was nearly forgotten in the new situation.

'And the good news?'

'I've found his phone number and address in Naomi King's address book.'

'I thought she'd died.'

'The niece had the address book and she let me copy Alan's down. Oh, I just hope it is the current address and not just another red herring.'

'There's only one way to find out.'

'Yes. And now I want your advice. Do I phone or do I write?'

Roz thought for a moment. 'Writing might be better, less of a shock.'

'I'm just terrified he'll drop dead before I can get to him.'

'I suppose he would be in his eighties.'

'So? Which do I do?'

'Write. Straight away and first-class post. If he hasn't replied in a couple of days, you phone. Then at least the surprise won't give him a heart attack.'

'OK. I suppose you're right. I was hoping you'd say I should phone.'

'Then why did you ask my advice?'

'So that you could tell me I was wrong.'

'What have you got there?' asked George.

'It's a letter.'

'Well, yes, I can see that. I was asking because you seem more interested in it than in the rest of your post. And it doesn't look like junk mail.'

'No, it isn't junk mail. It's a personal letter.' Kate wasn't used to being questioned about her post. 'It's nearly half past eight. Shouldn't you be leaving? You know you hate being late.'

'If you go on like that I'll think you have something to hide. A new lover, perhaps.'

Kate folded the pages and slipped them back into their envelope. The action gave her enough time to think what to say.

'It's to do with the new book. I wrote to someone asking for information, and they've replied.'

'And you're not going to tell me who or what.'

'You know what I'm like when I start on a first draft. I don't want to discuss it with anyone. Not even Estelle.'

'This is the one set in the Second World War, full of passionate land girls?'

'Something like that.'

'So why is your letter from someone called Alan? He wasn't a land girl, was he?'

'How do you know he's called Alan?'

'His name is on the back page and you were holding it only

233

a foot or so away from my eyes. "I hope we can meet soon. Regards, Alan something." I couldn't read the surname.'

'You must be right. He has to be my new lover,' said Kate.

'As long as it's only that,' said George, getting up from the table. He pulled up the knot of his tie and put on his jacket. 'I'll be getting off, then.'

'Yes.'

The terrible thing is, thought Kate, that he's right. He means it. He'd rather I found myself a lover than believe that I've contacted the uncle of those two children.

What was it with these Dolbys? She and George had been as happy as anything just a couple of weeks ago. But as soon as she raised the smallest question about his family he went into a mood. The whole relationship was at risk, just because of a couple of evacuees.

No, I can't blame Chris and Susie, she thought. They're just the catalyst. It's because I doubt his version of events. The Dolbys have to be above suspicion, and I've challenged that assumption.

'It's a question of priorities,' said Roz. 'If you want George –'

'Yes, I want George.' Kate was definite about that.

'– then you'll have to give up trying to find out what happened in 1945.'

There was a silence while they both thought about it.

'He can't ask me to do that,' said Kate eventually.

'He wouldn't ask you. That isn't the way the modern man operates.'

'He'd go silent on me and keep his distance.'

'Silent and accusing,' confirmed Roz.

'Accusing me of what, exactly?'

'Of spoiling his own view of himself. Of questioning the honesty of his family.'

'Yes, I was working that out for myself this morning. Strange, isn't it? I'm sure our family tree's full of sheepstealers and con men,' said Kate. 'It wouldn't worry me if George presented me with a dossier of their misdeeds.'

'But we've never aspired to being pillars of this or any other society,' said Roz. 'That's the difference between the Ivorys and the Dolbys. Just think of those family portraits. Pillars, the lot of them.'

Kate grinned. 'What was that word again?'

'It was probably something like pillars.'

'Corsets,' said Kate. 'I think of them as rows of corsets.'

'But in spite of your vivid imagination you couldn't realistic-ally accuse them of criminal activity. Meanness and lack of charity, possibly. Narrow-mindedness and complacency . . .'

'Yes, yes. No need to overdo it. I get the picture.'

'But the sort of crimes that bring policemen to your door and cause a stir in the neighbourhood? It would be like accusing the Queen Mother of fiddling her expenses.'

'This is serious, isn't it?'

'Objectively speaking, yes. And from your point of view, if you're planning a future with George, even more so.'

'He's controlling my life and work, isn't he? Not by laying down the law or bullying me, but by manipulating me into doing what he wants. If I give in now he'll do it again.'

'He'll feel he's justified.'

'Perhaps I should just forget it.'

'Do you think you could?'

Another long silence.

'I could try.'

'The effort would show. And anyway –'

'– anyway, I've never managed to keep my curiosity in check for more than a few minutes at a time. We're talking years, aren't we? Decades, even. I'd never manage it.'

'I suppose you could carry on and find out what happened, and then bury it again.'

'I could confide in you.'

'I don't think I'm a very reliable confidante.'

'There would be this secret between me and George that we'd never refer to.'

'The elephant in the sitting room.'

'Just a baby elephant to begin with, but it would grow until it filled the entire house. There'd be no room left for the two of us.'

'Perhaps you're allowing your imagination to run away with you again.'

'But I would, wouldn't I? My imagination would work away in the silence until I'd turned George and his family into monsters.'

'So what have you decided?'

'I don't know.'

'Oh, I think you do.'

'You're right. The decision was made for me when I got the letter from Alan Barnes this morning.'

15

'He says,' said Kate, 'that he's been waiting for fifty-five years to tell his story and it's quite a relief to find that he can do so at last.

'He says that he's written a lot of it down, but that he hasn't been able to get so much done in these last few months and it might be easier if he could speak to me and tell me about it instead.

'He says that he's dying.

'He has leukaemia, he says. It's not progressing rapidly, but he's had it for a while now, and he thinks he's come round the last bend and into the final straight.

'He wonders whether I'd like to visit him since he's past being able to travel much himself.

'And he'll hand me over the material he's written down. He doesn't know if it will make much sense, but he'd like me to have it since I sound as though I care about what happened to Chris and Susie.'

'West London's a long way from here,' said Kate. It was true that she was doing much better recently and was starting to overcome her fear of wide spaces and crowds, not to mention closed spaces and one or two menacing people.

'I'll drive you,' said Roz.

'You would?'

'No problem.'

'Thanks. But when we get there I think I'll have to go in to see him on my own. We might be a bit overpowering as a twosome.'

'Fair enough. I'll find myself a coffee shop, or a pub perhaps, and you can ring me on my mobile when you want to be collected.'

'When did you get a mobile?'

'Last week. It's very useful, isn't it?'

'As long as you don't walk around with it permanently clamped to your ear. Or make phone calls that start "I'm on the bus".'

'I wouldn't dream of such behaviour. And you've still got yours, haven't you?'

'Of course.'

'So we're all set up. When are we going?'

'I'll go and ring him right away.'

'It sounds as though we'd better see him as soon as possible. With your luck, he'll slip away before we can get as far as the M4.'

'Don't even joke about it.'

Alan Barnes was prepared to see Kate the following morning. He sounded tired on the phone, as though he'd been fighting a long battle and was now ready to give in and retire from the field.

Hang in there until I get to you, she wanted to say.

'Thank you for agreeing to see me,' she said instead. 'We should be with you by nine-thirty. Is that too early?'

'I don't waste much time in sleeping,' he replied.

The next problem, Kate found, was to explain to George what she was doing. For a moment she wondered whether she could get away with not telling him. If she and Roz left as soon as he'd gone to work in the morning, she could be back before he returned in the evening. She could say she was spending the day with her mother. Not a lie, after all. And something any daughter might want to do.

But she'd be deceiving him. And he'd probably see through her. And once she started telling half-truths, the lies would follow and their relationship would founder in a sea of deceit and recriminations. That wasn't what she'd had in mind when she'd come to live at High Corner.

It had all started so well, too. For a moment there she'd thought she'd found the one man with whom she could happily spend the rest of her life. Maybe she still could. Maybe they could work this thing out.

She tackled him that evening – not immediately he came in through the door, but after she'd poured him a glass of decent wine and listened to what he had to tell her of his day. She waited, too, until they were sitting down to a meal that was good, but not so good as to hint that she was feeling guilty about something. The over-elaborate meal, after all, was the woman's equivalent of the man's bunch of red roses.

'I've found Alan Barnes,' she said.

'The children's uncle.' At least George didn't pretend he didn't know who she was talking about. 'When are you going to see him?' There was very little expression in his voice. He wasn't allowing his feelings to show, but she had a suspicion that under the smooth exterior he was feeling very angry, and with her.

'He's living in West London, so Roz and I are driving over there tomorrow. I'm hoping he can tell me the rest of the story.'

'And what will you do then?'

A good question. 'I'll file it away and get on with my new book.'

'But you're determined to dig up as much dirt on my family as possible before you do so.'

'You're assuming your family did something wrong, then?'

239

'I'm assuming that if that's what you're looking for, that's what you'll find.'

'I can't just hide away the evidence and pretend that nothing happened.'

'The way Sam and I did, you mean.'

One box hidden under the floorboards. Another pushed to the back of a seldom-visited cupboard. At least they didn't throw them away.

'Perhaps it would have been more honest if you *had* thrown Chris's stuff away.'

'Sam wanted to do that, but I said no, it wasn't right,' said George. 'We couldn't just pretend he didn't exist.'

'He was dead. And you've all done plenty of pretending over the years.'

'I know he's dead. But I didn't want to destroy the only pieces of his life that he'd left for people to read. Sam was right, of course. We should have stuffed it all on the bonfire and got rid of it.'

'Because you didn't want anyone else to read it, did you?'

'I didn't know that *you* were going to find it and spin it into such a story. You make Elinor sound like a monster.'

'Well, she was.' As soon as she'd said it, Kate knew she'd gone too far.

George put his fork down and Kate followed suit. She'd lost her appetite for linguine in a lemon dressing.

'She was a product of her age and class,' said George.

'I'm sorry. I got carried away.' And she didn't even have Emma's excuse of too much to drink.

'That's your problem. You can't let a subject drop.'

'I can't help the way I am.'

'And if you find something criminal did happen, will you go to the police?' he asked.

'That depends on the circumstances.'

'I thought you were working fearlessly on principle here. Personal considerations weren't entering into it.'

'There's no point in hounding the dead,' she said.

'But you wouldn't let my feeling for my family get in your way?'

'I have to find out what happened.'

'I can't stop you,' he said.

'No.'

For the rest of the evening George pretended to read a newspaper and Kate pretended to watch television.

Kate spent the night balanced on the far edge of George's large double bed. She didn't sleep much and when she did she was disturbed by hot, frightening dreams.

George was up at 6.30 the next morning, and out of the house by 7.15. Kate felt a powerful sense of relief when she heard the door close behind him.

Now she could concentrate on her coming meeting with Alan Barnes.

'I'll drive. You navigate,' said Roz.

'This is a new car.'

'New to me, at any rate,' said her mother.

'I thought you were permanently attached to the old yellow Beetle.'

'This one has better acceleration.'

'This one's very snazzy.'

'Where do you pick up such old-fashioned terms?'

'Cool, then. This one's really cool, Mum.'

Five minutes out of the house and she was already in a much better temper.

'I can get us into the western outskirts of London,' said Roz.

'After that you'll have to tell me where to go.'

Kate had the *A to Z* and after only a modest number of wrong turnings she managed to get them to Alan Barnes's address. Roz drew up outside the kind of semi-detached house that must have been put up by the million in the 1930s and then again in the 1950s.

'I'll be off, then,' she said, taking a good look at the house. It told her very little: it was just like all its neighbours. 'You've got my mobile number?'

'Yes.'

Now that she was here, Kate was feeling nervous. She wished she'd asked if Roz could come in with her. But no, it wouldn't do. She would have to deal with this on her own.

'You're sure you're going to be all right?' asked Roz.

'Yes.'

Kate walked up the short path and pressed the bell. Roz was still waiting at the kerb and she turned and waved at her. *I'm fine, Roz. Really, I'm fine.* If she repeated it she might convince herself.

Roz waited until the front door opened and Kate had disappeared inside the house before driving away.

Alan Barnes had turned and was leading the way into the sitting room at the front of the house. His back was thin and the skin above his collar was a translucent white. His ears stuck out from a meagre crop of wispy grey hair.

'I don't live in the whole house,' he was saying. 'Just these two downstairs rooms and the kitchen. Then I have a shower and a lav to myself.'

'Very nice,' said Kate, her mind on the coming conversation.

They sat down cautiously, each perched on a chair as though ready to fly at any moment.

She wouldn't have recognised him from the photograph in

Chris's box. Any trace of youth, and even of life, had been erased from his face. The fat had melted away so that it looked as though the skin covered only bone and the essential muscles and blood vessels. His lips were thin and oddly dark in colour.

'You've seen what you were looking for, have you?' he said, returning her stare. But he had been judging her face, too, Kate knew. She hoped that what he saw was satisfactory.

'You know why I'm here.'

'You'd better tell me how much you know.'

It was as though they were each fitting their thoughts into the minimum number of words so as not to waste any of Alan's remaining energy.

He smiled at her then, and the smile resembled a dead man's. 'You needn't worry. I'm not leaving this earth just yet. I've got a good week or two left in me.'

Kate was reminded that people described death as a process rather than an event. And the process was far advanced in Alan Barnes.

'I'm living with George Dolby in Cavendish Road, Oxford,' she said. 'I know that his house was called High Corner, Armitage Road, until the nineteen-sixties, when they renumbered the houses. Your nephew and niece, Christopher and Susan, were evacuated to Oxford in 1944 and were billeted on Elinor Marlyn, who owned the house.

'They weren't particularly happy there, but things weren't really so bad. But then Christopher started to suspect that Miss Marlyn was involved in various criminal activities – from black marketeering to spying, I gather. This may just have been in the imagination of a boy at a time when he was under stress, but then again it may have been based on fact.' She stopped and looked at Alan. 'You don't really believe she was a spy, do you?'

'No.'

'I didn't think so.'

'Go on with your summary.'

'In February, 1945, Chris was run over and killed by a delivery van driven by Danny Watts, who was an acquaintance of Miss Marlyn's.'

'He was a little spiv, involved in the black market.'

'Yes, I gathered that. In late November, 1945, Miss Marlyn herself died in an accident that might have been suicide, although nothing was proved. Danny Watts fell off his bicycle one night when he was drunk and was drowned in the river.'

'Not bad,' said Alan Barnes. 'I didn't know that about Danny Watts. When did it happen?'

'I'm not sure exactly, but not long after Elinor's death, I think. Probably later that same winter.'

'I only met him the once, but I didn't like the little bugger. He probably didn't deserve to die, though.'

'But Elinor Marlyn did?'

'That's for you to decide.'

'I found various belongings of Chris's while we were clearing out parts of the house. I brought them with me. I thought you might like to see them.'

'When you say "we", do you mean the current owner of the house is a friend of yours?'

'We live together.'

'So he's a Marlyn.'

'He's a Dolby. If I have it right, Elinor's sister, Sarah Marlyn, married George's grandfather, Robert Dolby. Elinor left the house to her niece, Sadie Dolby, and Sadie in her turn left it to her nephew, George.'

'Great believers in the ties of family, those Marlyns.'

'So I'm discovering.'

244

'And you live with this George.'

'Yes.'

He sat in silence for a moment, as though considering something. Kate was afraid he was going to decide she wasn't to be trusted.

'I want to find out the truth,' she said. 'I can't go on living with George while we both pretend there's nothing wrong.'

'And if the truth reflects badly on his family?'

'I'll have to face that. If George can't accept that I know about it, I'll have to leave.'

There, she'd faced it. Here, in this neat little suburban front room she had admitted that she and George might be going their separate ways.

She handed over the two boxes with their sad little collection of children's treasures.

'That was my knife,' said Alan. 'I gave it to him in January, 1945.'

He lifted up the rabbit in silence and looked at it, then placed it back in the biscuit tin. 'Poor little Susie,' was all he said.

'You'll find a private notebook of Chris's, and one or two letters from his mother,' said Kate.

'I'll look at them all later on,' he said. 'But for now I'll tell you a bit about the background. Only as much as you need to understand the story, though. Then you can have the stuff I've written out.'

'Thanks,' said Kate. At last, at last.

'But first, be a good girl, and get us both a cup of tea. You'll find all the makings in the kitchen. Milk's in the fridge.'

'Chris and Susie were my brother Harry's kids,' said Alan.

'He'd married Sheila when they were both too young to

know better, but the marriage had been a success in spite of the fact they were both children, really. They weren't well off and the digs they lived in for the first few years of their lives together were cold and damp. Black fungus in the bathroom growing big as field mushrooms. Condensation streaming down the scullery walls. Well, you know the sort of place I mean.

'There was consumption in Sheila's family – one sister had already died of it. It was common in poor families in those days. Things are different nowadays, thank the Lord. Anyway, Sheila started to develop the symptoms, too. And the disease really seemed to take hold when she had the second baby. They shouldn't have thought about starting a family, really, but Sheila would say how babies were God's gift and you shouldn't try to stop them. I expect Harry talked sense into her after they had Susie.

'And then, while Susie was barely out of her pram, the war started. Harry and I both joined up straight away. I don't like to say this about my own brother, but I reckon he was glad to get away from the coughing and the sick room. It's a terrible responsibility for a young man.

'Harry went marching off to war, as he called it, before I did. He was sent to France with the British Expeditionary Force – you'll have heard of that? And he never came back. He was officially "missing, believed killed", but I knew he was dead all right. We were close, Harry and I, and I'd have known if he was still alive.

'Sheila didn't want to move out of Reckitt Street, where she and Harry had lived. I think she imagined that he'd come home one day, out of the blue, and just knock on the back door to be let in. She wanted to be there when that happened, and not out in the country somewhere, hiding from the bombs.

'So she stuck it in London, with the kids, all through the

bombing, until the summer of 1944. We all knew that the war was coming to an end. With the Yanks in on our side, the result was inevitable. It was only a question of time. At that point, the disease took another turn for the worse. TB's like that. She could be all right, or nearly all right, for months on end, even a year once, but then it would take hold again. She couldn't cope with the kids any more, and she didn't want them to see her as ill as she was. It was upsetting for them. I know that.

'Consumption. TB. You don't hear much about it nowadays, but in those days it was a killer. Maybe with proper care and trips to the seaside, or to Switzerland, she might have survived. All we had was the windows thrown open night and day and whatever decent food we could get hold of on top of the rations.

'She was dying and she didn't want the children to see her getting worse all the time. She longed to have them with her, but she wouldn't do it. She didn't go to Oxford to see them there, either. There was a belief at the time that you should shield children from the realities of life. But the children knew all the same. Probably what they imagined was worse than the reality. Probably felt it was their fault. We kept her illness secret because it was easier for us, but we fooled ourselves that it was for their sake.

'I'd been away, too, of course. I was out in North Africa when I was captured. I won't bore you with the whole story, but I ended up in a prisoner-of-war camp in Northern Italy. And then, one day, we were free. Our guards had scarpered. Several thousand Allied prisoners on the loose, trying to get back to Allied territory.

'We had no food, no transport, and we had to make our way south through the mountains. I'm sorry. You'll have to forgive me for a moment.

'Where was I? Oh yes. Back in England with a permanent

hunger for food that could never be satisfied, and hours, when I should have been sleeping, filled with nightmares.

'So I left those kids, Harry's kids, down there in Oxford where I thought they were safe, away from the bombs and the TB, and the reality of their mother's approaching death.'

Alan Barnes looked steadily into Kate's eyes. 'What happened after that you can read in the manuscript.

'What about Sheila?' Kate asked gently.

'She died. She lasted till the June, then she passed on. It was heart failure took her in the end, the doctor said. It wasn't like me, dying at the proper age. Sheila, she was only thirty-one. That's no age to die, is it?'

'It's too young.'

'And the dreadful thing is that, after she died, I felt relief. I missed her, of course, and it was another link with Harry gone. But I felt free for the first time since the beginning of the war. I'd picked up some bad habits over the previous few years that didn't fit me for civilised society. I liked to eat at the kitchen table and I preferred it with no cloth on. I liked to wash under the cold tap instead of using the bathroom. And I could roam the streets at night instead of staying cooped up in my room.

'I had a few friends who'd been through the same as me. We used to go out and get drunk together whenever we wanted and there'd be no one to grumble about it when I got home.'

'And Susie?' asked Kate. 'People told me that she'd returned to London when she came out of hospital, but no one seemed to know what happened after that.'

'Susie was as much a war casualty as Harry or me. I couldn't cope with her as well as Sheila when she came home from Oxford, so for those last few months I found her some foster parents. Oh, they were good enough people, and they weren't doing it just for the money. They did their best for her, I really do believe. They were relatives of some neighbours of ours, and they lived out Blackheath way. And after Sheila died, it seemed sensible to leave her there. It was no fun for a child, living with a bachelor like me.

'But she never really forgave me. It seemed to me that when she got to fifteen or sixteen she was always looking for some man to give her the love she felt she'd missed out on. You could see it in her eyes when she looked at you. She was accusing me of something, or rather she accused me of lacking something that I should have offered her. So she went elsewhere for what she thought she needed. You'd call her precocious, I suppose. There are other names for it which I shan't mention.

'She married when she was nineteen or so. He was a Canadian and they went back to Toronto to live. I think she expected it to be like a fairy tale, but nothing ever is. I used to write to her at Christmas, but I didn't always get a reply.

'And then I got a short letter to say she'd died. She'd have been twenty-seven. Even younger than her mother.'

'How did she die?'

'She was riding pillion behind some tearaway on a motor-bike. Not her husband, of course. She wasn't wearing a helmet and when he skidded and went off the road, she didn't stand a chance

'I don't think she was happy, even in Canada. Maybe she'd have been different if she'd had two parents to bring her up. Maybe not. She never had Chris's strength of character. It was always as if you had to reassure her that she was worth loving. Poor little kid.'

'Shall I get us some more tea?' Kate asked. 'You must be thirsty after all that.'

'You get us a fresh pot. You know your way around by now.'

When she got back with the tea, she found that Alan had

brought out the notebook he had spoken about. She poured them both a cup of tea and offered Alan a biscuit from a packet she'd come across in the kitchen. When they'd settled back in their chairs he pushed the notebook towards her.

'Here, take it,' he said.

Kate looked enquiringly at him over the thick bound note-book he had laid on the table in front of them. Black with a red spiral binding.

'It's a diary,' he said. 'What they call a confessional diary. Plenty about my thoughts and feelings, not too many details of visits to the dentist. I was in the hospice as a day patient and they provide you with everything you need there. Thai massage and a woman to talk to you about death. The counsellor – that's what she called herself – told me it might help. She said I wasn't to write for anyone except myself. No one else should read it. If I liked, she said, she would see to it that it was destroyed after my – well, afterwards. It would help with the pain, she told me. It might help me to face up to the fact of – I might stop denying what was going to happen.'

Kate stayed silent. If she interrupted he might change the subject.

He shrugged. 'I'm supposed to face up to the fact that I'm dying,' he said after a while. 'I know it, of course. I've known it for a long while now. It was the actual words I ran away from, just as I ran away from what I saw there at High Corner: two little kids, looking to me to save them. I was all they had. Their only hope.'

'You did what you could. You had your own demons to deal with then, too,' said Kate.

'Maybe. But all I could do was pick up the pieces afterwards.'

'Is it all in here?' she asked, tapping the book.

'Most of it. You want to know what happened to Chris, and

how Elinor Marlyn died, and why, don't you?'

'Yes.'

'It's in there.'

'How did you find out what really happened? I've been round asking people and I can't get much further than the story that appeared in the paper.'

'I got it out of Susie in the end. When you get to the end of the diary, and there are still questions to ask, then phone me. I should be around for another week or so, at least.'

He smiled his death's-head smile and Kate tried not to flinch.

She opened the cover and looked at the first page. What could you say when a man handed you the record of his life? The writing was so neat! Each letter carefully formed, so unlike her own careless scrawl.

'It wasn't written for anyone else, so you'll find it hard going in places. And there are long sections where I'm just railing against Fate. You can skip them if you like.'

'I doubt whether I'll skip any of it,' said Kate.

'You're wondering how an ordinary working man like me got to be so articulate,' he said.

She nodded. Yes, she had wondered.

'It was the prison camp. Chieti first, then Fontanellato.' He saw that the names meant nothing to Kate. 'Northern Italy,' he added. 'You know the worst thing about it? The boredom. There was nothing to do for hours every day except read, or go to the lectures that the officers laid on. I'll give them their due – they passed on to us all that they remembered of their expensive educations. They gave it to us for free, us graduates of the local elementary school. I've always thought learning's an uncomfortable business. It means making yourself like a child again. Looking stupid. But discomfort wasn't the problem in that camp: boredom was. When you're as bored as I was, you'll set your mind to conquer anything. We talked about everything – History, Greek and Latin. Mathematics and biology. And politics. We spent hours discussing Marx and Engels. So that was my college, Kate Ivory. That's where I learned to develop my ideas and express myself. See what you think of the result.'

She wasn't sure whether to take that last remark at face value or whether it was ironic. She picked up the notebook and placed it carefully in her bag.

Alan was watching her. 'Like I said, it's not a single, coherent story. I wrote it in fits and starts and I put down what occurred to me, in no particular order. But you're a writer. You'll make sense of it.'

She phoned Roz and met her in the pub on the corner.

'Thank goodness you're driving,' she said. 'I need a large gin and tonic.'

'Did you get what you were looking for?'

'Yes, I think so. I won't know till I've read the account he's written.'

'So you'd like to go straight home when you've drunk your gin.'

'I'd like to go back to Agatha Street. I don't want to read Alan's diary at High Corner, I'd rather be in my own place.'

She was sitting on her favourite velvet sofa when she started to read. There was no sound from the neighbouring house to disturb her. The Frightful Fosters were apparently away for a couple of days. Roz had poured her a glass of Sauvignon Blanc and then disappeared to her own room.

I still wonder whether I should have seen what she was up to right from the beginning. Does that make me partly to blame for what happened?

It's a painful thought to live with in the small hours of the night . . .

PART 3

LONDON AND OXFORD, 1945

1

When I reached the station after my visit to the children at High Corner, night had fallen. The platform was crammed full of people and they looked as though they'd already been waiting a while for the London train. It drew in fifteen minutes later and I managed to find myself a seat in a crowded compartment. The guard had pulled down the blinds and we were really closed in. When the train door slammed behind me with a final *clunk* I could imagine that someone had turned a key in the lock. How I hate that sound. It makes me want to scream – really scream – and never stop. This was what had kept me away from Oxford, if I'm honest. Not the cold and the discomfort, but the way I felt when they shut me in. I closed my eyes and tried to sleep through the long miles of black countryside.

As we reached the outskirts of London I could only imagine the herds of barrage balloons floating in the night sky like bloated silver pigs. But I could hear the muffled, stuttering roar of a rocket overhead. So many of them were coming over that they weren't bothering to sound the air-raid sirens any more. The murmured conversations paused briefly and then resumed. The train slowed to a crawl, stopping and starting as though evading the doodlebugs.

Conversation grew louder. A man spoke to me, tried to draw me in.

'If your number's on it . . .' someone was saying.

Maybe ours wasn't, but some poor bastards copped it. We

heard the thunderclap of an impact over on our right. Maybe I'd find devastation when I got back to Reckitt Street. Nothing but a pile of rubble. No house. No Sheila. All my past life gone for good.

For a moment the prospect of starting from scratch with no baggage to carry seemed sweet.

As the train lurched forward a package fell from the rack, catching me a clip on the head.

'You all right, mate?' someone asked.

'Mustn't grumble.'

That exchange summed up my life, I reckon.

As I walked home through the dusk I saw this girl sitting in her front room. She was perched on the edge of a chair at the table. Her hair was hanging down on her shoulders instead of being pinned up. She was wearing a blue dress – Alice blue, they used to call it. And she was sobbing her heart out. I know I should have stopped. Should have knocked at the door, asked what was wrong, what I could do for her. The scene was so clear, and I realised then that the windows had all been blown in. When you looked carefully you could see there were just a few ragged shards sticking to the edges of the frames.

I heard someone, her father most likely, shouting from the open doorway behind her.

'Don't get excited!' he was instructing her. 'Just do what I tell you!'

She wasn't listening. And none of what he was saying was making any sense, anyway.

When I called in at the corner shop for half an ounce of tobacco, 'It was her birthday,' someone was saying.

I don't know why that should make it any worse, but it did.

* * *

258

I've had a letter from Miss Elinor Marlyn telling me the children are thieves. But whatever happened down there at High Corner, there's more to it than that.

It's not that I'm making excuses for them. What they did was wrong. But people like Elinor Marlyn never go hungry – not really hungry. Oh, I know they may skip a meal and get a bit peckish. They may think they're putting on too much weight and deny themselves a few treats for a couple of weeks. But day in, day out, lasting for weeks, the sheer boredom of grey mince and beige mash, of an inch cube of sweaty mousetrap cheese, a scraping of bright yellow marge on gritty beige bread – they know nothing of that.

Oh, I know we're not starving or anything – *I* should know that if anyone does – but there's never quite enough somehow, and certainly not of the things you might enjoy eating.

We think about food all the time. It has taken over from the weather as our normal topic of conversation. And it isn't just people like me, ex-POWs who have experienced starvation, it's everyone. You hear them in the shops and in the pubs, in the bus queues and down in the air-raid shelters talking about it: food.

So you can't really blame the kids, can you?

We were alike, you and I, Christopher. Sent away to do our duty, then fucked up by the enemy. We thought we could return home when it was all over, but we couldn't. 'After the war' – that was our anthem. It started every flight of fancy, taking us away from a present that was unbearable, into a future where everything would be as we wanted it. But there was no past to return to, was there? It no longer existed. I'm not sure now that it ever did. But somehow by repeating that little phrase we entered a communal never-never land. I suppose the modern equivalent is, 'When I win the lottery'. What is it they say? You're more likely to die before the next draw than you are to win the jackpot.

After the war, that's what I repeated to myself through the weeks and months. 'When I get home.' But they'd dropped bombs on my home, ripped the sides off the houses so that you could see right in to how people lived, all the small details of their lives. They shouldn't have been exposed to the public view – like catching your grandmother on the lavatory. I believe that happened, too, in Tanner Street. Old Mrs Beavis, caught with her directoire knickers round her ankles. Poor old thing was never quite the same again afterwards, but maybe that was the way the blast deadened her hearing, so she was never quite sure what people were saying about her.

You're just one more shadow on my life, Elinor Marlyn, waiting for me round corners, lying in wait in the dark at the top of the stairs, a ghostly example of the banality of death, the futility of revenge.

You remind me, with that smile of yours, just how alike we are. When I look in the mirror – and that's something I only do when I really need to – I see your face just behind my own. Joined for ever, as we never were in life, by that other act of consummation.

In my imagination you're younger than when we met, and I'm older, though not as old as I am now. And we meet as equals, because we understand.

When I came home from Italy, and nursed Sheila through those last months – though the Lord knows I wasn't much of a nurse! – and watched the landmarks of my boyhood disappear beneath the rubble of the bomb sites, I learned to cling to my few possessions, the small corner that was left to me and to which I still felt I belonged. I'm not being very clear here, am I? But this corner of the Borough, this battered house in an embattled street was *mine*. I'd have fought to the death to defend it. I know it wasn't much, just four rooms and an outside privy, but it was the most important spot in the world to me. I'd dreamed of it every night in that camp, and I longed for it every day when I was on the run. It was what kept me going through the days when I had nothing to eat but some raw vegetables stolen from a field and once, in desperation, a paper bag I found snagged on a fence. You'd laugh, Elinor, wouldn't you? Oh yes, I know your name now, and in our conversations I call you by it, the way I never would have done in real life.

Our houses were very different, but the feelings we had for them were the same. House, family, tradition. We both valued them and in the end it's what led us both to do what we did.

I could feel the pride coming off you that very first time we met, like waves of heat from a furnace. It was evident in the polish on the floor, the sheen on the paint, the pictures on the wall. I thought at the time it was all about money, but it wasn't only that. Of course you needed money to keep the place up. You wouldn't fill it with lodgers the way I'd have done if I'd had to. No, you wanted to keep it the way it was when your grandfather first handed it over to his unmarriageable daughter. A sign to the world that you were important, that you meant something in the community. You wanted your portrait up there with the rest of them, the City Aldermen, the Mayor, with all their gold braid and haughty expressions.

Miss Marlyn. That's how you first introduced yourself, and a Miss Marlyn would live in that house for ever, that's what you believed. And in the meantime you'd live there in your solitary glory, not sharing your house with anyone. That is, until Chris and Susie came along. They were the least of the evils on offer.

Hand-picked. Nice, clean children. No lice, no scabies, no bedwetting. Well, not much, anyway. And you'd have wet the bed, Elinor Marlyn, if you'd gone through what they had, and seen how they left their mother coughing her guts up every morning.

I'm getting angry. Getting carried away. That won't do, will it? No, you and I know how to control ourselves, Elinor. We don't lash out on impulse, we plan it and prepare. It? Revenge, Elinor. A dish best eaten cold, as they say. Your crime arose out of pride; mine out of revenge. I might have sympathised with you if you hadn't chosen those particular kids to take it out on. That was your only mistake. You'd have got away with it, if it hadn't been for me. And I've got away with it ever since.

Do I regret what I did? No, not really. The only evil thing I did, as I see it, was to cut you down when you were at your peak. You thought you had so much to live for, once the war was over and you could live openly in the style you had purchased for yourself. But I ended all that for you and you never lived to see the lawn and shrubbery restored, the pictures back on the walls, the windows sparkling in the sunlight. You robbed me of the niece and nephew who meant all the world to me. I robbed you of your triumph.

We sat and talked for a while, you and I, though I believe you knew from the moment I walked in what I had in mind. You wouldn't have screamed for help, though, would you? You wouldn't give in to the fear. You were still strong, physically, but you used words to attack me.

'I don't know what their father was like,' you said, 'but Christopher was like you, Alan. Too sharp for his own good. I couldn't order him to do what I wanted, nor could I frighten him into it. Things have changed in my lifetime. I've lived through two world wars and after the convulsions and blood-letting, the country was never the same again. We were fighting to keep things the way they had been, and twice we failed in that endeavour. Things will never be the same again, and it's men like you, Alan, who stand for everything we've lost, the pitiful things we've gained.'

I must have looked my enquiry.

'When I was young, people like you knew their place. If they had brains, they hid them. If they had initiative, they buried it – or joined the Army and got promoted to Sergeant.'

She saw me smile at this.

'Your nephew was the same. He didn't know his place.'

I spoke then. 'And what was his place?'

'He had no business prying into my affairs.'

'The affairs of his betters?'

'If you like to put it that way.' She sounded as though she always thought of herself as better than the likes of Chris and me. Well, she would have done, too.

'And then he defied me. He looked straight at me, the way an equal would, and he let me know he believed I was lying. He shouldn't have done that.'

'But you *were* lying.'

'There you go. Stepping out of your place again.'

But she was laughing at herself, I could tell, when she said that. It was that glimpse of self-awareness in Elinor Marlyn that made me like her, in spite of everything. In spite of everything she did.

She hadn't been expecting a visitor and her hair was looser than she usually wore it, the knot on her neck slipping down her back, the strands of hair escaping from the band that held them. Her hair was quite curly, I saw with surprise. And she must have washed it recently because it shone like the coat of a healthy animal under the light. Another of her 100-watt bulbs, I remember thinking.

'Well, what's on your mind, Alan?' she asked then. Our hands were only a couple of inches apart on the table. The angle of the light on her face didn't flatter her age, but it showed up the precise lines of the bones beneath the skin, and the fineness of the skin itself with the blue veins just below the surface.

And if I'd said that I'd come to make love to her? What would she have done then?

I suppose she'd have laughed out loud and told me to mind my place again. To remember who I was and how I shouldn't look at someone like Elinor Marlyn even if she was more than ten years older than me.

'I've come to kill you,' I said. 'An eye for an eye.'

'You're blaming me for Christopher's death.' The way she said it, it wasn't a question.

'Oh yes. And for ruining Susie's life.' I could see the sneer on her face when I said that.

'Susan lacked moral fibre,' she said.

'She saw you.'

'I know that.'

'She saw that you were driving, not Danny Watts. Oh, he was behind the wheel, all right, but you grabbed it from him. You took control and you steered the van straight at Christopher. He didn't have a chance.'

'And you found all this out from dear, dim little Susan?'

I wasn't going to rise to the bait. 'That box you gave her was an antique. Tortoiseshell inlaid with gold. I found it when I packed up her belongings for her. No one gives a child a valuable object like that unless there's a good reason. I got the story out of her in small pieces, over time. She told me about the people she'd seen, and the van that arrived at night with blacked-out headlights. She didn't know what it carried, but I could fill in the blanks. You could give her a square of sweet-smelling soap, or a pretty little box, and she'd have been your loyal friend for ever. But Chris was getting worried about it, wasn't he?'

'Why on earth do you think I would need to do all these things you accuse me of? Why should I run the risk of discovery and even imprisonment?'

'I read the newspapers. Your stocks and shares were nearly worthless. Even your house had lost value by the end of the war. You needed the money. You couldn't face life without it.'

'You think I planned Chris's death?'

'No. You can't have done. I think Susie ran into the road without looking and Chris went after her to pull her back. Danny was trying to avoid Susie, but you made him kill Chris. And Susie saw you, leaning over to the side and with your white hands clenched on the steering wheel.'

'So why didn't she tell what she saw?'

'You bribed her.'

'She allowed herself to be bribed with a silly little trinket.'

'Weren't you afraid she'd tell what she saw one day?'

'She was too frightened of me. She wasn't like Christopher. He had determination. She hadn't. She'd tell everyone how kind I was, and forget about the food on the table, just because I gave her a little sliver of soap. Her approval was easily bought. And I knew she'd always wanted that little box. I'd seen her greedy eyes looking at it in the cabinet in the drawing room. I should never have allowed her in there. But even if she'd spoken, no one would have listened to her story, or believed her if they had. Children were generally taken to be natural liars in those days.'

She made the assumption sound quite reasonable.

'And Danny Watts? Weren't you afraid of blackmail?'

'Danny had great hopes of me and what I might bring into his life.' She was mocking me again, forcing me to use my imagination. I doubt whether there was ever any sort of relationship between them, though. She was just leading me on. 'And what could he say? He was at the wheel. I leaned across, on an impulse, just to help him avoid the boy. They wouldn't take his word against mine. Why should they? I'm a Marlyn from High Corner and he's just feckless Danny Watts from the hovel next door. I paid his fine and gave him a little more besides to keep him sweet. What more would he want?'

'He'll bleed you dry.'

'I don't think so. If he goes to the police he'll have to explain what we were doing in the van, and he wouldn't want them looking too closely into his own illegal deals.'

'If you were so successful with Susie and Danny, why didn't you think of bribing Chris?'

'I knew what he was like.' She paused. 'He was like you, Alan. I couldn't make you do what I wanted, and I couldn't make him do so, either.'

She'd changed again. She was no longer the woman who had taken on Chris as an equal and defeated him. She was no longer the woman flattering me and considering, however remotely, my seduction. She was just a selfish old woman who wanted her own way and would let no one, not even a couple of children, defeat her. I think it was her contempt for Susie that really made my mind up for me.

'So you killed him because you couldn't face telling people that you'd lost your money. All those investments that had cushioned you from real life for so many years dropped their value in the war and put you on a level with the rest of us.'

'I was never on your level.'

'No, you weren't. I wouldn't deal in stolen petrol and car tyres. I wouldn't take scum like Arthur and Danny Watts into my home so that I could have good food on my table. You must have made a fortune out of your various deals.'

'I had some capital left and I used it. I won't be poor again and neither will the niece who inherits this house from me.'

'You knew you'd have to pay one day.'

'How melodramatic, Mr Barnes!'

I just looked at her. Her hazel eyes didn't blink and she didn't drop her gaze.

'How do you intend doing it?' she asked. She still had her old arrogant manner. She didn't really believe I would kill her. 'It's not so easy once you actually look your victim in the eye, is it?' She was still staring at me as she said it, as though I was the victim and not her.

But there she was wrong. It's difficult the first time, but even then, the desperation carries you through. You know that one of you has to die, and you're not going back to that prison camp. When there's an open door with hell standing behind it, you don't go back. You go forwards, whatever it takes. No, after that first time, it's not so difficult. And I'd already done it three times, maybe four. It comes back to me at night, in my dreams, but during the days I can forget. However, Elinor Marlyn knew nothing about any of that. Here in Oxford they could watch the convoys moving through, they could see the aircraft in the skies, but they were free from the daily fear of death. It existed all right, they knew that, but it wasn't happening *here*.

She blinked at last. Maybe she read a little of what was running through my mind in my expression. Maybe not.

But I knew how to do it, all right. That's what they teach you in the Army: how to kill people. And in the prison camp and afterwards, while I was making my way down through Italy, I learned how to kill without waking up the neighbourhood. But for you, Elinor, I wanted something that would fit the crime you committed.

I'd made my preparations before coming into the house. Everything was ready for her.

When I got up from my chair, and stood behind her, she must have known what was going to happen. Not *exactly* what was going to happen, of course, but she knew. She recognised someone with as strong a will as she had – not in every corner of my life, but in this one thing, I was more determined than she was.

She didn't scream. She had dignity, I'll give her that.

Quick, hard pressure on the carotid artery. Not enough to kill, not enough to bruise, but enough to render her uncon-scious. By the time she was herself again I had the gag round her mouth and was fixing the cords round her wrists. She kicked out at me while I tied her ankles, landed a blow on my cheek I had to explain away for the next few days.

I didn't hurt her. The bindings weren't tight enough to mark her skin. I didn't want her to suffer, I just wanted her to die. I knew the bonds wouldn't hold her for long, but then, they didn't have to. As I worked I could smell the soap she used: carnation with something of pepper behind it, something delicately fragrant that had been unavailable in the shops since before the war. She must have kept it – hoarded it, I told myself – wrapped carefully in tissue paper at the back of a drawer. Or maybe one of her black-market friends gave it to her as a Christmas gift. But that perfume – carnations, strawberries, a bit peppery – brings her face back to me as nothing else can.

She shouldn't have given a sliver of it to Susie. She should have known that I'd always recognise it and know where it came from.

I opened the back door and the door into the garage, then hefted her over my shoulder and carried her out to the van. It was a small delivery van – maybe the same one that killed Chris, who knows?

I didn't need a light, so there was no chance of anyone seeing us from the road. Not that there were many casual passers-by in a road like that. I had taken careful note of the lie of that garage and so I could work fast to push her into the driving seat and close the door against her. I took the starting handle and cranked the engine. She was wriggling and squirm-ing again by then, trying to get her hands and feet free, but I knew enough about knots to know that the ones I'd tied would last long enough while I did what needed to be done. The engine putt-putted into life and coughed blue smoke into the garage.

The garage was a very small one. It fitted that van with only a foot to spare on every side. The passenger's window was partly open, enough to let in the fumes, not enough to allow her to wriggle out. The air was getting thick by then and I closed the garage door and went back into the kitchen to wait.

That was the difficult part, just sitting in the kitchen and watching the hands of the clock move round. When I considered I'd waited long enough, I went outside and took a very deep breath. Then I pulled open the garage door, ran to the van and removed her bindings and her gag with three quick cuts. I'd brought a good knife with me. I was out again within two minutes, closing the door behind me. I'm good at moving around in the dark. You get used to that when you're on the run.

I'm glad I couldn't see her, couldn't even smell the exhaust fumes and the indignity of death. Back in the kitchen I gulped air into my lungs, air that was still tinged with the smell of carnations.

And that was it, really. I made sure I'd left no traces in the house. I took the cut cords and gag away with me, and I melted out of High Corner and down Armitage Road as secretly as I'd arrived.

Not that the neighbours would have wondered too much. There'd been no shouting for help, nothing to wake the neighbourhood. And I reckon I wasn't the only man who turned up at that back door and asked for admittance. There was something too knowing in the way she'd sat there with her hair loosened from its knot and the light slanting down on the smooth planes of her face. Elinor Marlyn knew what she was doing, I reckon.

And just for a moment it was worth it. Then reality broke in and I knew that hers was just another sad, dead body like the ones I'd seen in North Africa and Italy during the war. All that waste of life, and I'd added to it again.

It didn't bring back Chris or help Susie. It didn't satisfy my anger for more than a matter of seconds. And the regrets have stayed with me for years.

Though I killed you, I've kept your secret, Elinor. Your house is still in your family, it still belongs to your blood. There was no loss of dignity for you, Elinor Marlyn. I didn't betray you. I just brought you what you deserved.

PART 4

OXFORD, 2000

1

George was carrying on a one-sided argument. He and Kate were in the garden. It was odd, she thought, how little time they'd spent out there in the months she'd been living at High Corner. Maybe she was the one who had wanted to spend all her time inside and George had just gone along with her. Maybe he just wasn't interested in gardens.

She knew what he was saying, what he was trying to persuade her to agree to and she wasn't really listening. She'd heard his arguments more than once and she'd already made up her mind.

Something landed on the back of George's shirt and he twitched a shoulder to remove it. Whatever it was stayed in place. George carried on talking. Kate moved back a step and saw a shield bug, very green against the white of George's shirt. She reached out her right hand and flicked it gently into her left palm. Its scurrying feet tickled slightly. She opened her fingers and the shield bug flew away, its wings working so rapidly that they became transparent and she could see its chestnut-red body. George, unaware of the tiny drama, was saying something about forgetting the past, remembering only the present and what they both had. He was speaking even faster now, but the very rapidity of his words made them as transparent as the shield bug's wings, and she saw the truth behind them.

'I'm coming home,' she said on the phone to Roz half an hour later.

273

'Oh good.'

'You think we're going to be able to share the Agatha Street house quite amicably, do you?'

'No, it isn't that, Kate. We don't need to share. We'd only get on one another's nerves after a week or two. I was going to tell you that I'm moving out in a month's time.'

'Where are you going?'

'I've bought a house of my own.'

'Where?'

'In East Oxford. One of those little streets between the Iffley Road and Cowley Road.'

'Those houses may be small but they still cost a fortune. Where did you get the money?'

'I didn't steal it, if that's what's worrying you.'

'Good.'

'The thing is that I did rather well for myself with your computer. Did you know that you can deal in shares on the Internet?'

'I'd heard about it but I've never tried to do it.'

'You should, you really should. It's much more fun than betting on the horses.'

'More expensive, too.'

'But so lucrative once you find out what you're doing. And with so many helpful websites telling me what to do and who to back, I couldn't go wrong, could I?'

'Ah—'

'What's that funny noise you're making?'

'I'm groaning.'

'You can stop worrying, Kate. I'm fine. And I'm going to continue that way. Do you want me to help you pack? No? Come home as soon as you can. This afternoon if possible. I'll put a bottle of wine in to cool.'

* * *

'Hello, Emma?'

'Is that you, Kate?'

'Yes. And I wanted to tell you about George and me before anyone else does.'

'You're not getting married, are you?'

'No, it's—'

'I'm so glad. It would have been an awful mistake, for both of you.'

'Do you think so?'

'Not that you weren't very well suited in lots of ways, of course.'

'Of course.'

'But you're not very materialistic, are you, Kate?'

'I always thought that was one of my nicer traits.'

'I expect it is. But the Dolbys are very down-to-earth people. They believe in property and investments and things like that. In the end George would have found your attitude too flighty.'

'Yes, I expect you're right.'

Kate was only too pleased to have separated from George without permanently damaging her friendship with Emma. Her feelings at the break-up she could keep to herself. For the moment she didn't want to share them with anyone.

'You and Sam are getting on all right, are you?' she asked.

'Well, of course we are. Why do you ask?'

'You were having a tiny difference of opinion about babies last time I saw you.'

'Oh, that's nothing. We've decided on a compromise. That's what married couples do, Kate. We'll have one more child and then we'll call a halt. We're both happy about that.'

But if that was so, why had Sam had that look of desperation on his face when she'd seen him cycling down Headington Hill that morning?

'Come and see me in Agatha Street one day next week,' said Kate.

'Do you mind if I bring little Jack with me?'

'No, of course not. I look forward to seeing you both.'

She could always remove the sticky fingerprints afterwards with a damp cloth.

She called round at the vicarage to say goodbye to Elspeth. It seemed more polite than a simple telephone call.

'I shall miss you,' said Elspeth. 'I did enjoy just being able to pop in to see you.' Today she was wearing a buttercup yellow shirt with tangerine Capri pants.

'I shall miss you, too,' said Kate. 'Life won't be nearly so colourful without you. But you can always journey across Oxford to visit me.'

'One always says that, but one never does,' said Elspeth.

'You have your parishioners,' said Kate. 'They keep you busy, and I'm sure they're all very friendly.'

'They're not the same thing.'

'And anyway, I assumed you had a secret lover. He must keep you amused.'

'What?'

'When you came to the Centre for Oxfordshire Studies with me, you disappeared for two hours without saying where you were going.'

'I didn't realise you'd been puzzling about it ever since.'

'Well?'

'I was checking a reference in the Bodleian.'

'Not for two hours. And you turned up at the library with a

cheerful smile on your face. The Bodleian never has that effect on me.'

'I'd been to the chiropodist, that's all. I have trouble with my feet.'

'Oh.' Well yes, that is something you'd be secretive about.

'So you see, I really will miss you.'

'There'll be somebody else,' said Kate. There was nothing so comforting as a good cliché, she'd always found. 'And I've brought back your cassettes. They came in very useful at the end.'

'Did you manage to find out all you wanted about that little boy?'

'One never finds out everything. But I think I know most of it by now.'

'I thought you'd be taking a file of evidence down to the police station. You were very determined about it, you know.'

'I wanted the answers to my questions, but it wouldn't be any use going to the police now. Death has got there before the detectives. There's only one person from Chris's story who's still alive, and he won't be around for much longer than a month or so, I should think. So there's no point in dragging up the old scandals.'

'That all sounds very mysterious.'

'No, it's all just very sad, I'm afraid.'

'I'll be starting on my own novel soon. That should keep me occupied.'

'At least you've got the plot register to help you.'

'I shall read it avidly.'

'I'll have to go, I'm afraid. I still have some packing to do.'

'Goodbye, Kate.'

* * *

'Hello, Estelle?'

'Yes.'

'It's me. Kate.' Baffled silence at the other end of the phone line. 'Kate Ivory,' she explained.

'Ah, Kate. Good.'

'I'm ringing to let you know about the new book. You asked me to give you a progress report, remember?'

'Excellent.'

'Well, like I told you, it's a story set in World War Two. The heroine is a young woman, only about twenty-two, who has lived a very secluded life. Her father's a vicar.' For a moment she thought Estelle was going to say something, but there was silence at her agent's end of the line.

'Estelle?'

'Yes, dear. I'm listening.'

'And when she's called up – and young, unmarried women were, you know – she takes a job as Billeting Officer. Then she meets this dashing young naval officer . . .'

'Yes, dear?'

'What do you think of it so far?'

There was something that sounded suspiciously like a yawn at the other end of the line.